Now that her te
doubt the wisdo

been too hasty.

She could appreciate what a surprise her appearance must have been to Greg when he'd been expecting his father's fiancée. Maybe she should own up before things got out of hand...

The kitchen batwings suddenly flew open, announcing the arrival of the subject of her thoughts. "Do you have anything a little more...?" A pointed pause, as cold eyes travelled from the top of her head to the red tips of her enamelled toes before disdainfully settling on her face. "...suitable to wear? We've been invited to my sister's for dinner. She's looking forward to meeting you."

I'll bet, thought Raven, sliding off the barstool. Suddenly, any thoughts of stopping this farce disappeared with the condescending tone of Greg's voice.

"Of course, Greggie, I have this simply divine black gown that Brad absolutely adores. I'll wear that, shall I?" She tilted her head so she was gazing up into his face. Presumptuous oaf, she smiled, gritting her teeth at the same time.

"There's no need to dress for dinner."

Greg spoke as if to a child, or more likely an imbecile, Raven thought.

"Perhaps something a little tidier than...than what you have on now." He seemed to stumble trying to find the proper words. "And shoes. It would be appropriate to wear shoes."

Raven couldn't help it. She laughed. This was fun. And it really served him right, after all. Slipping quickly into her part again, she replied, "Of course, I'll wear shoes, Greggie, if you think that's really necessary."

Worlds Apart

by

Anne Ashby

Worlds Apart

Cover Art by *Tina Lynn*

The Wild Rose Press
PO Box 708
Adams Basin, NY 14410-0708
Visit us at www.thewildrosepress.com

Publishing History
Last Rose of Summer Edition, 2010
Print ISBN 1-60154-722-6

Published in the United States of America

Dedication

To Loree Lough—whose encouragement
gave me the confidence to pursue a dream.

Very special thanks to Kathleen, whose friendship
and latent interpreting skills smoothed
my transition into the American lifestyle.

Thanks also to Ray, Coanne, Trish and Barbara
for capturing times
when Greg spoke with a Kiwi accent.

Prologue

"I can't do this," Raven Titirangi gasped, staring at the airline ticket in her hand.

"Why not?" grinned the man seated at her hospital bedside. "Didn't your mother teach you not to look a gift horse in the mouth?"

Raven frowned. "My mother taught me lots of things, like always being on the lookout for lecherous old men—"

Brad Collins threw back his head, his shout of laughter drawing glances from others in the hospital ward. Raven felt a swell of affection. Since meeting Brad during the annual Rollercoaster Fun Run around Auckland's North Shore, life had been so different. The tall American tourist said he had spied the advertising for the fun run and joined the thousands of runners pounding the pavement. By the time they'd crossed the finish line, Brad and Raven had established an easy rapport that had continued to grow, and very soon he'd worked his way into her family's hearts.

"Look, honey..." He leaned forward grasping her clenched fingers. "You work too damned hard. You need quiet time to recuperate. Listen to what the doctors said. You need to rest or this surgery could take a long time to get over. If you stay at home, you won't rest." He pressed on as if aware of her mounting hesitation. "Joy said you have an extended leave of absence from school to recuperate, so there's no reason why you can't go. You know I'd like you to come to America permanently, so why not take this chance to visit Ellicott City and see what you think of the place? I have my own quarters so you won't need to bother Greg, unless you feel like being sociable. Our house actually borders onto a state forest with hiking trails you could use to build up your strength again. And if you feel up to doing some painting, I have a sunroom that would be ideal for you to use as a studio."

He's ticking off everything he knows I'll find irresistible, Raven realized.

She looked up from their entwined fingers. What he suggested sounded very tempting. She knew she had to slow down and give her body time to recoup, but how could she accept this offer? She had her obligations here—still, a holiday in America, all expenses paid, staying in Brad's home, it sounded wonderful, relaxing, and carefree. Almost what the doctor would order...

No, she must not be tempted. Her mother had enough on her plate without taking over Raven's maternal responsibilities as well.

"All you're really doing is going over for a couple of weeks before us. What could be the harm in that?" he pressed.

"But without the boys?"

Brad continued as if she hadn't interrupted. "It will help to put some colour back into your cheeks. I'll make all the arrangements, have Greg or Abby pick you up in Baltimore, and look after you until we arrive. Perhaps if you feel up to it, you might want to help with some of the wedding arrangements, make sure everything suit your mother."

Brad didn't stop long enough for Raven to speak. Instead, he slipped in the coup de grâce: "I've talked this over with your mother already and we have it all sorted out. Between the two of us we can take care of everything here."

Finally Brad paused. Raven guessed he was uncertain what further arguments he could use to sway her. He knew she would not willingly expect Joy and him to look after her sons. A small smile crossed her lips as she realized he'd probably heard her quote 'they're my responsibility' on more than one occasion.

"Raven, you must realize that without your health you're no good to your boys or yourself. Take it easy for a while!" He sighed, looking quickly over his shoulder, before returning his eyes to her face, entreating, "Please."

"Your reinforcements are arriving." Raven tried to keep the amusement from her voice as she sighted the familiar woman entering the ward. Brad's head swung around and his face lit up with the sweetest smile.

Raven watched her tall, slim mother approaching the bed. Joy smiled apologetically at Brad. Still attractive even as she approached her sixties, there was now a glow about her that thrilled Raven. As a child Raven had often dreamed of her mother remarrying, but it had not happened—until Raven had taken Brad home that day on the promise of a 'home-cooked Kiwi meal.' Within a short time she could see that Joy had found someone she could love. Raven hadn't been surprised when they had shared the news that they intended to marry.

"What kept you?" Brad asked, concern marking his face. "I saw some parking spaces along the road before you dropped me off."

"Yes, but it's a one-way street. By the time I got around the block they'd all gone. It doesn't matter. I finally found one lone car park down Grafton Road." Raven watched the love soften her mother's face as she touched his cheek before turning to her with a smile.

"Hello, darling." Joy leaned over and kissed Raven. "How do you feel today? You still look awfully pale to me, although it's such a relief to see you without those tubes."

Not for the first time Raven thought of how frightening her collapse must have been to her mother. *Thank God Brad had been there to help Mum cope with her grandsons and her fears, through those long terrifying hours when my life hung in the balance.*

"I'm feeling much better, thanks, Mum. The doctor said I'd be able to come home within a week."

"That's good news. The boys will be so happy. We'll bring them in later today. Brad and I wanted to talk to you alone, so we came a little early."

Raven tried to glare at the concerned face. "Yes, I've been hearing already, Mother. You two are ganging up on me, aren't you?"

Joy didn't even have the grace to look ashamed although her lips twitched at the almost unheard of formal address. "Of course we are, darling. Maybe two of us can talk some sense into you. You wouldn't listen to me before when I said you were doing too much. No one can continue burning a candle at both ends. Something had to give and it was your health."

"Mother, appendicitis isn't caused by overwork, you know."

"Of course it isn't," Joy acknowledged, "but you must have been ignoring the warnings your body was trying to give you. I suppose you told yourself it was a torn muscle or something?" She sniffed disparagingly, shaking her head. "Anyway, I don't want to listen to excuses. I can manage the boys until we all join you."

Using her sternest school-teacher voice, eyes glittering with determination, Joy continued. "Take that ticket and get on the plane to Maryland, Raven. Stop arguing. Brad and I are quite competent, you know." Her eyebrows arched defying argument. "We'll see you in a couple of weeks."

As if she could read her daughter's mind, she

added, "I spoke to the boys last night and explained you need a holiday."

"But—"

Brad cut in guilelessly, "They were really happy with the idea if it means you getting back to your old self. Especially when I suggested we might be able to spend a couple of extra days in L.A. on the way over."

Raven couldn't help it. Laughter bubbled up even though her stomach hurt and she had to clutch it firmly. "You old reprobate! Mum, how on earth could you fall for someone as sneaky and underhanded as this?"

Joy looked across the bed at Brad, her eyes twinkling. "Just fate, I guess."

Brad tore his eyes from Joy's and back to Raven. "Go, Rae," he urged. "I promise everything will be okay here."

Tears welled up in Raven's eyes.

What would life have been like if I'd grown up with him as a father? Still, soon he will be my father. Well, stepfather, she corrected herself, but that was good enough. And seeing the change in her mother over the last month made her heart swell with love and gratitude.

She placed her hands on either side of his face. "Brad Collins, I love you. If you'd been a few years younger, I'd have given Mum a run for her money." Raven missed the glance that flashed between Brad and Joy as she hugged him tightly. Just as well. She'd never have consented to go to Maryland, had she known Brad's ulterior motive.

Chapter 1

Greg Collins stared at the computer screen in disbelief. Fingers went up to massage his tired eyes and he read the message again. The words were the same. He felt as if he couldn't breathe. His chest was tight, as though wrapped in unexpandable mesh.

Dad, getting married? He shook his head. There had to be some mistake.

No, the words were not ambiguous in any way; his father's email was quite direct. He intended to marry a New Zealand woman he'd met while on vacation. The wedding would take place here, in Ellicott City, and Greg and Abby were to arrange everything for an April date.

Greg snorted. The old fool. What is he thinking?

His knuckles whitened as he waited for the printer to spit out a copy of the offending message. Obviously, some woman was trying to get her hooks into his father, and Greg intended to make sure she didn't succeed.

Greg admired his father, depended on him. He considered him intelligent and very astute. Greg couldn't imagine him being taken in by some sorry story—but even considering such a major step as another marriage without a word to his children? It was totally out of character. Something smelled fishy...

His father never advertised his wealth. Perhaps this woman had discovered his worth somehow and saw Brad Collins as a way of feathering her nest.

Well, we'll see about that. Grabbing the paper from the printer, he slammed out of the house.

****

As he swung into the driveway of his sister, Abby's modest home, the tires of his four-wheel drive squealed, and protested again noisily as he braked. Picking up the printed email from the seat beside him, he jumped out of the truck, slamming the door behind him. Racing up the front steps, he kept his finger glued to the doorbell until the front door swung open.

"Where's your mother?" he demanded brusquely as he brushed past his young nephew.

"Greg—" Abby hurried out of the dining room, her face paling with concern. "—what's wrong?"

"Have you read your emails today?" he growled.

She clutched his arm. "Oh, no," she cried. "Something's happened to Dad?"

He tossed the paper at her. "You're right about that," he fumed, barely acknowledging Tony joining them in the foyer and sliding an arm around his wife. Suddenly, Greg felt contrite as he watched Tony's arm tighten to support Abby's slumped body. He hadn't meant to frighten his sister.

"What's he thinking? He must have lost his marbles," Greg railed, after Abby and Tony had read the email. He missed the questioning look that passed between them. "What should we do?" He swung around to Abby.

"I'll deal with dinner. You look after Greg." Tony squeezed Abby's arm.

Abby grimaced, dragging Greg toward the privacy of the den.

Greg hung back. "Hey, Tony, Abby, I'm sorry." He scrubbed his hand across his face. "I was so worried about Dad, I never gave a thought to the time. Abby, finish your meal..."

"My meal can wait."

"No, this can wait, eat while it's hot."

"What are microwaves for? I'll nuke it later.

Come on."

"But…"

"Forget it, will you? This is far more important. You want to tell me what's upset you so much?" Abby asked as she leaned against the closed door.

Greg swung around and looked at her in astonishment. "You can't tell me you approve? What on earth is he thinking?" he muttered as he paced across the small room. "He's sixty years old, for God's sake, how can he even consider marrying again?"

"Maybe he's thinking of himself, for once in his life?" Abby suggested calmly.

Greg could only scowl.

"You have to admit, he's always put family or the business first before. Remember all the excuses he had for not taking this vacation in the first place?" Abby paused thoughtfully. The silence caused Greg to look at her closely.

"You know," she continued, "I think it's nice that he's met someone."

"Met!" He exploded. "We're not talking met. He's talking about marrying the woman! We know nothing about her and—"

"It's really got nothing to do with us, Greg."

He swung around. "Of course it has." He stopped. "You already knew!" he accused.

"I did not know," Abby shot back. "But didn't you ever wonder that although he intended to tour New Zealand and Australia for three months, he never managed to get past Auckland? As far as I can judge by his emails and postcards to the children, he's never left the city." She smiled slightly at Greg. "Even a fool would have to wonder about that."

Greg had never wondered. But then, he hadn't had much time to think about anything but work these last busy weeks. The only time thoughts of his father had entered his mind had been when he missed Brad's input or advice about some problem or other.

Greg dipped his head sheepishly.

"Okay," he acknowledged, "so I haven't given the Old Man much thought lately. But marriage, hell..." His fingers tugged through his hair. "I bet she's only after his money."

Abby smiled sadly. "Greg, you're never going to trust another woman, are you? We're not all like Sybil, you know."

He glared at her.

"Dad's still a very good-looking guy."

Greg was speechless. He'd never considered whether or not his father might be attractive to the opposite sex.

"He's just a gullible old man who's probably going to be taken to the cleaners if we don't do something."

"You know what, Greg?" Abby's voice had hardened. "If you were Caleb's age, I'd say you were acting like a selfish little brat. Dad's been a wonderful father. He must have been so lonely since Mom passed away, and if he's found someone he loves, well I say good luck to him."

Greg stopped pacing, staring at her in bewilderment. He'd expected Abby to be as worried as he was. Can't she see this might be disastrous for Dad? "But she'll be after his money—"

"Come on, Greg. Dad's no fool. I doubt if anyone could take him for a ride. And anyway, big brother, who cares about his money? He can't take it with him when he dies. I don't want it. Tony and I are quite happy the way we are. That only leaves you." She glared at him, hands on her hips. "You already have all the money one person could ever need in a lifetime. Why should you care about Dad's?"

"It's not the money," he growled, horrified at the picture his sister was painting of him. His concerns hadn't come across as being that selfish, had they? "It's the principle of the thing, Abby. I don't want him to get hurt." He turned earnestly to his sister. "Look, I know how it feels. A relationship built on material things doesn't last, and somebody always gets hurt. I'm not willing to sit by and see that happen to someone I care about." He sucked in a deep breath and pledged, "If she is after his money..." He left the threat unsaid.

"Why not just give her the benefit of the doubt until we meet her?" Abby suggested gently. "You might be doing all this worrying for nothing. She's probably the loveliest lady. If Dad's fallen for her, I'm sure she's very special."

Greg detected a slight hesitation in her words, and breathed a sigh of relief. He wasn't being totally paranoid, not if Abby was worried too.

"Let's just wait and see, shall we? When does he say she's coming?"

Greg leaned over, picked up the page from a side table and skimmed through the lines of his father's newsy email. He read aloud. "Raven—" he scoffed. "Raven. What sort of name is that?" He continued, "—has been ill, and needs a rest, which she won't get here. I have convinced her to take a vacation before the wedding, and have a quiet look around. I so hope she likes Ellicott City. I want her to be happy there. I've told her to settle into my apartment and make use of my car."

Greg snorted. "I'll make sure she's happy, all right," he muttered. He continued skimming: "Friday night. She's arriving on Friday." Two days away. "He's done this on purpose—giving us no notice." His hand raked through his hair again. "Raven. Bet she'll be just like a raven, a black bird of evil."

"Honestly, Greg. Now you're being too silly. How can a person take on the personality of a bird?" Abby reasoned crossly. "But if you're determined to pursue that analogy, perhaps she's like the ravens as some of the native tribes of Alaska see them. I remember helping Caleb with an assignment this past fall. They look on the raven as the creator of the world. I believe they're held in very high regard for their courage and shrewdness. Perhaps Dad's Raven will portray those characteristics."

"Shrewdness, for sure; but more likely doom and disaster."

"Perhaps she should stay here with us," Abby offered. "I doubt if she'll enjoy the type of hospitality you sound like you're going to be offering."

Greg was adamant. "She's staying at the house with me."

"Dad wants her to use his apartment, Greg, and if she's been ill—"

"She'll stay in the main house, where I can keep an eye on her." He noticed Abby's concerned frown but was not about to change his mind.

"Don't you go doing anything stupid, Greg. Dad would never forgive you."

Greg's eyes narrowed, his jaw clenched. "Of course not. I would never do anything to upset Dad." He knew exactly what he intended to do. "Oh, I'll be the most perfect host you've ever seen."

****

Raven flopped down on the edge of her bed amidst a suitcase and variety of items she was trying to decide whether to pack or put back in her dresser. A week out of hospital and she still didn't feel much stronger, she still couldn't get through a day without collapsing into bed for a rest.

Today was no exception. She sighed despondently. For someone used to running up to ten kilometres each day, plus often having a squash game or a workout at the gym, the idea of not being able to even get through a sedentary morning without carking annoyed her so much she sometimes felt like screaming. She let her head fall back onto the pillow and swung her legs onto the bed. She would just lie here for a minute, collecting her energy.

****

Through the drowsiness she heard whispering. It never ceased to amaze her that children could make more noise whispering than grown people made talking normally. She stretched, enjoying that last moment of semi-oblivion before she would be forced to open her eyes.

"If I don't get a kiss soon, I'm not moving."

Suddenly two pairs of arms were wrapped around her neck and a set of lips was pressed against each cheek. She held the wriggling bodies tightly for a moment before opening her eyes.

"Hi, guys. How was school?"

She listened attentively as they plied her with stories of their day, each trying to outdo the other. At seven, Tane's sensitivity already showed as he occasionally allowed five-year-old Scott to control the conversation. Raven smiled. Three months since starting school, Scott was still proudly excited to share his day's work with his mum.

Raven closed her eyes, lamenting how fast her babies were growing up. All too soon they wouldn't need her any more. Her hold tightened just a little. She never got over how much happiness they gave her. While she knew she'd never stop missing Chris, watching his sons grow up happy and healthy had dulled much of the pain.

Time heals. She could almost believe that now. She never ceased to thank God for these two little boys, and be eternally grateful she and Chris had decided to start their family almost immediately after they had married. They'd both been only children, and had dreamed of filling their home with the noise and bedlam associated with large families.

But that wasn't to be. They'd had just four years together before a drunk driver took Chris's life—such a needless, senseless loss. But Raven couldn't maintain her anger against the other driver, a young family man whose life had also been devastated by the accident and his own stupidity. God counselled forgiveness, and although it had taken some time, she found her forgiveness had not only helped that driver but her as well.

Painting and her boys had been her salvation since.

Stopping an argument between her boisterous sons, Raven sent them outside for a few minutes to play before they'd need to begin their homework.

She headed for the fridge and began to prepare tea. As she worked, she found her thoughts wandering to Brad and her mother. She was so happy her mother had found someone new to love, although she wished Brad was a Kiwi. Then he wouldn't be taking Mum all the way across the world to live.

Joy had raised Raven alone, and then, with no thought for herself, had willingly stepped in to help when Raven's world had fallen apart. Raven could never repay the sacrifices her mother had made for her, and she was thrilled to see the happiness radiating from Joy since she'd met Brad. Her mother deserved all the happiness that he could give her, and more.

Thankfully Joy didn't seem fazed to leave all she'd ever known, her family and friends, her home, her country. Not something Raven would do. No man could ever tempt her to leave these shores. But Joy seemed content to know they would visit often. And Raven had to accept Brad's reassurances, no matter how much she'd miss her mother. It was time for Raven to sacrifice something—her mother's company—and she would never let on how hard that was going to be.

As she arranged the pots on the stove, Raven pushed her selfish feelings aside. *Joy should never have had to be alone for so long. We weren't created to live alone,* she mused. Maybe one day I'll...

She quickly diverted those thoughts too. She wasn't on the lookout for another man. She'd already experienced the best.

No, she was quite happy with her life the way it was.

Wasn't she?

****

Raven watched Joy and Brad closely, drinking coffee after their meal. Raven was aware of her mother's nervousness.

Nervous? Her mother? Never! Joy Henderson was the most confident person Raven knew. Years of dealing with teenage students had probably helped develop that confidence. She'd never seen her mother anything but in total control; yet now she was even fidgeting, twirling a teaspoon around in her fingers.

Raven's eyes slid from Joy to Brad. The two of them kept making furtive eye contact, then hurriedly looking away. His hair was quite messy, as if it had suffered numerous finger combings.

Her mother's coffee cup clanked against its saucer. "We've been organizing ourselves for next week." Again the spoon twirled around. "The weekend, of course, will be no problem." Raven was ticketed to depart Friday evening. "We've been thinking that maybe..." The cup went to her lips and down again. "Maybe it would be easier—" again the pause, and nervous look at Brad, "—if Brad just moved in." The last phrase came out like a rifle shot.

Raven's eyes went from one concerned face to the other. They're worried about my reaction, she realised. They were a different generation. While her mother might seem very modern and 'with it,' Raven guessed that Joy was feeling uncomfortable about living with Brad before marriage. *What can I say that would ease their concerns without embarrassing them further?*

"Actually, I was wondering if I could suggest that. It would be the most sensible thing to do." Raven chewed the inside of her lip to stop the smile. They were so cute. She suddenly felt years older, as if she was the parent offering advice, or even vindication.

"But the boys..." Brad began, clearing his throat. "We don't want to be sending the wrong signals to them."

Raven smiled, grateful for their concern. "They'll be fine. I'll have a talk with them and explain."

She reached over and clasped her mother's hand. "I think it's the most wonderful idea." The relief was apparent on her mother's face.

"Oh, Mum!" Raven quickly rounded the table and hugged her mother. "I'm just so happy for you. It's been so long since you had someone to love you like you deserve to be loved. I just wish you could have met Brad twenty years ago. You grab every moment of happiness with both hands and hang on tight, Mum, and don't let go, ever."

Joy looked closely at Raven. "You're right, if only I had met him twenty years ago," she agreed fervently, "when I was like you, a young widow with a young family, lonely and afraid to love again—"

Raven withdrew sharply. "Mum, I'm not afraid." She took a deep breath, collecting her wits, dismayed at how her mother had turned the conversation around. "Don't start on me. Just because you're in love, don't think everyone else should be, too." She spoke lightly, taking any heat out of the words.

"Oh, Rae, don't give up on love like I did. I loved

your father dearly, but he never wanted me to spend my life as I have. All the months he fought the cancer, he worried what we'd do, how we'd cope without him." Her intensity stilled Raven's attempt to move away. "How I would cope without him. He wanted me to find another mate and enjoy life to its fullest. He made me promise I wouldn't reject the possibility." She caught at Raven's arm. "If Chris had had the opportunity—he wouldn't have approved of the way you're shutting love out of your life either."

Raven turned from the table. Staring out the kitchen window, her voice took on a defensive tone. "I am not shutting love out. I have the boys to love, and you—"

"Don't be obtuse, Raven," Joy cut in sternly. "You know what I mean. You can't go on grieving for Chris all your life. He'd have been appalled that you're burying yourself in the boys. You can't take the place of a father in their lives, you know, even if you are being Super Mother."

Her tone softened. "You need to make a life for yourself. The boys will be grown all too soon, and you'll be left a hollow shell. Relax your guard, darling." Joy moved behind Raven and gently touched one of the hands clenching the edge of the bench. She glanced past Raven to where Brad sat. "I still can't believe I've fallen in love again. You will too, darling, if you'll take the chance. Just don't lock up your heart. You have to start living again—not just going through the motions."

Raven saw tears in her mother's eyes. She had long known how her mother felt, but Joy had never put it so plainly before. Raven would never doubt her mother's good intentions or the wisdom of her words. Occasionally—very occasionally—Raven had begun to wonder if there wasn't more to life than what she was experiencing.

She turned and hugged Joy for a long moment. "Don't fuss over me so much, Mum. You're starting out on a whole new life. Don't clutter up your happiness worrying about me. I'm fine."

Joy looked at her, a sceptical expression on her face.

"I am fine, really. I've long passed the grieving stage. I'll never stop missing Chris, or wanting to share things with him, but I know I have to get on with life." She paused, suddenly realising that she actually believed there could be someone else out there for her. That while she may have lost one soul mate, there might be another. She'd never really considered the possibility before. Had her recent brush with death caused her to realise that life was all too short as well?

"I know, Mum. I do understand." She paused, suddenly uncomfortable with the charged atmosphere, and sought to lighten it. "It's just that I've never even seen another man who twitches the old heart strings."

Still trying to ease the tension filling the kitchen, and reassure her mother, Raven grinned as she hugged Joy's shoulders. "You stole the one I had my eye on," she teased. "Okay, okay, if it'll make you feel any better, I hereby pledge to you that if I ever meet someone who looks as good as Brad, I'll think seriously about him."

Brad moved to join them, his arms encircling mother and daughter in a tight hug. Raven felt her heart swell as the emotion threatened to overflow. She blinked rapidly, secure in their love.

Trying to cover up her heightened emotional state, Raven again resorted to humour. "Now, to return to our previous conversation—" She slipped away from them toward the door, throwing over her shoulder at Brad, "Has Mum assured you that the boys are really heavy sleepers?" She waited just long

enough to see Brad grasp the significance of her statement and watch the colour sweep up into her mother's face before skipping out of the room.
****

Raven couldn't help feeling excited. She'd never really travelled overseas, just a five-day honeymoon in Australia. She'd dreamed of taking her boys to Disneyland one day, but money wasn't that plentiful.

Her mother and Brad had taken the boys to the airport playground while Raven joined the check-in queue at Mangere International Airport.

Finally it was her turn. The handsome clerk in the crisp uniform of the national airline wore a huge smile, teeth flashing against his brown skin. "Good evening. Welcome to Air New Zealand. Could I see your ticket and passport, please?" Raven flicked through the handful of documentation and handed over the required paperwork. How sick he must get of repeating the same old phrases to hundreds of travellers a day, and yet his ready smile and welcome seemed for Raven alone. Raven heaved her suitcase onto the scales and waited while the clerk fed her information into the computer.

"I have a nice surprise for you, Mrs. Titirangi. You've been upgraded." White teeth flashed at Raven's gasp. "You'll have a much more pleasant flight, with a little more leg room," he said, winking conspiratorially. He stapled the luggage receipt to Raven's ticket and handed her the packet. "You have a six-hour layover in Los Angeles before your plane to Baltimore. Your baggage has to be collected and taken through customs by you." He went on to explain the whereabouts of the terminal she'd need for her domestic flight, assuring her that she was a confirmed passenger for the onward journey. "Your boarding call will be at eight-thirty. Make sure you're at gate eleven at least ten minutes before then, please, and have a wonderful flight." Again the smile flashed before he dismissed her in favor of the next person in line.

Raven moved toward the escalator, bemused. She'd heard of people being upgraded to better seats when travelling, but had never dreamed it might happen to her.

It's a sign, she thought. This flight might just be fun. The holiday might be fun. She was going to enjoy herself from now, and not worry. The boys would be fine. They hadn't seemed the least bit upset about her leaving before them. Of course Brad would spoil them, so they were probably counting on having quite a fun time without her. Besides, what could happen in a couple of weeks?

She placed her papers into the zipped side-section of her travel bag and, throwing it onto her shoulder, headed for the children's playground with a lighter frame of mind.

Dumping the small backpack down beside the table where Brad and her mother sat, she slid onto a seat. "You'll never believe what happened. I got upgraded!"

Her eyes quickly searched the playground until she spotted her sons, and then swung back as her mother spoke, her voice edged with concern. "I hope it means you'll be able to get some sleep. I still wonder if this is too soon. Maybe you're not well enough yet to be rushing off to the other side of the world."

Brad reached out and covered Joy's hand. "I thought you were happy with Raven going."

"Oh, of course I am. It's just—I thought she'd be stronger by now."

"Don't be such an old worry wart, Mum. I'm as strong as a horse." She smiled across at Joy. "Look, it's after seven and I'm still awake. You know that's an improvement." Raven dropped the humorous tone as she realized how concerned her mother was about the upcoming flight. "Seriously, Mum. I feel so much better each day. I don't have any pain, and I've managed to knock my midday sleeps on the head. Well, for the last two days anyway," she appended honestly. "I can feel my muscles screaming to get back to normal. Within a few days I'm going to check out that circuit through the bush Brad mentioned."

"For Heaven's sake, don't start running through the bush!" Joy was aghast. "You would have no one to help you if you felt faint."

"It's called a forest," Brad inserted carefully.

"I don't care what it's called," Joy snapped playfully at Brad, and turning back to Raven. "I want you to promise me you won't go running in the bu—in the forest."

"I promise. But I am starting to feel like I could do something extra...not too much, though. I'll be fine, Mum, really, don't worry."

Brad consulted his watch. "What time is your boarding call, Rae?"

"Eight-thirty." Raven waved for the boys to join them.

"You'll want to have a little time after you go through Immigration to look around the duty-free shops and get to your departure gate. Shall we go and get the boys something to eat now? Then it'll just about be time for you to head through."

"McDonalds, McDonalds, McDonalds!" chanted the boys, jumping up and down beside him.

"Pardon. What did I hear?" Raven warned, looking sternly at the excited children.

She was not taken in by their attempt to look angelic; keeping a straight face was difficult as they stood straight and tall in front of their new grandfather.

"Yes, please, Brad." Scott's normal impish grin was firmly under control.

"Thank you, Brad," Tane added.

"You don't have to pretend to be angels, he already knows you're not." Raven stood. "But never forget your manners." She opened her mouth to continue as the boys joined in to recite the often-heard adage: "Manners maketh the man."

"Why, you two little ratbags..." Raven's fingers reached out to tickle them both. "Now let's go."

Time whizzed by, and all too soon Brad suggested it was time for Raven to leave.

She clung to her two boys. "I'm going to miss you guys so much!"

They hugged her tightly for a moment, then began to squirm.

"You be really good for Nana and Brad, won't you?"

"We're going to call him Granddad," Tane whispered close to her ear. "Do you think he'll like that?" Raven glanced up at Brad, who stood behind the boys with an arm around Joy.

"I think he just might," she said, smiling. She stood up to enfold her mother and Brad in a big hug. "Thank you so much. You've both been wonderful these past few weeks. I would never have managed without you."

"Of course you would," Joy scoffed, blinking to fend off tears. "Now off you go, and have a good time. No worrying about the boys." She glanced down at their shining faces. "We're going to be fine, aren't we, guys?"

"We sure are, Nana. Mum, do you know it's only fifteen more sleeps and we're going to America?" piped up Scott.

"Yes, I know. And I bet you can hardly wait."

"It's going to be so cool! Brad's going to take us to a fun park that's much bigger than Rainbow's End."

"I'm going on all the fast rides again and again, even if I get sick," added Tane.

"Not if I'm sitting beside you, you're not," Brad cut in.

Raven grimaced at the image. She shook her head, pretending to rebuke Tane, but her look caressed him and Scott before she bent to give them one last hug.

"I love you. See you in eighteen sleeps."

She rushed through the entrance to the Immigration area, not turning to wave until she was almost out of their sight. She didn't want the boys to see her tears, not when they were so excited and saw her trip as a forerunner to their own. She caught her breath in a sob. This was the first time she'd ever willingly left them and she'd miss them so much!

****

Joy watched her daughter disappear behind the large gray partition, knowing how she was feeling, understanding because she was feeling the same. She sighed, realising that she was probably being silly. Raven would be fine. This break was what she needed to get back on her feet. Still, she said, "Do you think she'll be all right?"

Brad's arm squeezed her shoulders. "She'll be fine. Don't worry about her."

"That was wonderful of you, arranging the upgrade." She looked at him closely. "You did arrange it, didn't you?"

"I knew she wouldn't accept anything but the cheapest fare. You know she wanted to pay for her and the boys. It was only my insisting that getting married at home had been my idea, so it was my responsibility to make sure your family was able to attend the service. Otherwise she'd have insisted on using all her savings to pay for the damned tickets." He hugged her tight against him. "This way she thinks she's had a lucky break, and we'll know she is getting a bit of extra attention and a lot more comfort during the flight."

"Thank you." Joy laid a gentle hand on his arm. "You're a very kind and thoughtful man, Brad Collins." She smiled up at him. "What have you told your children about her arrival?"

"Just that she's been ill and needs rest. Greg will take good care of her. Don't worry. He's had a few hard knocks, but he's a good boy. He and Raven will hit it off, I'm sure," he said, shrugging conspiratorially as they followed the boys up the escalator. "You know what she said: If she ever saw anyone who looked like me, she'd give it some thought." He grinned. "You've seen the photo of Greg, but Raven hasn't."

Joy couldn't help laughing. "You old matchmaker." Then her motherly instinct came to the fore. "Raven's not going to get hurt, is she?"

"I don't see why. They're exactly right for each other. All we have to do is hope they can see that." Brad's voice firmed in a mock threat. "They'd better! I don't want to take you away from your family."

Joy looked up at him. What a wonderful man, so gentle and considerate. "I've made my decision, Brad. It has no conditions attached." Momentarily she forgot Raven as she studied his handsome face. How was she supposed to continue to act normally when the anticipation of tonight was awakening all her senses?

Brad's face tightened as he read the message in her eyes. His arm squeezed her close against his side and he murmured, "Not long now, darling."

They called the boys and headed towards the observation deck so they could see Raven's plane depart Aotearoa. They both knew they must spend this next little while with the boys, making sure they were content without their mother. It was already well past their bedtime and they'd be asleep long before the car pulled into the garage in Devonport.

And *fortunately*, they were very sound sleepers.

Chapter 2

Greg entered the terminal at the Baltimore-Washington International Airport feeling about as relaxed as a tightly wound spring. He'd allowed himself ten minutes to spare. Any longer and he knew his agitation would increase tenfold.

He acknowledged that he'd never been a very patient man. He liked to stay busy, needing something to fill every second of the day; never allowing for dreaming or introspection. Looking back was too painful and dreams of the future were for fools. And Greg was no fool.

He headed for the nearest monitor and quickly ran his eye down the listed flight arrivals until he found the one he was waiting for.

Damn. His fists clenched. It had been delayed and was not now due to arrive until eleven-thirty. He consulted his watch, forty-five minutes. Not so long really, but to Greg, an eternity. How would he fill forty-five minutes in an airport, especially when he was already winding himself up to meet this woman?

He moved toward the gate where she'd be arriving. All the stalls and shops were closed and deserted. Only the long corridor in between showed signs of movement as people hurried along its narrow length, heads down, eyes fixed as they moved to their destinations. Perhaps it was the time of day, but their voices seemed hushed and muffled as they scurried one way or the other along this never-ending corridor of glass.

His mood couldn't have been more different from

the muted, passive surroundings. The words pounded in his brain with every step, gold digger, gold digger, gold digger. He was prepared for her if she showed just the barest sign of materialism— well, he was just the man to dish up her just desserts.

Finding an empty seat near the gate, he slowly sank onto it. He checked his watch. Less than five minutes had elapsed. He centered his thoughts on the woman he was waiting for, his soon-to-be stepmother. He still believed his father must have taken leave of his senses, or he'd been hoodwinked. Greg scoffed at the idea this could have been motivated by mutual love.

Love! Such an over-rated emotion.

His sister had been less upset than he had expected. In fact Abby had almost welcomed the idea, and that had surprised him. They'd always been close, tending to think alike on most topics. Yet this time she'd disagreed with him strongly.

That had given him pause for thought. He'd spent some time over the last couple of days trying to analyze his feelings, to determine why he was so against the idea of his father remarrying. Some of the thoughts that came to mind appalled him, causing him to look at himself more closely, and he hadn't much liked the picture he'd seen. He found himself trying to bury his distrust and rely on Abby's intuition. If she was right, then this woman did not deserve a hostile reception.

His father rightfully expected the family to embrace his new bride-to-be and do everything they could to make her feel at home. Greg sucked in a huge breath of air. He was going to try, for his father's sake, but it would not be easy to pretend a welcome he didn't feel, or hide the distrust he felt.

Greg glanced around at the others waiting for the delayed flight. His eyes were drawn to a woman sitting across from him, trying to subdue a clearly excited and very impatient young boy.

"How long now, Mama? How long until Daddy gets here?"

Greg couldn't hear her reply, but noticed her somewhat embarrassed glance as she tried to quiet his exuberance.

Greg looked away but found his attention drawn back to the boy. His gut tightened as painful memories invaded, memories he never allowed to surface during his busy days. But sometimes they still caught up with him while he slept and couldn't control where his mind went.

Would Ethan have acted like that, been so impatient to see his dad? Would he have been so vocal and demanding? Greg found his thoughts moving further. Would his boy's hair have been that sandy blond? Ethan's eyes had been blue...

Greg leapt to his feet and strode to the huge window, fists clenched in his pockets. He stared into the darkness, blinking rapidly. For God's sake, it had been six years. Why did he have to start remembering now? That was from another time, another life. As his deep breaths calmed him, he turned and glared across the waiting area at the child willing himself to forget, pushing the agonizing memories into a place where he could at least pretend to himself they were forgotten.

He checked his watch again. Time was slowly ticking by, but oh so slowly. Pacing down the corridor a little way, he paused to look into some of the shop windows, not seeing anything but the reflection of his face. The cold emptiness he saw in the eyes staring back at him caused him to hurriedly look away.

At last the plane arrived. Greg moved back to the waiting area slowly, his mind returning to his father's bride. What would she be like? His father had not described her at all, so he had no idea whom he was looking for. Was she tall or short, big or small, dark or fair?

Oh, definitely dark. He knew that. What else would someone called Raven be but black-haired? But how old was she? He supposed in her fifties. Perhaps he should have brought a placard with her name on it. He'd seen that done many times. Then he scoffed at the thought. If she was going to marry Brad, there was no chance she would fail to recognize Greg as his son.

Greg couldn't help but notice the first person up the walkway and past the empty security counters was 'Daddy'—a young man in a crinkled suit, whose briefcase fell to the floor forgotten as he swung his son into his arms. Greg tore his eyes away, but not before noticing the father was obviously as eager to be reunited as the boy had been. Again his fists clenched, envying the young man.

He quickly forced his eyes into the shadowy depth of the tunnel, trying to determine which passenger was Raven. Perhaps her hair was no longer black, but gray, or even white. He made to move forward as a lone woman came through, but her eyes were drawn to another group who called her name. There were suited businessmen, a couple of families, and a very nice young woman who caught Greg's eye for a moment and gave him a knowing smile. Greg found his eyes following her, enjoying the sway of her bottom as she walked off down the corridor towards the escalator. He was still watching when a voice penetrated his thoughts.

"Greg? Hello, I'm Raven Titirangi."

He swung around, ready to make some inane welcoming remark and stopped, aghast.

****

It had been a long flight. Well, two flights really, but still less than twenty-four hours since she'd left

Auckland. In fact, it was now only three hours later than when she'd said her good-byes; by the clock, that was. But she had never known a day to take so long. She'd left Auckland convincing herself she'd enjoy this whole experience, but the pleasure and excitement had slowly diminished.

The first flight had been fun. Perhaps excitement had caused sleep to elude her, but now she was paying for that. She'd considered the sleeping pills in her bag, but had avoided them. Now she wished she'd taken some. At least then she might have been feeling less washed out and drained.

The wait in Los Angeles had dragged, with her trying to stay awake for fear of missing the boarding notice when it came. Then this last leg, to Baltimore, had been a killer. The flight had been delayed due to equipment problems. Then her assigned seat had been beside an older lady who was inclined to chatter, so Raven never managed to get a wink of sleep during this five-hour flight either.

Her visit to the toilet shortly before landing had confirmed what she'd suspected. She looked terrible, pale and drawn, hair a frizzy mess and clothing wrinkled and grubby. Oh well, not much she could do about it. She sighed, moving slowly through the tunnel, her eyes trying to distinguish the people waiting.

She stopped near the end of the tunnel. Leaning against the wall for a moment to catch her breath, her eyes flew upward as she uttered a quick prayer. "Please let them be as nice as Brad."

He'd told her not to worry, that either Greg or Abby would meet her. She'd half expected to find her name plastered across a piece of cardboard so she'd know them. As she heaved her bag onto the other shoulder and pushed away from the wall, she knew she didn't need a placard.

Brad's look-alike stood there—a much younger Brad, but a nearly exact duplicate just the same. No wonder Brad had told her not to worry! She could see Greg's eyes flickering over the passengers as he looked for her. It was such a relief to see him there, to know he was just like Brad. This is going to be all right.

She paused near him, watching as his eyes followed a Barbie-doll type. She smirked a bit as she noted his gaze travelling up and down, then centering on Barbie's bottom with its exaggerated sway.

Raven had a moment to study him. He was a little taller than Brad and wider across the shoulders. His hair was lighter too, now that she looked more closely. The blond length of it curled down under his collar. The darkness of his coat was a perfect foil to show off his fair hair and tanned face. As it was late winter here, Raven realised that his face probably stayed that shade or maybe went even darker in the summer. She couldn't see a freckle anywhere. Surely that was unusual with such fair hair. At home almost every light-haired person had at least a few freckles. Hers were scattered across her nose.

"Greg? Hello, I'm Raven Titirangi."

She watched a lock of hair fall across his forehead as his head swiveled at her words. She noticed a small scar, cutting through his left eyebrow, giving him a vaguely rakish look. He looked incredibly sexy.

Wow, she breathed, astounded where her thoughts were taking her. She looked up into his eyes. *They aren't like Brad's at all. What colour are they? Not green, or brown, or even hazel, but a mixture, with some yellow thrown in as well. Intriguing is what they are.*

She pulled herself up. *What's the matter with*

me? It's a long, long time since I've had these sorts of thoughts about a man.

This is Brad's son; don't be crazy!

He was looking at her with such a strange expression. *Oh no! He hasn't guessed what was rushing through my mind, has he?*

****

Greg sucked in his breath, his chest tight. He knew he was staring, even as he watched the smile disappear and uncertainty grow in her expression. He saw her hand slowly falling back to her side, but he couldn't speak.

This could not be happening. It had to be the brunt of some cruel joke. His father couldn't be considering marrying this—this girl. He stumbled over the word.

She looked young to him, and he'd just turned thirty-three. This had to make her thirty-five, maybe even forty years younger than his dad.

His gaze slid to her breasts as she shrugged her bag higher onto her shoulder. The movement caused the material to stretch across them, outlining the shape that had previously been disguised by the pale blue sweater she wore. He couldn't help but notice their round fullness before his eyes guiltily returned to her face.

She was tall, only a few inches shorter than he. Her hair was fair, darker than blond but still definitely fair. Its short cut surrounded her face with soft curls that looked like they had a mind of their own. Somehow the windswept look didn't seem the least bit untidy.

He couldn't help but notice the way she stiffened her back and lifted her head a fraction higher as she endured his stare. Her full lips tightened under his gaze.

Her eyes were brown, with flecks of green dancing in them, but they seemed rather lackluster, he thought. Then he noticed her skin pulled tight across her high cheekbones and remembered she'd been ill; she probably was still recuperating. The few freckles across her straight nose accentuated the pallor of her face. He almost forgot his animosity for a moment as he wondered if she was as close to collapse as she appeared.

Something told him that she would not ask for help.

"I'm sorry," he spoke quickly, embarrassed by his bad manners. "I was expecting someone—"

What can I say? Think of something, quickly. I can't say 'someone older, much older than you.'

"Umm—someone dark," he finished lamely.

He wasn't surprised when she looked confused. He surely was!

"Your name. I—I expected you to be dark."

Raven's voice was indifferent. "I had black hair as a baby."

Greg's arm quickly snaked out to grab hold of her as she swayed. "Are you okay?" A stupid question, her derisive upward glance told him. She was far from okay. He was surprised how frail she felt under his arm, how she sagged against him despite her attempt to remain upright.

"Here, sit for a minute." He helped her gently into one of the chairs, his preoccupation with the coming marriage replaced by growing concern for Raven's health. "I'll be right back."

****

Raven closed her eyes, leaned back against the seat, and tried to steady her breathing. She felt so weak. This is embarrassing! Not a good start at all.

Her mind drifted for a second, and she saw those eyes again. The sort of eyes one could get lost in, mysterious and oddly compelling. Don't be so ridiculous, scolding herself as she made an effort to keep her own eyes open.

31

What was wrong? Something was definitely wrong. Or was her brain even fuzzier than she realised? No. Greg's welcome was less than warm. She could feel antipathy radiating from him. Her lips tightened. She'd been relieved and comforted by the sight of him, but now she admitted ruefully, this was not Brad. He might look like Brad but it appeared that's where the similarity ended.

She watched his approach from further down the corridor, accompanied by an airport porter pushing a wheelchair.

For goodness sake, I'm not getting into that thing. Even if I'm a bit tired, I'm not decrepit. Yet. She tried to sit herself upright, but quickly sank back into the chair and watched him through half closed eyes.

She observed the way he walked, placing each foot on the ground, and then rolling forward onto his toes, adding a spring to each step. Is he an athlete? He surely had the body for it. Maybe basketball, that would explain the bounce—or was that hard body just the result of years of physical work? She knew from Brad that Greg enjoyed hard work, preferring to spend his day on the building sites, not in the office. Whichever it was, there was nothing wrong with that body.

The porter pulled the wheelchair close beside the seat and Greg gently helped Raven into it. She felt his strength as he steadied her but she was surprised by his gentleness. There was an air of impatience about him as though her weakness annoyed him, and yet his compassion was clearly evident.

Almost as if he guessed how disquieting this was to Raven, he smiled as he tried to lighten the atmosphere. "This has sure got to beat walking."

They entered the elevator, then down to the baggage claim area. At least with the porter accompanying them, conversation was not necessary and Raven had a chance to collect her thoughts. While Greg's attention was all anyone could expect from a stranger, Raven was very concerned. There was a tension about him. She had not imagined the way his face had tightened as she had introduced herself. What had he expected? What has Brad said about me? Something seemed wrong, but what?

As they waited near the luggage carousel, Greg attempted to make small talk, asking about her flight, talking about the time differences, jetlag. Raven kept flexing her fingers, trying to stay alert. Even as waves of tiredness rolled over her, she knew she must pay careful attention, trying to figure out what was wrong, listening to every nuance of his voice.

"How's my father?"

"Oh, he's wonderful." Raven's voice softened. "I think he's looking forward to coming home, though."

Aware of the coldness with which he surveyed her through narrowed eyes, she kept her voice neutral.

"So why didn't he travel with you?"

Raven looked up at him, puzzled.

Why? Why on earth would he want to do that?

"I don't understand..." she began, but was prevented from saying more by the sudden push of passengers crowding around the carousel. Conversation was impossible as people jostled around, grabbing their suitcases. Greg leaned forward and seized the suitcase Raven indicated and carried it to just inside the exit. The porter followed, expertly manoeuvring the wheelchair through the crowd.

"Wait here," Greg commanded. "I'll get the car."

"I'm perfectly capable of walking, you know." Raven felt the need to assert herself as she began to lift herself out of the chair.

A firm hand on her shoulder forced her back. "Stay there," he ordered. "It might be worth putting on a coat if you have one. It's about thirty degrees outside."

She didn't much like the condescending tone in his voice, but before she could retort he'd passed through the automatic doors. Thirty degrees, she mused. They still used Fahrenheit over here. With a frown she gradually recalled the equation she learned as a child and converted the temperature to Celsius. Wow. Definitely time to dig out the coat. Auckland had been at the end of an unusually hot summer when she'd left.

Have I been optimistic, expecting a friendly, warm welcome here? She took a deep breath, trying to rationalize the coolness of her reception. Oh well, perhaps thirty degrees wasn't so cold after all. It wouldn't be as chilly as the arctic depth in his eyes.

****

As Greg pulled up beside the large glass doors, he could see her sitting exactly where he'd left her. At least she can do as she's told, he thought as he saw she now wore a warm ski jacket. He tried not to appreciate how much that deep shade of blue suited her, how her cheeks had acquired some color, how perfect her features were.

He pulled himself up short, his breath catching in his throat. He had to bury any inappropriate feelings of attraction. Bury them very deep. This woman is going to be my stepmother. No matter how much he might disapprove, he would never hurt his father.

"All ready?" he asked unnecessarily as he slipped a hand under her elbow and helped her to her feet. Tipping the skycap, he picked up her suitcase and led the way out the door, carefully keeping his hand on her arm. He heard her gasp as the freezing air hit them and felt her shrinking into the folds of her jacket as she hunched herself against the wind. Quickly he helped her into the car and shut the door. After tossing the suitcase into the trunk he slid behind the wheel and started the engine.

Drawing a blanket off the back seat, he carefully tucked it around her knees. "The car will be warm in just a minute."

"Thank you." She snuggled into its warmth. "Do we have far to go?"

"About thirty minutes. Traffic shouldn't be a problem at this time of night."

Raven felt very awkward again. "I'm sorry you had to come out so late," she said stiltedly.

Greg shrugged. "It's what Dad expected."

He might feel sorry for her, but he couldn't bring himself to pretend she was welcome here.

He had to know. He couldn't hold back the questions any longer. "So how did you come to meet my father?" he asked as he pulled onto I-195.

"We actually ran into each other, literally." She almost chuckled. Again her voice seemed to soften. Although he couldn't see her face clearly now, he imagined her eyes had softened too.

"We were on a fun run and kinda tripped over each other. They're always a real mess at the start. Brad and I got tangled up, then ended up pacing each other the whole race. We really hit it off. He's a lovely man." She turned towards him. "You're very lucky."

She continued, not knowing that with each sentence she was tightening the tension within him. She talked quietly of his father's caring and generosity, of how helpful he had been, and how his kindness had changed her life so much.

Greg hadn't noticed her voice slowing down, her words becoming slurred. His hands were clenched on the steering wheel, fury mounting with each syllable she uttered. It was obvious to him what she meant: His father's wealth had changed her life, his generosity was the kindness she spoke of.

"Is that why you're marrying him? Because of his generosity?"

From the corner of his eye he noticed her head had turned away from him, and he heard a weary sigh. She murmured something unintelligible. He realized she had finally given in to fatigue. Raven was sound asleep.

Even as the car pulled to a stop in the garage she still did not move. Greg looked down at her for a moment. She looked so young and defenseless.

How looks could lie, he thought as he retrieved her suitcase and took it into the house. He moved straight up the stairs and into the guest room Manuela had prepared. Glancing around, he knew everything would be in order.

Putting the suitcase down, he headed back to the garage to waken her.

"Raven. Raven." He was damned if he was going to call her Ms. Titirangi. He wasn't sure if he could pronounce it properly anyway. He bent over and shook her. "Raven, we're here."

He was surprised at how vulnerable she looked as she opened her eyes, like she was uncertain where she was, who he was.

Then she must have remembered. She pulled away from his hand, and he saw the wariness that came into her expression.

"Here, let me help you." He could tell she hated having to accept his support, but realized she was intelligent enough to know it was necessary, for the moment at least.

He escorted her to the bedroom, showed her its connecting bathroom, and told her quietly, "Sleep as long as you need to. If you make your way down to the front foyer when you feel rested, you'll be able to find Manuela, our housekeeper, or me. Goodnight, Raven. Sleep well."

Tomorrow would be soon enough to tackle how he was going to deal with her.

Chapter 3

Raven woke up feeling woolly-headed. She looked around, searching for something recognizable. Nothing looked familiar, and for a split second she felt a rising panic. Then she smiled at her own silliness. She was at Brad's house in Ellicott City. Greg had left her in this lovely room, suggesting she should rest here as long as she needed.

The white painted walls, with soft green curtains complemented the eiderdown on the large bed she'd snuggled into. There was a dressing table with a large mirror across from the bed, and intriguing lamps on the night stands at each side of the bed. She found herself frowning up at the ceiling. Where were the lights?

There were no lights. Her eyes flew to the wall next to the door. There was a light switch, but no lights. How weird.

Raven stretched, easing her body gently, waiting for any telltale signs of strain. When she felt nothing, she knew sleep had rejuvenated her. She felt almost like her old self.

It had been a long time since she'd slept this late. She looked at the watch still on her wrist, and then realised she had not reset it since Los Angeles. How many hours is Baltimore behind Los Angeles? She couldn't remember but it didn't matter really. Since she'd probably slept for hours, it might well be afternoon.

She swung her legs out of bed and dug her toes into the luxurious carpet. It was then Raven noticed a cloth-covered tray sitting on a small table near the door. She moved closer and found a jug of orange juice and a glass. Also, in an airtight container, two large iced buns. Raven could see a jam-like filling in each, one lemony and other some berry flavour. She shuddered at the thought of eating them now. Even though they looked very nice, and she felt ravenous, they were definitely not suitable for breakfast. She didn't care what time of day it might be, her next meal would be breakfast. Still, how thoughtful of someone to bring the tray to her room. She hadn't heard a sound.

As she sipped the orange juice she reached out a hand to the light switch. She frowned. It was already on. Intrigued, she switched it off, and grinned as one of the bedside lamps illuminated. Must be a two-way switch, she mused as she headed to the bathroom. Running her fingers down the wall until she felt a switch, again in the 'on' position, she flicked it 'off', then gasped as the blazing light allowed her to see the elegance of the room. She couldn't remember even noticing last night. In one corner there was a large triangular spa bathtub. A shower cubicle stood in the opposite corner, while matching white vanities ran the length of the room. Raven had only seen such opulence in movies, or decorating magazines. Never had she experienced it firsthand.

A huge mirror covered one entire wall. Raven grinned at herself. What a holiday this was going to be—five-star accommodation, no less.

Moving back into the bedroom, she hurried over to the window, eagerly looking out from what she guessed would be the side of the house.

Her eyes widened in amazement. The area was as perfect as any park. Lawns square metre upon square metre, neatly trimmed and interspersed with tall dormant trees, shrubs and empty worked beds, probably for spring flowers. A high hedge, amassed with yellow flowers, bordered the garden as far as she could see. Concrete pathways meandered through the area. She noticed a number of wooden seats, some under the larger trees while others were dotted around making the setting even more park-like.

Raven leaned closer against the glass, trying to see around the corner.

What a truly lovely site, she smiled. Joy was going to love this garden; although, she may have to compete with professional gardeners to potter around out there, Raven suspected.

She turned from the window and surveyed her open suitcase on a luggage stand at the end of her bed. No point in staying up here, lovely though the room was. She needed to socialise with her new 'family' and generally test the water.

She remembered a little of the ride from the airport. She had nervously chattered about Brad and how she'd met him. But then, she realised guiltily, she'd fallen asleep. She must apologise to Greg as soon as possible. Falling asleep on one's host at their first meeting did not make for a very good first impression—especially when the first meeting hadn't gone that well anyway. She must do everything possible to improve the situation before her mother's arrival.

She sighed. Time to make a move. She took her toiletries from her suitcase and headed for the shower.

The warm water felt like heaven. She'd fallen into the bed last night after removing only her outer garments, not having the strength, or the inclination, to think about anything but sleep. But now, oh the water was so refreshing! Raven held her face up into the spray and savoured the gentle needle pricks against her skin.

Her body was benefiting from the watery

massage, but her mind could not relax. There was something wrong, and it hadn't just been her imagination. Greg seemed to resent her. She closed her eyes and visualised him. He'd been kind to her, she remembered, when he'd rushed off for the wheelchair, but there was animosity there. She sensed the lack of welcome, even through his impeccable manners. He did not want her here.

Why? Did he dislike the idea of his father remarrying so much that he would react this way to anyone associated with a new Mrs. Collins? Raven had to find out straight away whatever was causing this and get it smoothed over before Joy arrived. Nothing must blight her mother's happiness.

Raven turned off the shower and quickly dried herself, absently noting that the small scar from her operation was getting less noticeable, just as the doctor had assured her it would. She tried a couple of gentle stretches and smiled as she felt no strain. Great! Maybe tomorrow she could try some real exercise.

Not sure of the dress code within the house, Raven slipped on black jeans and a bright red shirt. She dismissed her running shoes and instead slipped on a low-heeled pair of black dress shoes she'd brought for evening wear. They gave her a little added height, and a sense of increased formality to the more casual clothes she'd chosen.

She sat in front of the dressing table mirror and looked at her hair. A mess as usual, she thought. If only she'd thought to bring her dryer. Even as the thought came to mind, she dismissed it. The appliance wouldn't have worked over here anyway, not without a power converter.

Oh, what does it matter? She ran her fingers through the damp curls and let them fall, hoping they looked like they'd been painstakingly placed. She quickly applied moisturiser to her face. Central heating meant the room was at a lovely temperature, but her skin and throat felt dry. Raven poured herself another glass of orange juice.

She studied her face in the mirror for a moment. No makeup, she decided; didn't want to give the impression she needed to 'paint' her face before setting foot out of her room. She didn't do it at home.

She stood and did a little pirouette. Yes, a definite improvement on her attempt to tidy herself on the aeroplane before landing. She took a deep breath and headed for the door, absently noticing it opened the wrong way. She glanced at the light switch, flicked it on and off again. It was upside down. She'd known about the cars, and Americans driving on the wrong side of the road, but not upside down light switches and back to front doors. *What else am I going to find different?* She grinned, filled with the confidence that she was about to begin a wonderful holiday. She felt great. Excitement lightened her feet as she ran down the stairs.

Raven stood at the bottom of the stairs, looking around. There was graciousness about the house. It must be huge. The foyer was bigger than their whole lounge at home. The staircase, wide and with intricately carved banisters, swept up from the foyer to the second floor landing she'd just left. She paused to study the large sculptured window at the half landing, her artist's eye appreciating the way the sun's rays were captured in the glass sending multicoloured reflections down into the foyer. The wooden floor gleamed under the brightly coloured floor-mats that were scattered across it. Again, Raven got the impression of wealth and elegance. A large chandelier, its many lamps too numerous to count, dominated the area.

Her eyes were drawn to the framed oil paintings on the white walls. Nothing she recognised, but they were originals, not prints.

Not for the first time she wondered about Brad's status. He seemed so down to earth and ordinary, but sometimes she'd suspected he was a lot wealthier than he led them to believe. Already she knew, with what she'd been able to see out her window, and in this foyer; this was not the home of a man who 'ran a small construction business'.

She had no idea which direction to take to find anyone, and was hesitant to open any of the closed doors she could see. Just then, a phone rang close by. She moved toward the noise and was approaching an ajar door when she heard a voice answer. Greg's, she was sure.

"Where have you been?" she heard him demand. Then after a pause, he said, "Yes, she arrived safely. Yes, I took care of her." Another pause. "No, she hasn't come down yet. She was pretty wiped out, I guess."

Raven lifted her hand to tap on the door, not wishing to eavesdrop on this one-sided conversation, but something stayed her hand for a moment.

"What's wrong? I'll tell you what's wrong! Abby, she's younger than you. I doubt if she's twenty-five."

Raven was chuffed to have so many years taken off her age, even as she caught the dismayed tone in his voice.

"Of course I'm sure. I was waiting for some middle-aged woman to get off the plane and suddenly this fox was talking to me. I tell you, she isn't as old as you. No way this is a love match, Abby. How can Dad even think of marrying someone like that?"

Raven gasped. How had this happened? Greg was talking to his sister and they had definitely got hold of the wrong end of the stick. They thought *she* was going to marry Brad. No wonder Greg's reception had been cool! Raven smiled as she pushed the door slightly. She'd clear up this

43

misunderstanding straight away...

Raven could see the back of Greg's head. He was sitting behind a large desk, but had swung the chair around facing the window, the phone pressed against his ear. His constant jerky movements clearly showed his agitation.

"There is no way someone like her could be physically attracted to a man of Dad's age. For God's sake, he could almost be her grandfather! We have to do something to stop this wedding. She's obviously after his money, or whatever else she can get out of him."

Raven froze. Someone like her! She listened unashamedly now. What gave him the right to make assumptions about her?

"I don't know. Okay, I guess. She has legs that go on forever. Bet she knows how to use them, too. Inveigling an old man into believing she loves him. It's disgusting."

"What was she wearing? How do I know? Cheap blue jeans and a sweater." Again a pause while he listened. "I can recognize decent clothing when I see it." Raven felt the blood rush into her face as she glanced down at her clothes. They may not be designer, but they were clean and tidy.

"Her luggage couldn't have cost more than a couple of hours' wages, either."

The arrogant snob!

How dare they discuss her like this? Even if they had somehow misunderstood Brad, they had no right to brand her as a gold digger. Decent people would have waited until they'd met her properly, asked her outright why she was marrying Brad. One thing for sure, now Brad's wealth was no longer in question.

She took a deep breath. Someone quiet and shy might not have coped with the derision in Greg's voice. But Raven had had to learn to be strong and stand up for herself. She wasn't about to allow anyone to assume such things about her. If her mother arrived and encountered such snobbery, her happiness with Brad would be in jeopardy. Raven was in no doubt her mother would sacrifice her new life if Brad's children weren't completely happy about their marriage.

Raven backed out of the room quietly, dismayed that they seemed to be dismissing their father's feelings with so little regard.

A plan was already formulating—she'd show them a thing or two about good manners and politeness. They seemed to be sadly lacking in that department, even if they did have money.

So they think I'm an unsuitable wife for Brad? I'll show them unsuitable! By the time they meet Mum, they'll be so relieved that Brad is marrying her and not me that they'll welcome her with open arms. Mum is not going to be subjected to any of this contempt! If Joy caught even the slightest whiff of disapproval—Raven had to make sure Joy seemed like an angel sent from heaven by comparison.

She rushed back up to her room, forgetting her new lack of fitness. She had to stop and catch her breath for a moment. Being puffed out by a short flight of stairs—damn, when would she be back to normal?

Rummaging through her suitcase Raven found a workout crop top, one that really wasn't suited to the middle of winter. There was quite a bit of midriff between it and the top of her jeans, but she threw it on quickly. It was one of her favourites, and it had seen many washes. She was sure Greg would recognize it as being well-worn. She kicked off her shoes and rumpled her hair. Raven paused to take some calming deep breaths. She was so angry right now, she might blow it if she didn't calm down. Otherwise she'd overplay her hand in an attempt to get back at him.

"Arrogant swine," she muttered as she counted to ten for the second time.

It was then that she noticed the rings on her hand. A woman about to be re-married would hardly still wear her previous wedding band. The fingers of her right hand caught hold of the jewelry and gently twisted them around her finger. She had never considered taking them off before, they were so much a part of her.

No. Taking them off could not be an option, she decided. But as she headed for the door, something stayed her movement, and as if there was someone else guiding her fingers, she watched the two rings slip off her left hand and onto her right finger. They felt strange and heavy there.

Her left hand was now desolate and bare, a white band around the skin where the sun had not reached for so many years. Raven flopped onto the bed, feeling very strange. Was this something that she'd needed to do? Acknowledge that Chris was part of her past, and could never again be in her present? Was it time for her to move on?

No!

She needed more time to consider the emotions and ramifications of no longer being a married woman. Was she ready for that? Would she ever be ready?

For now she could elect to reason she had removed her wedding band because of her need to smooth things out for her mother. She had to play this part to the hilt, or it was not worth playing at all. It was as if she was an actress, in a role that required no rings. That was why they had to swap hands.

Yes, that was all.

She got up and headed out the door.

Raven paused halfway down the stairs and

listened carefully. The house was silent. She moved down further and took a deep breath.

"Co-eee!" she called at the top of her voice. She smiled grimly as she heard the sudden bang coming from the room he'd been in.

Good, she thought, *I hope he's hurt himself.* She visualised him falling off his chair, although whether he had, she would never know. She saw him hurrying towards her out of the corner of her eye, as she appeared to study the paintings on the walls.

"Oh, Greg. Gidday." She reached out her hand and, grasping his, pumped it up and down. "It was so nice of you to come out and get me last night. I'm so sorry I fell asleep. I've been ill, you know," she gushed. "These are really cool paintings. Are the artists famous? I don't recognize any of them, but they look like they might be quite valuable."

She had to remember to talk really fast. Americans talked much slower, and she might be able to frustrate him if he had trouble understanding her.

"I'm an artist myself, you see." She couldn't quite bring herself to flutter her eyelashes at him.

"Oh, what a beautiful house Brad has! I'm going to love living here." She slipped her arm through his. "Do you live here, too?" Raven knew full well the house was actually Greg's now, and that father and son had recently adapted the rear wing into an apartment for Brad. If she hadn't been so annoyed, she would have laughed at the expression on Greg's face. She had him dumbfounded.

"Oh, I hope you don't mind me not wearing shoes." She surreptitiously watched his gaze fall to her bare feet as she moved away from him to examine another painting. "I hate shoes. They're so restricting, don't you think? I like to feel free." She almost tripped as she tried to do a pirouette on the edge of one of the carpet squares, but thankfully he seemed to be captivated by her toes. The red enamel tips do look kind of cute, she thought, twitching them a little.

Just as she was wondering what she could do next, a large woman scurried around from the back of the stairs. Raven heard doors swinging closed as the woman moved toward them.

"What on earth is all the noise about, Mr. Greg?" she demanded. The woman's tone suggested a high degree of familiarity, despite the apron tied around her ample body.

Before Greg could say a word, Raven jumped in. "Gidday." She held out her hand. "You must be Manuela. Brad's told me so much about you and Jorge. Did I pronounce the names correctly? I hope so. I'm Raven Titirangi. Please call me Raven." She slowed her speech a little and stopped the gush. She was annoyed with Greg and Abby, but there was no reason to offend this woman, whom Brad treasured so.

Manuela took the offered hand, a puzzled expression on her face. Raven realised she would have to be very careful. This lady was a very intricate part of the family, and if she guessed Raven was playing a game, well, her sympathies would lie with Greg and Abby.

"Was it you who brought the tray to my room? Thank you so much." The gush was back, just toned down a little. "I really needed a drink when I woke up. That was very kind of you. I'm afraid I never ate the cakes, though," she told the housekeeper apologetically. "It felt like breakfast when I woke up, a bit too early for cake. I would like to try them later though, if that's okay?"

Raven felt the need to keep on Manuela's right side. Joy would be closely involved with the housekeeper after the wedding and it was so important that Raven not cause any real feelings of animosity.

"Of course." Manuela smiled. "Mr. Greg, haven't you offered your guest anything to eat?" Raven was surprised he didn't seem to mind the chastisement in the housekeeper's voice. "Come with me." She bustled Raven around through batwing doors and into a huge, airy kitchen.

As Greg followed behind them Raven smiled, catching his muttered "Who could get a word in?"

"Now, what can we get for you?" Manuela moved towards the fridge. "Some coffee first? Pour her a coffee, Greg."

Raven was pleased to forestall that. She had no intention of having him wait on her. "No, thank you. I don't drink coffee."

"Don't drink coffee?" Manuela sounded horrified. "How can anyone live without coffee, especially first thing in the morning?" But her smile took any derision out of her words. "Would you like some more juice then?"

"Thanks, that would be lovely."

"What else would you like? Fresh fruit, perhaps?"

"Oh, that would be divine." Raven had noticed a frown gathering on Greg's face as he sat quietly drinking coffee. She hoped he believed the girl he'd picked up from the airport had been quieter due to exhaustion, and this was the real Raven.

"This bench top has the most amazing colour." She ran her fingers across the hard surface, genuinely admiring the depth of shades visible in the stone. "It's not granite, is it? Is it synthetic? They've done a great job making it look like real stone."

The haughty look down his nose told her what she already knew. The bench was definitely natural. And probably very expensive.

Still caressing the cool surface, she hitched

herself further up onto the stool beside the breakfast bar. Twiddling her toes again, she made sure they were clearly visible to Greg. Sure enough, his eyes were again riveted to her red nails. She smiled. This might get to be fun yet.

"This is a lovely kitchen, far bigger than mine at home. And you have so many electrical gadgets. Bet you could cook almost anything in a kitchen like this."

It might be fun, but it wouldn't be easy. She had to keep thinking of inane things to prattle on about, if she was going to give him the impression she was some empty-headed bimbo looking for the easy life.

Jumping off the stool, she headed for the window. "I can't get over all the dead trees. Do they have some disease or something? Are you going to have to cut them all down?" She glanced over her shoulder in time to see an incredulous look pass between Greg and Manuela. Had she overplayed that a bit too much? She swung back into the kitchen. "Oh, silly me," she said, giggling. "They're deciduous trees, aren't they?"

Greg's eyebrows rose, as if surprised she would even know the word. Raven's lips compressed. She wanted Greg to think she was different from whom she really was, but he needn't think she was completely without brains. "It's just that our bush is evergreen. I've never seen deciduous bush...whoops...I mean forest. Brad told me it's called a forest. It looks so strange, all dead and bare."

She was never one to miss an opportunity. "It must look wonderful in the autumn. I can't wait to see all the colours." She heard Greg's gasp and continued to hammer home her point. "I don't see too many of the trees from my room. I'd love to wake up in the morning and be able to look out the window at the autumn colours. I'm sure it will look so lovely.

Does Brad's room overlook the forest?"

Her lips twitched as Greg slammed down his mug and left the room, banging the batwings so hard they hit the wall. She felt herself blush a little as Manuela turned from the bench with a variety of cut-up fruit arranged on a serving plate.

"If you would like to come this way," Manuela beckoned.

"Oh, couldn't I have them here, with you?"

Manuela eyed her closely as she placed the plate on the breakfast bar. Raven realised she'd let her voice revert to normal. In her desire not to be relegated to a formal dining room where she'd have to eat alone, she had forgotten to broaden her accent. But she'd been alone long enough during the last couple of days and hadn't wanted to eat alone again.

Raven actually found it quite easy to talk to Manuela. She just remembered to throw in lots of gushy words, like super, wonderful, lovely, and divine; and to keep the subjects very impersonal.

Without Greg's unusual eyes trying to bore into her very soul, she found herself relaxing and enjoying the time chatting with Manuela. She met her husband, Jorge, when he came in and joined his wife for coffee. Raven learned the couple had immigrated to America from Peru as newlyweds. At first Jorge had worked with Brad's construction crew, but now concentrated his efforts working around the house and substantial gardens that surrounded it. Raven noticed he had quite a bad limp, and wondered if he'd suffered some work-related injury that curtailed his construction work.

Manuela proudly boasted that she had been Brad's housekeeper for almost thirty years, joining the family as a twice-a-week cleaning lady and gradually increasing the workload as Brad's lifestyle prospered. She had watched the children grow up and marry, had helped out when his wife became ill, and pitched in even more when the woman passed away. Manuela and Jorge now lived in an apartment above the garage, moving there after their youngest son left home to join the Marines. Their elder boy was a foreman, working for Brad.

It took Raven very little time to realise that while Brad might employ them, they considered themselves very much part of his family.

She'd have to be very careful. Upsetting these people could cause heartfelt repercussions. She guessed that their approval would be very beneficial in her effort to ease Joy's arrival.

She sensed that Manuela would not condone this act, no matter what the justification. Already, Raven knew it would be seen as dishonest. Raven cringed a little at the thought. She too, was basically a very honest person. Now that her temper had cooled, she began to doubt the wisdom of her actions. Perhaps she'd been too hasty. She could appreciate what a surprise her appearance must have been to Greg when he'd been expecting his father's fiancée. Maybe she should own up before things got out of hand.

The kitchen batwings suddenly flew open, announcing the arrival of the subject of her thoughts. "Do you have anything a little more—" There was a pointed pause, as cold eyes travelled from the top of her head to the red tips of her enamelled toes before disdainfully settling on her face. "—Suitable to wear? We've been invited to my sister's for dinner. She's looking forward to meeting you."

I'll bet, thought Raven, sliding off the barstool. Suddenly, any thoughts of stopping this farce disappeared with the condescending tone of Greg's voice.

"Of course, Greggie, I have this simply divine black gown that Brad absolutely adores. I'll wear that, shall I?" She tilted her head so she was gazing up into his face. Presumptuous oaf, she smiled, gritting her teeth at the same time.

"There's no need to *dress* for dinner."

Greg spoke as if to a child, or more likely an imbecile, Raven thought. "Perhaps something a little tidier than...than what you have on now."

He seemed to stumble trying to find the proper words. "And shoes. It would be appropriate to wear shoes."

Raven couldn't help it. She laughed. *This is fun. And it really serves him right, after all.* Slipping quickly into her part again, she replied, "Of course I'll wear shoes, Greggie, if you think that's really necessary."

"Can you be ready in thirty minutes?"

"Of course. Whenever you say. Shall I meet you in the foyer? Oh, whoops! I haven't reset my watch." She un-strapped it from her wrist. "What is the time anyway? I don't want to keep you waiting."

Consulting the gold watch on his own wrist, he said, "Five-of-four."

Raven looked up in surprise. She hadn't realised there were ways of telling the time that she wouldn't understand. "I'm sorry, I don't understand. Is that before or after four?"

Greg's eyes narrowed and Raven realised in her surprise, she'd forgotten her accent.

"Five minutes before four o'clock." He spoke slowly, pronouncing each word separately, then turned and left the kitchen.

Raven felt her hackles rising still further as she busied herself resetting and replacing her watch.

I'd love to get him in New Zealand, she thought uncharitably. *I'd soon make him feel like a fish out of water. Arrogant pig.*

"Don't worry about what you wear, chica. People see beyond clothes."

Manuela's tone was gentle, and Raven smiled gratefully. "What do you think would be suitable, Manuela? I don't want to cause any extra hassles."

"Do you have a blouse perhaps instead of that tee-shirt? And you need a sweater. It'll be warm in the house, but it's a little cooler than you're used to outside, I think. Your jeans are fine, that's all the girls wear nowadays. Don't go worrying about Miss Abby. She's a friendly girl. You won't get any grief from her."

"You're very kind. Thank you, Manuela."

Raven stopped her act. She guessed this was a very astute woman; she might have already seen beyond clothes. Perhaps while there seemed to be no harm resulting, Manuela might be prepared to keep her own counsel.

****

Greg paused halfway down the stairs, surprised to see Raven sitting demurely near the front door.

Demurely? Whatever made me think of that word? This woman is as far removed from demure as the moon from the earth!

That voice. How long could he stand having to listen to that terrible twang? He all but shivered.

He stayed where he was, watching her. She sat straight and still, waiting quietly for his arrival. Nothing like the woman he'd left in the kitchen. He doubted she would know the meaning of quiet or demure.

Some sixth sense seemed to make her aware of him. He saw her head lift, her eyes following him as he moved further down the stairs. He hoped she didn't realize he'd been studying her. As he got closer, she stood, her face catching the light.

Greg drew a breath. She was pretty, no denying that. Too bad her character isn't as attractive.

He couldn't help but notice her legs again. They do go on and on, forever—what man wouldn't appreciate her womanly form? He tried to justify finding her body so attractive while harboring those other dark thoughts about her.

"I didn't expect you to be ready yet," he admitted. The designated thirty minutes wasn't up.

"It's rude to keep a man waiting." She looked up into his face before he gestured her into the depths of the house towards the garage.

That would have impressed Dad, Greg thought. Brad's attitude towards clock watching was almost an obsession.

Greg couldn't bring himself to compliment her on her appearance, not after the way she'd dressed earlier. But he had to admit she was now quite appropriately clothed. He liked the way those jeans molded tightly around her bottom. His eyes stayed on her swaying hips as they moved through into the garage. Opening the car door for her, he found his gaze captured by the movement of her long legs as she got into the car.

Are those legs unusually long? Or is it just the tightness of her jeans making them seem that way?

Slamming her car door with more force than necessary Greg stomped around the front of the car, irritated by his thoughts.

He could think of nothing to say as he was trying to concentrate on driving, instead of those legs. *Does she have to keep moving them?* It was distracting, to say the least.

"This countryside is so different from home."

Could I have gotten used to that awful voice already? It doesn't sound quite so grating as earlier.

"You've come from the summer too, haven't you?" He'd follow her lead. Polite social chat was no problem for him. He often had to socialize with strangers. Liking someone wasn't essential to maintaining polite conversation.

She nodded. "Does your sister live very far

away?"

"Only about five minutes," he answered. Did he discern a note of anxiety in Raven's voice? Perhaps she was nervous about meeting Abby. Good. She hadn't shown any such hesitation with him. Was she used to being able to exploit men, but found her relationships with women harder to manipulate? Greg gave a satisfied smile. She'll have to be good to outwit Abby.

"Are you warm enough?" he asked, bending forward to adjust the heating.

"Yes, thank you."

His smile turned to a frown. Now she is acting like a polite schoolgirl. What is she up to?

Chapter 4

Raven was nervous. She wasn't sure how this evening would go, whether she'd be able to fool Brad's daughter. The role she'd undertaken was so unlike her natural character that she'd need to carefully consider every word and move. Could she keep it up? With Greg it had seemed easy, he'd rubbed her the wrong way and she enjoyed the challenge. But with Abby too? She wasn't sure if continuing the lie was the best way to ensure Joy's acceptance here.

Raven found herself drumming her fingers against the leg of her jeans but hastily stopped when she saw Greg's eyes take in the nervous movement with a slight smile on his lips.

He knew! He knew she was nervous about the meeting with his sister. She hastily started humming a song, making sure her fingers moved with the rhythm. If nothing else, she'd enjoy showing him a thing or two.

Raven surveyed Abby's house as they pulled into the driveway. This place looked huge too, but she was beginning to realise that houses were much bigger over here. It was smaller than Brad's but equally well-maintained, with neatly clipped lawns and shrubs. Quickly opening her door, she swung her legs out of the car as Greg came hurrying around the front bonnet. She ducked her head to hide the smile as she saw his grimace of annoyance. She'd remember that—he hated having his gentlemanly manners ignored.

The door of the house opened and Raven got her

first sight of Abby. She looked very relaxed and sure of herself as she waited at the top of the steps. Raven was surprised to see that she did not look anything like Brad or Greg. She had expected another carbon copy, but this woman bore no resemblance to the men except perhaps around the eyes.

Raven found herself looking as closely as possible at those eyes. Did she detect a shy welcome? Somehow she couldn't imagine any sister of Greg's to be shy. Or welcoming. Better take it carefully. She hesitated for a moment, again wondering if she was just making matters worse. But Abby had not appeared to be arguing with Greg earlier on the phone. She probably felt the same way as he did, that anyone marrying Brad was just after his money. Raven took a deep breath.

Lights, camera and action!

"Gidday, Abby, I'm Raven." She strode up the front steps hoping she looked more confident than she felt. "It's so nice to finally meet you. Your dad has told me so much about you, I feel like I know you already." She pumped Abby's hand, smiling fully into her face. "I sure hope we can be friends."

She quickly relinquished Abby's hand and grabbed Tony's when he appeared behind his wife. "And you must be Tony. Wow! What a hunk." She gazed at him for a moment, then turned to Abby and nudged her playfully on the arm. "Bet you have to keep your eye on him, aye, Abs?" Her laugh was quite natural. She couldn't help it. Although they appeared to be trying to keep up a polite front, the expressions on their faces were hilarious.

She had definitely made an impression.

Abby seemed at a loss, although Raven suspected she would rarely be in such a position. Tony gallantly offered Raven his arm and escorted her into the house with a flourish that seemed to suit the absurdity of the situation.

"What a lovely house, Abby. I just love this entrance. It's so light and sunny. Are all houses so big in America? I know I've only seen them from the street, but they seem huge. We don't even have a foyer at home, seems such a waste of space." She smiled at Abby. "That's if you don't have the space to waste, of course." She added a giggle for good measure.

"Thank you," Abby responded to Raven's compliment, but was stopped from saying anything else by Raven's acknowledgement of Abby's two children.

"Hello, Caleb." Raven held out her hand to the dark-haired boy who was almost as tall as his father. "How's your ice hockey going this season? Your grandfather told me you're very good." The boy flushed at this praise. "He's really missing not going to your games. I reckon it'll be one of the first things he does when he gets home. He's so proud of you." Raven smiled naturally at the boy, who returned the smile with a sheepish grin.

"Thanks, Miss Raven. I miss him being there too. It's so much quieter."

Raven laughed.

"And this little beauty must be Vikki." Again Raven shook hands, this time with a girl whose mass of curly blonde hair surrounded a cherub face. Raven knew her to be eight, yet she looked much younger. She hid a little behind her mother but willingly took Raven's hand.

"Or do you prefer to be called Victoria?" Raven leaned over toward the pretty shy face. "Victoria is such a beautiful name. You know I always said if I'd been blessed with a daughter, I would have called her Victoria."

Careful, careful. Her act was slipping.

She straightened. "My great-grandmother was

called Victoria. She was named after the Queen, of course." She forced a giggle. "Although I don't suppose Americans would name someone after the Queen."

"Hello, Miss Raven. I don't mind what you call me." She smiled shyly. "You're very pretty."

"Why, thank you my dear." Raven dropped a small curtsey. "So are you."

Raven looked straight at Abby. "Do they have to call me that? I'd much rather they just call me Raven, if you didn't mind."

"It's considered impolite for a child to call an adult by their given name," Greg cut in coldly. "Especially when they've just met."

Raven glanced over her shoulder and replied, equally coldly. "Oh, but surely that doesn't need to apply to me. I mean, I'm almost family, aren't I?" Raven felt a thrill at the way his nose flared. Then she looked back at Abby. "I would much prefer it, if you wouldn't mind."

"Of course they may call you Raven, if you're sure—?" She touched Raven on the arm. "Now please, come in and make yourself comfortable." Abby led the way into the living room.

"What can I get you to drink, Raven?" Tony asked, moving towards a small cabinet in the corner. "Wine, gin and tonic, vodka and orange—?"

"Oh, no, thank you. Maybe some juice or water if that wouldn't be too much trouble."

"Perhaps you'd prefer a soda?" Abby offered.

Raven frowned. "No, thank you. I don't like soda water very much." *Fancy offering her soda to drink. Weird, but who am I to question their choice of drink.* "Really, water would be fine, thanks."

Abby was confused, too. Raven could see that. "Soda—like cola, I meant, not soda water..."

Raven accentuated her giggle. "Oh, I'm so sorry. I didn't understand. Again." She glanced at Greg.

"I'm sure Greg must be getting sick of me not understanding." Another giggle. "But I'm finding out already that we don't really speak the same language, Yanks and Kiwis."

Raven made a show of slapping her forehead. "I've really done it this time, haven't I? I've insulted you all. I'm so sorry." This wasn't part of the act. Raven was really concerned that she'd hurt their feelings. Insulting people's heritage was something she would not stoop to. She looked around them all and found no visible signs of upset. In fact, they appeared to be amused.

Except for Greg, of course. His face would probably crack in two if he attempted a smile. But looking closely, even he seemed to look less stern. Or maybe she was just getting used to seeing him.

"You're not offended being called Yanks?"

"No, not at all," as Tony answered Raven breathed an exaggerated sigh of relief. "Just surprised. The word Yankee has pretty much fallen out of use since the Civil War."

"Oh. I guess it's only used outside America, then."

Abby laughed lightly. "You might get some funny looks though, calling yourself a Kiwi."

Raven looked at her blankly.

"Here, 'kiwi' is a fruit," Abby explained.

The light dawned. "Now I understand. In New Zealand we'd never refer to a kiwifruit as just a kiwi. We already have enough kiwis!"

Now it was her hosts turn to look bewildered.

"Well, first of all, a kiwi is New Zealand's national bird. It's also a slang term to call a New Zealander. Then our national Rugby League team is called 'The Kiwis'. So there's really no room to add the kiwifruit as well." Raven suddenly felt uncomfortable. "I'm sorry, I didn't mean to start lecturing." She glanced around, embarrassed.

"You weren't lecturing," Abby soothed. "We want to learn as much as we can about you, and about your country. I know Dad has fallen in love with it."

Raven was surprised to see no sign of malice in Abby's attitude. She seemed genuinely interested. Although she'd said it was New Zealand Brad had fallen for, not her. Raven sipped her drink, unsure how to continue. She had to make sure these people would not blight Joy's happiness in any way, but already knew her act wasn't the way to go about it.

But how could she correct their mistaken assumption?

Vikki, who edged along the sofa toward Raven, filled the awkward pause in the conversation. "I've never heard of a kiwi bird. I know what a raven looks like though."

Raven smiled down at the girl, thankful she'd spoken. This would give her a few more moments to decide which course of action to take.

"We don't have ravens in New Zealand, except me I guess." She smiled again. "But if you could give me a pencil and piece of paper, I'll show you what a kiwi looks like."

Vikki hurried away, returning just as Abby was apologizing for her.

"I don't mind. I love kids." She smiled faintly. "Kids and drawing; they've been my salvation." She took the writing pad and pencil and began to draw. She was aware of conversation in the room but took no heed of its content. She did notice how Vikki's body crept closer and closer until she was sitting tightly against Raven's side, watching. She smiled down at the curly head and quickly finished off the picture, then handed it to Vikki.

"One day I'll tell you the Maori legend of how the kiwi ended up living on the forest floor, instead of in the high branches like the other birds."

Vikki was staring down at the drawing in her

hands. "I can keep this?" She looked up at Raven. "Really?"

Raven nodded. "Sure, but give it back just for a moment." She carefully balanced it where Vikki couldn't see her write an inscription on the top, 'To my new friend, Vikki' then moved down to the bottom right hand corner where she signed her nom de plume, Aroha.

"There, now take a gink at that." She smiled at the little girl's puzzled look.

"That's a funny word. I never heard anyone say gink before."

"Haven't you?" Raven teased gently.

"Is it like geek? I know what geek means, Tommy Butler's a real geek."

"No." Raven spoke quickly, guessing Vikki might be about to embark on a list of Tommy Butler's other failings. "It just means to have a quick look."

Vikki's eyes fell to the pad Raven handed her.

"Thank you so much. I'll treasure it forever," Vikki breathed.

The girl's awed expression silenced the others as she moved slowly across to her parents, her eyes never leaving the picture Raven had drawn.

"Mommy, Daddy. Look at my picture."

"But this is wonderful," Abby gasped. Then she realised what she had said, or more the tone she'd used to say it. Raven watched as the colour rushed into Abby's cheeks, not in the least offended by the surprise in her voice. The mere fact that Abby was so embarrassed by her own thoughtless tone, gave Raven more reason to think that perhaps Greg's sister wasn't tarred with the same brush as her brother. Already Raven recognised she was much more pleasant than he.

Raven spoke softly, trying to ease Abby's feelings. "Didn't Greg tell you that I'm a struggling artist?" She glanced at him, her tone hardening. "I was sure that was one thing he would have definitely mentioned."

"No. He didn't."

Greg's eyebrows merely rose a little at the angry look he was subjected to by his sister.

"That was very rude of me, Raven. Please forgive me," Abby said stiffly. She shuffled uncomfortably in her seat.

"Hey, don't worry about it. It takes a lot for me to get my knickers in a twist." As she had hoped, her unusual turn of phrase lightened the atmosphere.

"This is an extremely good sketch." Greg was now looking at the picture. "I have to wonder what it would be like if you actually spent some time on it." He looked at Raven with a puzzled frown.

Does he assume I lack talent as well as expensive clothing?

"I like birds. It's what I mostly paint." She shrugged off his comment.

"And this signature. What's it, A-r-o-h-a," he spelled. "Why use some fancy name instead of your own?"

"Aroha." She pronounced it for them. "It actually means love in Maori. Someone used to call me that. He was my most ardent supporter. Using it on my paintings is a way of thanking him."

"Another elderly benefactor?" Greg sniped.

"Greg!" Abby gasped.

Raven's uncertainty and sense of shame at her subterfuge, again disappeared at Greg's abrasive tone. His initial query had been quite legitimate. But the following comment had been nothing short of a declaration of war.

"I don't know whether you would call him a benefactor or not." Her reply was as sugary as a bowl of molasses as she glared at him. "He was my husband."

"So you making a habit of marrying your

64

benefactors, do you?"

Raven would remember later how his eyes smouldered, how they seemed to change colour. But right now all she could deal with was the suffocating anger. Before she could formulate an answer, he continued. "What did you do with this one, ditch him 'cause he ran out of money?"

Raven could feel the blood draining from her face. What a cruel thing to say, especially to someone who you were supposed to be welcoming into your family. She couldn't remember anyone ever speaking to her like this before.

She felt tears begin to well up in her eyes, but blinked furiously to stop them. She took a deep breath forcing calmness into her voice that she didn't feel.

"A drunk driver killed him, three weeks after his twenty-fifth birthday," she said matter-of-factly.

Raven was gratified to see some of the colour leave his face before she glanced at Abby, and saw the sympathy in her eyes.

"Perhaps there's something I could help with in the kitchen?" Keeping her voice steady was not easy, but she thought she managed it.

"What an excellent idea," Abby grasped Raven's arm. "I do need to check dinner." She spoke to the children over her shoulder as she pushed Raven into the kitchen. "Go downstairs. We'll call you for dinner."

Raven saw the look Abby sent Tony and heard Tony's quiet voice berating Greg as the door swung shut.

"Oh, what you must think of us," Abby despaired. "I don't know what to say." She turned from the counter and looked at Raven. "Please ignore Greg. He's not been himself lately—" She hastily tacked on "—nothing to do with you though. He just has a few issues to sort through."

Raven's eyebrows rose sceptically. She appreciated Abby's effort, but was certain the only issue Greg was worrying about was her.

"Forget about him." Abby was trying to drown out the raised voices coming from the next room. "Tell me about Dad. How is he?"

It took Raven a few moments to compose herself but soon she found herself talking naturally to Abby. With the commotion next door she'd forgotten her accent, and now that she remembered, it was too late. Abby was far too astute to be fooled by the sudden change.

Abby was very careful with her questions, obviously trying not to offend Raven. She never once mentioned the wedding, or her feelings about the age difference between Raven and Brad. Raven was happy to talk about Brad, explaining how they'd met and become friends. She described things they'd done, places they'd been—omitting only the fact that they'd been accompanied by her mother and her sons. She noticed Abby looking at her strangely at times and wished she knew what was going through her hostess' mind. She hoped she was giving the impression that she cared deeply for Brad. She wanted their minds set at peace about that, at least.

"You've let him know you arrived safely, haven't you?"

"Well, actually no. I was going to ask Greg if I could send an email home, but—"

"What is the matter with him? It's the first thing he should have offered."

Abby was clearly exasperated at her brother. She leaned through the living room door and berated him. "Why haven't you let Raven call home to say she arrived safely? I'm sure Dad is worried about her."

"I tried to call last night, but apparently he's checked out of his hotel. Believe me, I wanted to talk to him too."

Raven heard Greg's belligerent reply and smiled. Serves him right. If he had mentioned it to her, she could have given him the number to call.

Abby all but slammed the door. "Men!" she muttered, shaking her head. She reached into a drawer and pulled out a phone book. "I have no idea of the time difference, but if it's not too bad, you can call right now." She started flicking through the front pages of the telephone book.

"But an email will do, there's no need for me to make a phone call."

"Nonsense. I know Dad. He'll be worrying about you." She found the relevant page. "It says to add 17 hours. That means it's about eleven o'clock in the morning there." She gestured Raven toward the phone on the wall. "Just dial zero-one-one, then six-four and the number." She glanced up. "You do know where he is, I presume?"

Raven nodded. "He's at my place." She shrugged. "If only Greg had mentioned he'd tried to ring him up..." She found herself smiling, aware Abby realised that she and Greg were at loggerheads.

"There's another phone in the den," Abby hurriedly offered, "if you'd prefer privacy."

"No, this is fine. Thanks very much." Raven doubted that at eleven o'clock on a Sunday morning there would be anyone home.

Sure enough, she listened to the clicks of the connection, then the ringing tone before she heard her own voice on the answer-phone. She had composed a quick message in her mind and hurriedly repeated it. "Hi, just thought I'd give you a bell to let you know I've arrived in one piece. Slept the clock around and I'm feeling good now. I'm ringing from Abby's where we're having tea. I'll send you an email tomorrow, so make sure you check the in-box. Love you and miss you!" She hung up the phone and turned to see Abby taking a dish from the oven.

"What can I do to help you?"

****

Raven thought an easy camaraderie might eventuate, based on the time she and Abby had spent finalising the meal. Their conversation jumped around many topics—Raven's recent illness, the latest fashions, an interesting television programme, which amazingly they had both seen, plus differences between America and New Zealand. It seemed to Raven that Abby was in no hurry to serve the meal. In fact she seemed to be delaying it, enjoying just chatting with Raven. They were both laughing at a shared joke when Tony put his head through the door.

"Anything I can do to help?" he asked, with a fond smile.

"No. Go away." Abby's grin took any heat out of the words. "We're having a woman-to-woman here. You go and continue your man-to-man with your partner."

"Your brother, you mean?"

"No, he can be your partner tonight. I'm disowning him for a while."

"I'm not too sure he wants to talk to me either, after what I've been telling him."

Raven was deeply concerned. "Oh, please, don't go having arguments on my account," she appealed to them. "The last thing I want is to cause any friction."

Tony put a friendly arm around her shoulders. "Don't you go worrying. This is nothing. Good for the blood pressure you know, gets the adrenaline going."

He was laughing, actually laughing, as he left the room.

"Abby, please. I didn't want to cause any

problems. Don't you or Tony be angry with Greg. I don't need anyone to fight my battles." Her pleading voice suddenly hardened. "Believe me, I can take care of myself."

Abby stood back and studied her closely, a serious expression on her face. Raven maintained eye contact for some moments before Abby finally nodded. "You know, I think I do believe you. You've had to face a lot of sadness for someone so young. I guess getting through that must give you strength." She turned away and mused, almost to herself, "If anything happened to Tony, I think I would want to die."

"You might want to, but with children, you have to get on with life."

Abby swung around, astounded. "You have children?"

Raven nodded. "Two boys."

At the sight of Abby's shocked expression, she was compelled to ask, "Brad never mentioned them, either? Just what did he tell you about me?"

"Apparently nothing," Abby replied dryly, sinking onto one of the breakfast bar stools.

Raven dropped her head into her hands. Oh hell! This was getting too complicated. What was she going to do now? She had to come clean and tell them about Joy. Right now.

"Abby, there's been—"

"Mom, isn't dinner nearly ready? I'm starving." The door flew open as if it had been hit by a tornado and Caleb erupted into the quiet kitchen.

As Abby spoke absently to her son, Raven cringed. Abby was shocked by the existence of her boys. Her assumption must be that Brad was beginning a new family—one in which his step-children would actually be younger than his current grandchildren must be abhorrent to her.

As much as Raven had come to love Brad, she

69

was now very annoyed with him. If he'd thought to tell Abby and Greg something about his fiancée, this ridiculous situation would never have happened. Raven did acknowledge the mess she was now in was all her own making. Still, she apportioned some blame to Brad. What on earth had he said in his email anyway, that could have confused them into thinking she was the bride?

Raven came out of her reverie to find Abby dishing up some sausages into bread rolls and spooning on cooked onion, some green relish that looked like chopped gherkins, then applying what seemed like copious amounts of tomato sauce and mustard. This must be the *real* American hotdog, she guessed.

She watched Abby's face closely, looking for some sign of how she was feeling. Abby seemed to have dismissed Raven from her mind, for the moment at least, while she finished preparing the children's meal and sent Caleb downstairs with two large plates full.

"Shall I take these through to the dining room?" Raven asked, indicating the crockery serving bowls Abby had set out on the bench. She'd lost the moment to put things right. There would be an opportunity at dinner she hoped.

"Thanks, Raven." The smile Abby flashed her way held nothing but friendliness. "That would be a big help. If you would just start with the white one there," she indicated, "and then get a soup ladle from that drawer beside you. I hope you like clam chowder?"

Raven's smile was very tentative. "I've never tried it before, but I love seafood."

Abby seemed to realise Raven's uncertainty. She gently squeezed Raven's arm as she moved past to retrieve plates from a cupboard, conveying a sense of amiability.

"Stop worrying, Raven. It'll all work out in the end." Then she amazed Raven by winking solemnly. "Why don't we let Dad do the worrying? Oh, and Greg of course. He doesn't feel alive unless he's worrying about something."

****

There was an uncomfortable atmosphere around the table as the four adults sat down to eat. Abby and Tony tried to ease the situation by chatting with Raven, asking questions about New Zealand and telling stories about the family. They were trying to make Raven feel comfortable and it did seem to be working. She was joining in readily enough. The conversation was restricted to the three of them though. Greg felt too contrite to join in. He half-heartedly listened to Tony telling an exaggerated story of how he and Greg had met as teenagers, on opposing sides during an important hockey match. How their competition had been very physical and how they had both worn evidence of their clash for days afterwards, and then of their friendship, which had started the following year when both attended the same high school.

Why is Tony embellishing our escapades so much? Why don't they just stick to stories about themselves? Leave me out of their true confessions.

Greg swallowed another mouthful of wine. Raven seemed determined not to look at him, but could he blame her? He couldn't get her facial expression out of his mind. *How could I have said something so thoughtless, so cruel?* She had looked so devastated. He'd seen the shimmer of tears although she'd desperately tried to hide them. He was sure it had not been an act; his words had upset her deeply. He hadn't needed Tony's lecture, although momentarily he had tried to justify his behavior to himself and his brother-in-law.

Greg doubted if he'd ever felt so low in his life, to

71

attack someone when he had no idea of the situation. He shifted uncomfortably on his seat catching yet another of Abby's glares. No matter how much he watched Raven, her eyes never came near his end of the table. If he hadn't felt so ashamed and guilty, he would have been slighted to think any woman could ignore him so completely; he wasn't used to being ignored.

Oh, hell. He doubted if an apology would help anyway. There was no way he could take back the words he'd said or all the associated feelings he'd made no effort to hide. No matter how much he disliked the whole idea of this setup, he hated the way he felt now—regretting his extremely bad manners.

He still could not understand how he had actually let those words escape. Though he'd been thinking them he hadn't intended to actually say them aloud. Perhaps it had been the way she'd calmly answered every query as if she had nothing to hide, when he knew better.

She was hiding something, he would bet his life on that. And if it had anything to do with hurting his father—well, he was going to protect the Old Man at any cost.

He had no idea how recent her bereavement was, but he realized that her sense of loss was still very strong. Perhaps she was marrying his father on the rebound? That might explain why someone as attractive as Raven could contemplate such an unlikely match; she was looking for companionship to ease the loneliness. Perhaps marriage to his father seemed like a way to fill that gap.

After the first course, Raven and he were left alone at the table. Whether Abby had orchestrated this or not, Greg didn't know; but he hastily took advantage of their being alone to try and atone. Raven continued to ignore him as he stumbled through his apology.

"I don't know what I can say..." he began. Why couldn't she at least look at him?

"I had no right to speak to you that way." Damn it all. What more could he say? That he hadn't meant what he'd said? That would have been less than the truth. At least he'd managed to find out something about her through it. That he regretted hurting her? Yes, that's why he was feeling so low. He hadn't intended that.

Greg took a deep breath. "I'm sorry." His attempt seemed to be falling on deaf ears, and it was beginning to annoy him. "It was crass of me. I had no right to make such personal remarks."

Damn her.

If she never wanted to look at him again, who cared anyway? Let her go on ignoring him. He sat back in his chair, more than a little put out that she didn't seem to want to accept his apology.

He was surprised when she moved her head slowly around to face him. The brown in her eyes was smoldering, burning. Like chips of coal on a cold night, they seemed to burn into his soul.

"You're a very selfish man, aren't you, Greg?" Her voice held no real expression but he knew she was goading him.

The little fool, does she think she can take me on and win?

His voice was steel. "I don't believe you've known me long enough to judge me." As the words left his mouth, he realized how ludicrous the statement was, under the circumstances. It didn't need her raised eyebrows. He'd judged her, and with less evidence than he'd given her just now. "I'm only concerned for my father. He—"

"You don't give a damn about your father," Raven cut in, glaring.

Greg was shocked. Anyone who knew them was

aware of the bond between him and his father. How could she suspect otherwise?

"You're wrong. I do care about Dad."

"Ha!" Raven almost snorted with disbelief. "If you cared a toss about him and his feelings, you wouldn't be packing such a sad about me. You're the biggest berk I've ever met."

"Berk?" He had no idea what she was calling him but he knew it wasn't complimentary.

"Okay. Jerk, swine, selfish bastard, whatever. If what you feel for Brad is your version of love, I feel sorry for you."

His voice rose as he tried to straighten out this ridiculous conversation.

"I love my father—" he began only to be interrupted again.

"So do I, Greg. That's something you have to accept. So do I." Her voice had softened, saddened a little. He stared closely at her, having to believe her as she refused to break eye contact with him.

Her character seemed multifaceted. This woman now eyeballing him determinedly was nothing like she'd appeared earlier. The act in the car on the way over here had been different again. Who was she? And what was her game?

The suddenness of clanking dishes next door could mean only one thing: Abby had been listening, giving him time to try and make peace with their guest. He found he didn't mind. At least she'd know that he had done his best to apologize. She and Tony now scurried into the room carrying steaming serving dishes, which they placed in the center of the table. The smile Abby sent him was far easier to live with than the scowls he'd been getting all evening. He shrugged, indicating that he'd tried but didn't feel as if it had been very successful.

The atmosphere lightened as the meal progressed. Conversation remained convivial, where any hint of friction was unlikely. Greg was surprised that Abby was not plying Raven with more personal questions. She was very good at digging information out of people, yet wasn't making any effort now. Perhaps she's found out all she needed while they were alone in the kitchen. He hoped she had. He had a heap of questions he wanted answers for, but knew he would not get anything from Raven. Especially now.

Greg found himself watching her closely. She still kept her head turned firmly toward Abby and Tony, but he knew she was aware of his attention. He saw the clenched way she held her cutlery, her whitened knuckles.

He was even more confused now, because he believed her when she said she loved his father. How could someone so young and vibrant as this consider tying herself to an old man? What a waste!

He pulled himself up sharply before his mind started to wander. He must not allow himself to think of her as a desirable woman. As anything except his father's wife-to-be.

He watched as one hand slowly moved up to touch the small silver amulet hanging around her neck. Such a slender neck... His mind did wander.

What would her skin taste like under his lips? And those ears, peeking out from under the fair curls—would she shiver if he took that lobe between his teeth and suckled it?

"Excuse me." He all but threw back his chair and left the room, not caring about the surprised expressions his abrupt departure caused. He headed through the laundry and out the back door. Out into the moonless darkness, where the winter chill helped to calm his erotic thoughts.

Chapter 5

Although he made no sound and was out of her sight, Raven was aware of Greg the second he re-entered the room. It was as if there was an energy field around him, warning her to beware. She had no idea how long he'd been gone, where he had been, or in fact, if he was coming back. Nor did she care. She'd had enough of Greg-High-and-Mighty-Collins for one day. Her sense of humour had definitely deserted her where he was concerned. If he carried on like this with Joy—well, it didn't bear thinking about.

Abby, Tony and Raven had adjourned from the dining room and were now in the living room sipping their drinks and talking quietly. For once Raven regretted her choice of beverage, but knew she daren't ask for anything harder while she was still on medication from the doctors. But that didn't stop her from wishing she could blot out at least part of this evening.

"Oh, there you are, Greg." Abby acted as if there was nothing untoward about his behavior. Perhaps he was always this rude, Raven surmised.

"We were just telling Raven about some of the sights she might like to take in before Dad gets home." Abby was being so friendly and it seemed genuine. She was working hard to try and make the evening a success. Raven felt sorry for her and had been trying to meet her halfway.

But now he was back, and had the nerve to join her on a sofa when there were other places he could have sat. She risked a quick glare at him and was utterly unnerved to find his eyes on her again. She felt her teeth grating together. Damn and blast the man.

Suddenly her fevered brain took in what Abby was suggesting. She had to be kidding. No way, not in a million years. "You don't have any plans for tomorrow, do you Greg?"

Raven was pleased to see Greg looked equally unenthusiastic as Abby outlined her idea.

"I know the forecast is for a beautiful day, and Sunday is the only day to go to Washington." She smiled at Raven. "You can actually find a parking space on Sundays if you go in early enough." Abby could not be oblivious to the vibes coming from Raven and Greg but she continued anyway. "You know we would have loved to take you Raven but we're booked to spend the day with Tony's parents. His mother hasn't been well and I really don't think we should disappoint her. Go on," she urged Raven. "You'd like to see some sights of D.C., wouldn't you? Why not go and have a look at the Washington Monument, Lincoln Memorial, the Capitol Building, some of the Smithsonian? There's enough within walking distance of the Mall to keep you busy for days. It's a beautiful place. You would be able to pace yourself, depending on how you're feeling. There shouldn't be too many people either, not at this time of year."

Raven remained silent. To refuse would seem rude, and to tell the truth she had hoped to get into Washington a couple of times before she had to go home. From what she'd read there was a lot to see, and she did want to see as much as possible. But she wasn't about to commit herself to spending a day in his company. Even at the risk of sounding rude, she had to extract herself from this arrangement.

"Perhaps I could catch a bus or a train in. That would save Greg having to waste his day." She allowed her eyes to meet his. "I'm sure he has other plans."

Raven seethed as she watched his lips twitch. She had given him the lead and all he had to do was follow it. Instead, he seemed to be getting some perverse enjoyment out of the situation.

"I have absolutely no plans at all for tomorrow." The smile he threw at her held all the warmth of a winter snowstorm. "There are no buses or trains. Not from up here anyway. I'm afraid you'll have to put up with me as your guide, or miss out altogether."

Raven fumed, caught between her desire to sightsee and her lack of desire to spend one more minute than she needed to in his company. She hated the way he laid back in his seat, the smug expression on his face, as if he could read her mind. He knew she wanted to refuse. Suddenly she felt like he was holding all the cards and she was no longer in control.

What's happened to my plan? When had she stopped thinking about Joy and started this crusade for her own benefit? A throbbing lump wedged in her throat, momentarily hindering breath from entering or exiting her lungs. Tucking trembling fingers out of sight under her legs, her mind whirled and struggled with an unpalatable answer: When she'd realised this was a man who made her react, made her blood boil, made her feel alive; more alive than she had in years. This was her crusade now. It had become very personal, no longer having anything to do with Brad or Joy.

This was war. The most basic kind—between a man and a woman, a battle she had absolutely no experience with. One she didn't know if she could win. But she knew she was already in too deep to get out. She had to get a grip on herself. She had to stay and fight.

"Why, thank you, Greg."

She was pleased to see his body jerk upright. He'd expected her to refuse. Good. Now he was saddled with her for all day, and she'd make sure he fulfilled the role of 'guide' to the limit. "It's so very kind of you to offer to give up your Sunday for me."

Raven could not help but notice the hasty exit Tony made from the room, nor miss the crow of laughter that travelled through the closed kitchen door. Abby kept a straight face, although Raven caught the twinkle in her eyes and the teasing wink that came her way. Raven glanced at Greg and knew that he had seen the wink too, and was far from amused at the way his sister had manoeuvred him.

A scowl darkened his face and he stood abruptly. "If we're planning a long day tomorrow, I believe an early night is called for." He swung a moody look at Abby. "Dad would never forgive me if I let our guest overdo things."

"What a sensible idea, Greg," Abby replied, ignoring the tone in his voice.

Did they always talk to each other like this? Acting almost like wolves, each waiting for the other to pounce. From Brad's comments about his children, Raven had got the idea that they were extremely close. They didn't appear close now; they were at daggers drawn.

Once again Raven was aware of the twinkling in Abby's eyes as she hastily ushered them toward the front door. She was enveloped in a warm hug and then pushed through the exit with the promise of a phone call on Monday.

Even as she turned around to say thanks, she found herself facing the closed door. She gratefully slipped on the jacket Greg held out to her, and snuggled into its warmth. Shivered with cold as she moved slowly down the steps, she tried to distinguish the sound from within the house. Was that smothered laughter she'd heard from behind the door?

"I think I'd prefer to drive, if you don't mind." The sarcastic tone in Greg's voice alerted Raven to another faux pax. Her startled eyes slowly travelled from his, across the top of the car, down to the door she had just begun to open. She felt the blood rush into her face as she saw the steering wheel and was thankful the darkness of the night would hide her blush from Greg. He didn't need to rub it in. At home, this would have been the passenger side. How was she supposed to remember everything different about America when she had only been here one day?

She slammed the door with no regard to any possible damage to the car, and stomped around to where he was politely holding open the passenger door.

"Thank you." He made her so mad she was more tempted to stamp on his highly polished shoes than utter her appreciation, but she did manage to utter the words without actually choking on them.

There was total silence between them as they drove back to Brad's house. Not the companionable silence that can exist, but more like the silence of two animals which having stalked their prey, were now conserving their inner strength prior to the final attack. It was a very tense silence, one that Raven had no intention of breaking.

This night had been an eye-opener, that was for sure. She had not anticipated Abby's open friendliness, or her apparent willingness to accept Raven so unreservedly. Tony seemed very quiet, but there was no doubt in Raven's mind that he shared Abby's feelings regarding Brad and his intention to remarry.

But not Greg, he was a different kettle of fish altogether. *Is he against Brad's remarriage on principle, or is it just the bride he's taken exception to?*

Despite the heightened adrenaline that had been flowing, Raven suddenly found herself yawning. She was glad of the darkness within the car, yawning would be a display of weakness. She wasn't showing any smidgeon of weakness in front of this man. She stiffened her back, and her resolve, just as she recognised the house in the glow of the car headlights. Soon she could curl up in bed. Another good night's sleep and she would feel able to meet anything Greg might care to throw at her.

Still not a word was uttered as they climbed out of the car. Raven made sure she was quick enough to foil his intention to open of her door. She pretended not to notice that he had politely moved to help her exit the car. They entered the house and Raven headed straight toward the staircase. About to continue up the stairs without speaking, her conscience finally got the better of her. After all, manners maketh the woman as well as the man.

She turned to Greg. "Thank you for such an illuminating evening," she said making no attempt to keep the mockery from her voice. She didn't wait for a reply, but knew he remained at the foot of the stairs, watching her.

"Raven." His voice halted her as she turned at the half-landing. "Please be down here at eight-thirty, ready to go." He acknowledged her nod with one of his own, then paused for a moment as if considering how to phrase something. His eyes bored into her, and she gripped the handrail, waiting, not able to continue up the stairs. "Did you leave something at Abby's?"

Raven frowned, confused. She had taken nothing with her, save her purse, which hung on her shoulder.

Greg continued, after a lengthy pause. "Your

accent. You seem to have left it at Abby's."

The words made her eyes widen with shock. With all the emotion flowing around during the evening, she had completely forgotten to exaggerate her accent. She glanced away trying to think of a reply, but Greg did not wait for an answer or explanation. He moved towards the kitchen without another upward glance.

"Oh damn!" she muttered as she stomped up the rest of the stairs. Now she was right up the creek without a paddle.

****

Raven was ready to leave well before eight-thirty. She found herself taking extra care with her appearance, laying out three different outfits before heading for the shower. Now upon returning to the bedroom, she scoffed at her own vanity. What was she trying to do, attract the man?

She sank onto her bed amidst the laid out clothes, aghast. Was that what she wanted? For him to find her attractive? That clouded her plan to convince him she was about to marry his father, and yet she acknowledged its truth. For the first time in many years she felt an attraction for a man. She recalled his face easily to mind. Was that because it had woven itself into a misty dream last night? She couldn't recall anything about the dream, other than the certainty that Greg played a prominent part. His eyes: they were the feature that Raven found most attractive.

Attractive! What was she thinking of! Even if he had the face and body that could have graced any magazine advertisement, his personality didn't match up to what she would look for in a man.

But he wasn't just any man, he was Brad's son. And she had committed herself to spending a whole day alone, in his company. She shivered. Was she playing with fire? Was it an unconscious desire to be with him that had caused her to accept the plans for today?

She had achieved an affinity with Brad so quickly. Could she be attracted to Greg because he reminded her of his father? Or was this more basic, more physical?

One thing she knew: the emotions she felt about Greg were in no way similar to her feelings for Brad. Brad had taken the place of a kindly father; theirs was a very comfortable, caring relationship. Nobody would call whatever Greg and she seemed to be developing as comfortable.

She pulled herself up abruptly and looked at the time. Yicks. She'd better hurry if she wanted to have some breakfast before meeting Greg. She hastily dressed in a pair of jeans and a bright red shirt. She considered the warm woolen jersey she'd knitted last winter, and then quickly pulled it on. Perhaps if the day were going to be sunny, she'd be able to dispense with her jacket later in the day. She slid her feet into well-worn running shoes and was pleased to be able to tie them up without any sign of discomfort from her stomach.

A quick glance under the bathroom sink earlier had revealed a small hair dryer, which she now plugged in and used to fluff the ends of her hair into soft waves. Then on went some moisturizer and the barest amount of makeup, although she highlighted her eyes by applying her favourite shade of eye shadow. She grabbed her jacket along with her purse and camera as she sped out of the room and down the stairs.

Thank goodness he wasn't in the kitchen when she arrived. She still hadn't figured out how she was going to explain away her sudden loss of that awful accent. Should she bring it up and try to offer an explanation? Or say nothing unless he brought it up first? Oh, what a tangled web we weave...she never bothered to finish the proverb. She didn't need a bunch of old words to tell her she'd really messed up. The big question was what to do about it now.

She glanced around. There was no sign that anyone had already breakfasted. No coffee in the pot, no pans on the stove. She heard no sound from anywhere in the house, but expected Greg any moment. He didn't fit the bill of a man who would start the day without breakfast. She quickly checked the fridge and smiled gratefully as she spied a bowl full of chopped fresh fruit covered tightly with plastic wrap, and a jug of juice next to it. Manuela had placed these prominently so she could not miss them.

"Would you mind dishing me some of that, please?"

Raven was glad she'd not yet taken the juice from the fridge, for her fingers slipped on the handle at the sudden sound of his voice. The jug merely bounced onto the shelf, spilling only a drop. Where was her radar this morning? She hadn't been aware of him at all.

She carefully placed the jug of juice onto the kitchen bench and closed the fridge door. She kept her eyes averted from his as she glanced around for utensils.

"That drawer over to your left."

Raven got out some forks and spoons, and turned to find he'd placed two plates on the breakfast bar ready for her to serve the fruit. Meanwhile he quickly filled the percolator and switched it on. Within seconds the smell of coffee permeated through the kitchen and caused Raven's stomach to heave. She hastily poured juice into one of the glasses he'd placed next to the plates and drank it.

"You really don't like coffee, do you?" Greg murmured.

"Can't abide the stuff."

"Would you like some tea? I think Manuela might have some around here somewhere."

"No, thank you. Can't abide that, either."

While he kept the conversation to an impersonal level, she must try to be civil. She found herself waiting, nervously wondering if he would bring up the question of her accent, or more to the point her lack of accent.

"So what do you normally drink?" The content of the conversation couldn't be more impersonal and mundane.

"They say water is pretty good for you."

"You're not one of these health fanatics, are you?"

She watched as he settled down on one of the bar stools and started eating his fruit. Slowly she joined him, uncertain. While his attitude remained hostile she knew how to treat him. But now he was in a different mood altogether, perhaps not actually friendly, but with no obvious sign of animosity either.

Raven decided to follow his lead, talk about mundane things. "I wouldn't say it's fanatical to look after one's body," she answered, not realising until the words were out of her mouth that she was virtually inviting him to examine hers—which he wasted no time in doing. She found herself blushing as his eyes travelled slowly down, then up the length of her. His appreciation was obvious, although he made no comment.

"I work out every day. But I eat and drink whatever I want to. Luckily, I tend to like what's good for me."

"I'll just bet you do."

For the first time this morning, Raven looked at him closely. What does he mean by that crack? But he looked back at her quite innocently, smiling faintly. She realised that the remarks she'd made could have seemed coltish, so she thought perhaps it was time to leave that subject. All of a sudden her mind was a blank. This was embarrassing. This silence was crying out to be filled.

"What's that?" Phew, something to say. Raven didn't care if it was perfectly inane, she could now break the silence. Greg had reached over into the fridge and taken out a bread roll of some sort and was about to put it into the microwave.

"A bagel," he replied. "Don't you have bagels in New Zealand?"

Raven shrugged never having tried them, mainly because she didn't have a clue how they were eaten.

"Want to try one?"

"Okay. Why not? What do you do with it?"

"Usually you warm them up a little and then spread them with cream cheese. Let's see what flavour Manuela has bought this time—" He bent down to see further into the fridge.

Now it was Raven's turn to survey the body in front of her, or at least the backside of it. She found herself admiring the firm buttocks, how they tapered down to thick thighs. She liked the way the muscles strained against the material of his jeans as he moved.

She hastily averted her eyes and finished the last of the watermelon on her plate as he placed two packets of cream cheese on the counter in front of her.

"You can get all sorts of flavoured bagels. Some sweet, some not," he explained in a pleasant voice. "Try the plain cream cheese on these, they'd probably taste a bit funny with blueberry."

Raven watched him closely as he split his bagel and applied a large amount of cream cheese to the warm surface, then followed suit. She found herself smiling as she finished her first mouthful.

"That's quite—" She searched for a suitable word. "—different." Raven savoured another mouthful. "I think I could get to like this. I wonder what they would taste like with marmite on them," she mused aloud.

"Marmite?"

Raven felt her smile growing. "It's a yeast spread we use at home. It's as much a staple item in a Kiwi kitchen as I guess peanut butter is in an American's. Not sure how it would taste on a bagel though. I think the bagel might ruin it."

Without realising it immediately, Raven now thought how domestic the scene was there in the kitchen; just the two of them, preparing and sharing a quick breakfast, then helping to clear away the dishes. If a stranger had come upon them this morning, they could have been forgiven for thinking Greg and Raven were a couple. Choking a little as she finished her juice, Raven hastily dismissed the picture from her mind. She was surprised when Greg picked up a dishcloth and began to wipe down the entire bench surface they had used. Could this be the same Greg?

He caught her look and smiled wryly.

"If Manuela comes in tomorrow morning and finds a mess, she'll have me strung up."

Raven wasn't sure if she should trust the friendly tone of his voice. Was he just biding his time before he attacked her again? Better not allow him to lull her into a false sense of security.

"Raven." Greg's voice halted her as she started to turn towards the door, happy the kitchen was as they'd found it. She immediately noticed yet another change in tone and stiffened.

Oh no. Here it was. The inquisition. But she was amazed at his next words.

"I really am sorry about last night. I'd

appreciate it if you could try to forget what I said, and we could start again."

She found herself staring down at his outstretched hand. Was this some sort of trick? A leopard couldn't change his spots this quickly, could he?

He seemed to sense her uncertainty and smiled gently. "Well, could we consider a truce, at least for today? Washington's such a pretty city, and I'd like you to enjoy your first visit. I promise to be on my best behaviour."

Raven's hand seemed to rise to meet his almost of its own accord. "Okay, a truce for today."

She didn't smile, but watched his fingers clasp hers tightly for what seemed a moment longer than necessary. Even as he released her hand she could still feel the tingle that had shot up her arm, the warmth where his fingers had been.

"Have you got everything you need?" His voice wasn't rushed or breathless like she guessed hers would be. Hadn't he felt that flash of awareness, the electricity between them?

Obviously not. And if he wasn't aware of it, then she wasn't about to admit it, even to herself.

Raven nodded, and together they headed for the garage.

****

Now that he'd cleared the air a little, Greg decided he was going to enjoy showing someone Washington. Although he'd lived in Ellicott City all his life and visited the Capital many times, he'd never actually seen it through the eyes of a foreigner. It would be very interesting to see how Raven would react to the heart of his country. There were so many things he could show her. What would she like to see, he wondered? He glanced over at her and found her eyes darting around as she tried to take in everything around her.

"There's no hurry, you know," he murmured. "You have the rest of your life to see it all. Give yourself a few months and you won't find anything very exciting about all this. It's just typical suburbia."

He frowned as she quickly turned her face away from him, but not before he saw her biting her lip. What had he said that could have upset her now? Once again the feeling that she was hiding something perturbed him. He smiled grimly to himself, determined to find out what it was. After all, it must have something to do with his father.

He would do as he had promised, play the dutiful guide today. If he lulled her into a sense of companionable friendship, she might give herself away somehow. He would be alert to anything she did or said that might give him some idea what was going on in that tiny, little mind of hers.

"I think we'll head down the I-95. It should be a pretty quick run this early, and I'll bring you back a different way, maybe up Route One. It's one of the original roads, although it's not used so much now since they built the interstate in the sixties. You might be interested to see what America looked like in the fifties. Development along that road really slowed once the interstate was put in."

He was intrigued by the questions she asked as they drove. It was obvious she was interested in learning about the area, and seemed to be soaking up everything he could tell her. He found himself wondering, *was the dizzy blonde portrayal as much of an act as her fake accent had been?* She was displaying a very intelligent character. Some of the questions she asked he found he could not answer.

She seemed a little nervous at the size of the interstate, but settled back and relaxed when she realized there really was very little traffic on it at the moment. He noticed her flinching and even once shutting her eyes as yet another car cut in front of him without any warning. He made sure he kept a greater distance between himself and the car in front than he normally would, then smiled to himself at his unconscious consideration. He couldn't remember tempering his driving to suit anyone else before. Was it a desire to protect this woman who had apparently stolen his father's heart? He felt the guilt rise again, knowing he'd put his father's relationship with Raven right out of his mind. He didn't want to think of her and his father. Not ever. The mere thought caused his stomach to knot in a thousand places.

Coming out of his daze at the sound of her voice asking yet another question, he found himself telling her as much as he could remember about the Eisenhower interstate system. How the whole idea of linking all the states with a freeway system had been devised after the Second World War so troops could be moved quickly, if it was ever necessary to do so. And how President Eisenhower had ordered that the interstates must have long, flat areas every so many miles so they could be used as airstrips. He even explained how the odd numbered roads went north-south and the even numbered went east-west.

"You can't see very much of the city in one visit," Greg said. He steered them off the beltway that surrounded the city and headed down Connecticut Avenue toward its center. "Have you any ideas what you would like to see? Would you like to go to the Art Galleries? I believe the Freer Gallery is well worth a visit."

He hoped it wasn't his tone of voice that caused her to shake her head. While he appreciated fine art, he didn't know if he had the patience to spend the day walking around galleries. A little at a time, that was his motto.

"Would you mind if we look at all the really

tourist things? All the places I've seen on TV and in the movies—the White House, Jefferson Memorial, and Lincoln's too? I really want to stand up on those steps and look along the reflecting pond towards that tall thin obelisk. What is it?"

Greg couldn't help smiling. She was like a schoolgirl on an outing, excited and keen to see the reality of things she'd only seen in movies.

"That obelisk, as you call it, is the Washington Monument, honoring our first president."

"Whoops. Sorry." She smiled back at him, seeming to enjoy his teasing. "I know I'd like to see some of the Smithsonian, but it's such a lovely day, and I hate to waste all this sunshine. Would that be okay?"

"A walking tour of the monuments it shall be."

Greg found he was pleasantly surprised at her choice. Walking around the Mall with this beautiful woman on his arm would not hurt his ego one bit. He could already anticipate the envious looks he would get, as strangers assumed they were together, a couple, an item.

No. Greg did not mind her choice at all.

Chapter 6

Greg found a parking space very near the Mall. He was still smiling at Raven's reaction to the steam seeping up from the manholes along Seventeenth Street as he parked the car. She had grasped his arm in fright, convinced the Metro tunnels were about to explode. He glanced at her warily, but her sheepish smile assured him she hadn't minded his good-natured teasing.

His touch on her arm halted her attempt to exit the car. He could tell that she was eager to start sightseeing.

"Let's decide what we're doing before we brave the cold. What do you want to see most?" He leaned close to her as he reached under her seat to grasp a pile of maps that he brought out and placed on the seat between them.

What perfume does she have on? It's not familiar, but the essence is so sweet. He hastily tugged his mind back to where it was supposed to be. He had promised to guide her around DC, not the nearest boudoir.

"I know you've been ill, so maybe we'll need to take it a bit easy." He ignored her shaking head. "How about you tell me what you hope to see today, and then we'll plan how to manage as much as possible." He studied her closely, "Always assuming you continue to feel okay." He'd selected the map of downtown DC and folding it with the Mall uppermost, laid it on her knee.

"We're here. The White House is right there," he showed her on the map and then pointed through the windshield. "That's the closest you can get, unless you want to be here at five o'clock one morning to line up for tickets to get inside." He pointed again, this time behind them towards the Washington Monument. He continued to point out the sights on the map, carefully avoiding touching her legs. He needed to keep his mind off her legs.

"We can do all of these, can't we?" Raven had followed his finger as he picked out the sights she had mentioned on the way into the city. "It doesn't look far."

"It isn't really very far, but we might be pushing to see them all in one day, especially when you haven't been well."

"Don't you worry about me. I'm as fit as a fiddle. Let's go, shall we? I don't want to miss anything."

Greg had to smile at her eagerness. "I doubt if any of these monuments are going to disappear within the next few days," he teased, as they got out of the car and moved along the street until she could see the White House through the tall fence. He watched quietly as she lined her camera up between the rails, trying so hard not to notice just how shapely her body was.

"Come on." Greg tried to avert his thoughts. "If we're going to see all you want to, we're going to have to get moving." They headed towards the Washington Monument. Greg was careful to keep himself between her and a group of homeless men huddled around a vent at the corner of the Mall, but he was aware of her compassionate glance as they passed.

"Can't something be done to help those people?" she asked, looking back over her shoulder. "They look so lost, as if life has given up on them."

Greg was thankful he was with Raven. He had the feeling she might have approached the men, offering to help, had she been on her own.

"There are numerous groups trying, believe me." Greg assured her. "They'll gradually make a difference."

"It's so sad to see such hopelessness. How terrible it must be to have no family."

He was relieved when the lights changed color and he could lead her across the street, away from the reminder that life was far from perfect. They stopped under the Washington Monument, where he took the camera from Raven's hand and began clicking shots of her.

Next on Raven's wish list was the Jefferson Memorial, so off they went. Greg was sorry that they were too early in the spring for the famous blossoms that turned the Tidal Basin into a magnificent blaze of pink. The buds were beginning to form on the trees, but compared with the sight that would abound in a few weeks time the place was bare.

He was impressed with the pace that Raven set, but wondered if she'd be able to maintain it all day. He couldn't help but watch her, seeing how her body flowed as she walked. She was so light on her feet it was almost like she floated. There was no effort to her movement, as though body and mind merged together in the epitome of physical perfection.

Following behind her at one point, moving past others on the track, he'd realized that even after her illness—whatever it had been—she still displayed a perfect body. On a scale of one to ten, she was a twelve. Even through her jeans, he was aware of the way her muscles rippled as her legs moved. He found his eyes glued to her bottom, loving the way it moved, wanting to run his hand over it. Wishing he had the right—

For Heaven's sake. What's the matter with me? This woman is about to marry my father. He took a deep breath. *Okay, okay, Jefferson Memorial... Thomas Jefferson, what could he tell her about*

Thomas Jefferson? Author of the Declaration of Independence, third President, didn't he reorganize the Congress? Hell, history has never been my strongest subject.

As they moved into the dome, Greg realized Raven did not expect him to share his meager knowledge. Thank goodness. Instead, she was happy to move slowly around reading from the huge displays.

"He was quite a guy, wasn't he?" she whispered over her shoulder. "I've always meant to read up on him a little more."

"Dad's a bit of a history buff. You'll find plenty of books in the den. Please feel free to read any of them." Did he really need to make her feel like a visitor?

Yes, because he couldn't abide the thought of her marrying his father. Just for today he wanted to pretend she was just a guest, nothing more. That way he could at least attempt to enjoy the day.

Despite his efforts to take a rest at the FDR Memorial, Raven insisted on moving on. He watched her gait closely, in case she started to falter. He suspected she surprised herself as much as him with her endurance.

"I'm not going to cark out, you know." She grinned at him as she picked up the pace. "We can rest at the Reflecting Pond. It's very pretty there, isn't it?"

"Should I be pleased you're not going to 'cark out'?" he asked as he lengthened his stride to keep up with her.

"Very," she quipped back, "I weigh a damn sight more than a few four-by-fours. You'd probably end up with a hernia if you had to carry me back to the car."

Greg couldn't help but laugh as Raven teased him. As they left the Tidal Basin and walked

95

through the Korean War Memorial, he realized that he was thoroughly enjoying the day. Far more than he had thought possible. Wandering around the tourist sites of Washington would never have appeared on his list of things to do with a beautiful lady—he would have found other pursuits to follow. But today was showing him that life could be slowed down and still enjoyed.

If it was possible, Raven seemed to increase the pace as they approached the Lincoln Memorial. There was a look of total fascination on her face as she stood at the bottom and looked up at it. As she climbed the steep steps, he noticed she'd slowed down, and he lightly took her arm. At first he thought she would push him away, but then he felt her lean into his support, accepting she was obviously not as fit as she'd hoped. He was amazed at the look of triumph she wore as she looked out across the Reflecting Pond toward the Washington Monument and the Capitol Building. She silently handed him her camera and he knew she had achieved some sort of dream. He quickly clicked numerous photos, hoping some of them would capture the wonder in her expression.

"Ever since I saw the clip of Martin Luther King making his speech on these steps, I've wanted to come here."

He took her arm again as she returned from reading the towering inscriptions.

"Do you remember in *Forest Gump* how his girlfriend runs across the Pond?" he nodded as they slowly moved down the steps. "I always thought it was deep, like a lake—" Raven laughed a little self-consciously. "—until then."

Around the side of the Memorial Raven spied a hotdog stand and shyly requested they take a look. After an extended conversation with the vendor, Raven thoughtfully chose a Polish sausage and then insisted they sit under a tree beside the Pond. Not exactly what Greg would have chosen to eat for lunch, or to serve to such a gorgeous companion, but she seemed to be enjoying it.

Greg smiled at her as he bit off another chunk of hotdog. Completely against his will, he found himself liking her. She was nothing like he'd expect a gold digger to be. She seemed to enjoy simple things—look at what she'd requested for her lunch—and had shown great delight at seeing sights that he took for granted. They'd talked about a variety of things as they walked—movies, music, current affairs. Raven had even been able to comment knowledgably about the primaries that were taking place. One thing he knew for sure, Raven was no dizzy blonde bombshell. Whatever reason she might have for displaying such a personality yesterday Greg could not imagine.

****

Raven was very quiet after finishing her lunch. She was edgy as she studied the map on her knee. Her fingers were unsteady as she traced their route. He tried to see her face but she had it turned away from him and he couldn't make out any expression.

"We're close to the Vietnam Memorial, aren't we?"

"Yes, it's through the trees, you can just see the top of it," he pointed. "The black wall, see it?"

Raven nodded. Pausing for a moment, then with a very deep breath, she stood and pushed the map into the back pocket of her jeans. The movement drew Greg's eyes, and again he found himself appreciating the curve of her hip, the sway of her bottom as she moved. He rejoined her quickly, and was temporarily annoyed to see a group of young men approaching from the opposite direction actually turn to watch her as she walked away from them. But the envious looks on their faces restored his good humor, and his chest puffed out.

Today, this fox was with him.

Concentrating far too much on his libido, Greg wasn't aware Raven had stopped until he bumped into her.

"I'm sorry..." he began apologetically, but she seemed to be in a world of her own as she stared at the long black wall, its fifty-six thousand names of fallen Americans engraved into its length.

There were quite a number of people around; some checking the books near its entrance, some talking to the Vietnam veterans who were available to answer questions, others walking. One group was tracing a name from the wall onto paper. A few people were just standing, like Raven, as if overawed by the simplicity of the monument, or perhaps the magnitude of the loss.

Again he heard her taking a huge deep breath before she started to walk its length. Something told him to let her walk the path alone, following slowly many paces behind. The rows upon rows of names were enough to affect anyone.

His mind returned to Raven and he quickly scanned those along the walk until he sighted her. She was leaning against the chain fence near the end, and her stance warned him immediately that something was wrong. Very wrong.

Hurrying to her side, he was mindless of the people he pushed past. As he approached her, he saw tears rolling down her face. She was trying to control them, hide them, swiping her hands across her cheeks, but to no avail. Greg sensed her embarrassment and tried to shield her from prying eyes. Now he knew the reason for her tenseness, for some reason this memorial held a powerful significance to her.

"Let's sit over there." He put an arm around her shoulders and led her to an empty park bench out of sight of the memorial. He kept his arm in place, and after a moment when she hadn't pushed him away, gently turned her so he could clasp her in his arms.

What do I do now? She was a stranger, how did he comfort her. Instinctively he held her tight and gently rubbed her back. Were her sobs lessening?

He found he liked the feel of her body close to his, and for a second wished she were seeking something more from him than comfort. He could feel his heart pounding as he enjoyed the sweet smell of her perfume, the touch of her hair against his chin, the warmth.

Raven's move to withdraw from his arms bought him back from fantasyland with a thud. *What's the matter with me?* She needed comfort and support right now, not someone whose hormones were raging like a teenager's.

"Are you okay?"

"I'm so sorry." Raven had found a tissue and was blowing her nose. "I didn't mean to cry all over you."

"Think nothing of it," Greg replied gallantly. "Would you like to talk about it?" He wasn't sure if he should offer or not, but it seemed to be the right thing to do.

She moved a little on the seat, putting space between them. "My dad was a career soldier," she began very quietly. "Serving in Vietnam killed him."

Greg waited quietly, not sure if she was going to continue but loath to break the lengthening silence.

"Mum said he was so different when he came home. He was always getting sick. Any bug going around, he'd always catch it far worse than anyone else. I was two when they discovered he had cancer. He died a year later."

What can I say? Nothing came to mind so he just remained silent.

"A lot of Vietnam vets got cancer. They reckon it's because of the Agent Orange the Americans sprayed all over the countryside to kill the dense foliage. Those that are left are still fighting to get compensation." Greg faced the accusation in her voice, knowing absolutely nothing about the Vietnam War, but still feeling a sense of guilt and sadness at the possibility his countrymen could have been responsible for her father's death. Illogically, the thought filled him with remorse.

"I guess I was actually lucky. Some of their children had birth defects." There was another long silence, but when Raven spoke again the sadness in her voice was replaced with anger. "Do you know what really gets to me?" She swung around to face him. "What about all the others that are still dying because of that War? Do they get any recognition? Do they get their names on a monument? No bloody way. It's so unfair. For someone to give their life for their country and nobody gives a rat's."

He watched as color flooded her face and her eyes widened. He thought she looked even more beautiful, but her outburst suddenly stopped and she was left embarrassed. Jumping up, Raven strode a few paces away from him and kept her back toward him for a moment. When she turned he knew she was again in control.

"That was inexcusable." He noticed her difficulty swallowing and realized maybe she wasn't so much in control after all. "I apologize for my outburst, and for crying all over you." Would she normally have been this formal, or was it just because of who he was? "It's something I feel very strongly about."

"I understand." He didn't really, but wasn't about to admit he'd never felt that sort of passion, no matter how worthy the cause might be.

Greg checked the time, seeing it was getting late enough for them to call it a day and head home. Before he could suggest it, Raven had taken the initiative again.

"Can we walk this way? I don't think I could walk past there again today."

That was the end of her sorrow and anger. She'd buried those feelings, although he wondered if she could forget her outburst so easily. He followed her lead not wanting to embarrass her further, but he noticed the furtive glances she sometimes shot his way. She was no longer as comfortable in his company as she had been earlier in the day.

He was finding it hard to forget how warm she'd felt in his arms, how right it had felt for her to seek comfort from him. It would be even harder to forget how tempted he'd been to kiss away those tears, hoping to make her forget everything but him.

****

"Greg?"

He turned toward Raven as the garage door slid closed behind them. She was captivated by the friendly smile he threw her way. He was such a good-looking bloke and she would be less than honest if she didn't admit she'd enjoyed being with him today. She'd enjoyed the looks she saw other women giving him, eyeing him up like a prize piece of meat. But now she realised not only did she admire his looks, she believed she could actually like him as a person.

He had displayed a gentle caring spirit all day. She'd been aware of him trying to moderate their pace and knew he was concerned about her stamina. Her display at the Vietnam Memorial could have been so embarrassing, but he couldn't have reacted in a more sympathetic way. She would have felt so humiliated if he'd made an issue out of it. Crying all over him had been bad enough, she didn't need a third degree. She had been most impressed when he'd followed her lead and 'forgot' all about it.

The question she wanted answered was which Greg was the real one? The kind, friendly guide of today; or the sour, mean-mouthed brute from last night?

"Thank you," Raven said softly. "I don't know when I've had such a lovely day." She watched his smile broaden as she added, "You could make a living guiding foreigners around Washington if you ever get sick of building things."

She held out her hand, meaning to shake his as an extra expression of her gratitude. She found her fingers enveloped in his, not shaken, but held. He was rubbing his thumb across the back of her hand very lightly. Its effect was heart stopping, the whole of her hand burned. His touch caused an electric current to shoot through her veins.

She found her eyes locked with his. Those eyes mesmerized her. She watched as he leaned toward her, her eyes now on his lips as they came closer. She felt herself leaning too. Waiting, hoping...

Suddenly the garage door began to open and both Greg and Raven jumped back guiltily. Their eyes looked everywhere but at each other. They climbed out of the car in time to greet Jorge and Manuela as they pulled their car in beside Greg's.

Raven was grateful for their presence as their conversation filled the guilty silence. For an instant her eyes met Greg's, then flicked away. They knew what had nearly happened. They knew it would have been wrong. But that did nothing to dampen the desire Raven had seen in Greg's eyes. Nor, she was ashamed to admit, her own disappointment.

****

Greg had to straighten himself out, and soon. He'd acted like a bear with a sore head all day. Joan, his father's secretary and general Girl Friday around the office for many years, had finally threatened to resign unless he left her in peace. She'd sure been surprised when he'd decided to go home.

Greg grimaced. It seemed indicative of his lifestyle that she should have been so amazed. Joan's sharp-edged but kindly-meant comments had always fallen on deaf ears, but not today. Was it because today, for the first time in a long, long time, Greg felt like he had something to go home to? Or someone?

Greg flinched as he threw the internal garage door shut and it slammed on its hinges. It was all very well to want to see Raven again, but what good could come of it? She had wanted him to kiss her last night. He knew he had not misread the heightened tension in the car. That moment had dulled all his common sense because all he'd wanted to do was feel her in his arms again.

During the sleepless night, common sense had prevailed! She was going to marry his father. His father! How was he going to tolerate virtually living in the same house, seeing her day after day, imagining her with his father? He found himself shivering with distaste.

Damn! This is getting like some second-rate trashy afternoon television talk show: Son Lusts after Stepmother.

Greg ran his fingers through his hair striding towards his office. He had to figure a way to stop this wedding; or leave town, for a while at least. He couldn't imagine being able to live in such close confines while his body was screaming out with desire for her. He wouldn't risk hurting his father.

The trouble was he knew Raven felt something too, something that might well break Brad's heart. Again his fingers combed through his hair. She had no right even to consider marrying anyone, let alone his father; not when Greg's touch drew such a response.

As Greg entered his office he saw the object of all his thoughts, all his immediate problems, sitting behind his desk at his computer.

"What are you doing?" He hadn't intended his voice to sound so gruff, but from her guilty jump he guessed she hadn't been aware of him prior to his words.

"Manuela showed me. She said you wouldn't mind if I sent an email home." The defensive note in her voice caused him to grimace.

His hand returned to his hair. Again. And he sighed. "Of course I don't mind, Raven. I meant to show you last night when we got home." His voice petered out as their eyes met and held for a moment. Both remembered why conversation had not been resumed once they were out of the car...

Greg was intrigued to see color coming up into Raven's face before she hastily averted her eyes from his. *Oh, she remembers all right, she remembers wanting me as much as I want her.*

He noticed with some surprise that Raven became even more agitated as he moved around the desk behind her. Did she think he wanted to read her letter? Why would he be interested in whatever she wrote home? Home to whom? Brad? Or maybe someone else? He was intrigued, despite himself. *Has she said something about me?* He leaned closer, apparently to reach something on his desk but surreptitiously eyeing the screen.

He was right. She was very jittery.

"I'll be just a sec, then I'm finished," she spoke hurriedly over her shoulder, typing a few final words.

"That's okay. Take your time." He moved around the back of the computer so he could watch her. She looked tired today. Dare he hope that she'd had trouble sleeping last night too? Or was it just the after-effects of a full day yesterday? His loins stirred as he watched her furtively glance at him. She was aware of him, his presence affected her. The fingers that had been speeding across the keyboard now fumbled. He grinned as he watched how many times she had to correct mistakes. He moved toward a filing cabinet almost directly behind her, pulling out a drawer but not averting his gaze. She fumbled again seeming to know his eyes never left her, as if she was feeling them—as if she knew he wanted to let her feel much more than just his eyes on her.

"I'm just finishing..." Her voice sounded husky, sexy.

He took a deep breath, his hand going to his hair again. This was murder. How on earth was he going to deal with this?

Hey! Why did she do that?

Raven sent her email, and then deleted it. He quickly looked away as she glanced at him, as if checking to see if he'd noticed. He pretended to be searching through some papers lying beside the monitor and noticed her soft sigh. A sigh of relief? What had been in that email that she hadn't wanted him to see?

He picked up a letter and moved around behind her. "This needs to be answered right away. I missed it somehow. Are you finished? No, don't shut it down—I'll do it later."

Greg hustled her out of the chair and appeared to ignore her as he quickly sat down and began to type. He heard her murmur something as she moved toward the door, but didn't even acknowledge her leaving.

As soon as he could no longer hear her footsteps, he jumped out of the chair and crossed to shut the door. Returning to the computer, he cancelled his typing and threw the 'letter' he'd been holding—a flyer offering discounted carpet cleaning—into the trashcan. He'd had to think of something quickly to get her away from the computer before she had a chance to delete her message from the recycle bin as well. He didn't care about the ethics of reading other people's mail right now. He was going to find out what she'd been saying, especially when she'd gone to so much effort to ensure he wouldn't be able to read it. She was hiding something, maybe now he could find out what.

He felt like a guilty schoolboy as he brought up the offending email from the recycle bin. He kept his ears open, listening in case she returned to the office for some reason. He hadn't been this sneaky since he and Tony had pulled some of their girl-watching pranks back in school.

He wasn't really surprised to find the letter going to someone other than his father, but he didn't know whom. It just started with 'Hi'. However, the first words of the text caused him to suck in his breath and he watched his knuckles whiten as his feelings of guilt quickly changed to anger. Intense anger. His first impression of her had been right; she was a conniving little bitch.

Make sure Brad doesn't see this. She'd even typed it in capital letters for emphasis. Greg groaned. He'd wanted to find out what she was up to, but he'd no longer felt suspicious of her motives. Hell, he'd really enjoyed yesterday. He liked her, liked her a lot. Not just her body but also the type of person she seemed to be. He cursed, thumping his fist against the desk, wincing at the pain that flashed up his arm.

He'd had the premonition that she was only taking Brad for a ride. Why had he allowed himself to be hoodwinked? He was even more gullible than his father. He'd had some warning of her intentions and yet still managed to fall for her.

Jerking open a bottom drawer in the desk, he brought out a bottle and glass. He needed some fortifying before he read any further. Because he was going to read it—he was even going to make a copy of it and show it to his father when he got home. He would double any effort, do anything, to ensure that she could not hurt Brad.

The second glass of amber liquid didn't seem to burn his throat as much as the first. He slowly and deliberately screwed on the bottle top and replaced it in the drawer. Setting the glass down very carefully next to the bottle, he pushed the drawer shut. His fingers began to massage the bridge of his nose. He could feel his head beginning to ache unbearably, but he turned to the screen and began to read.

It took only a couple of lines for Greg to realize the reason she did not want Brad to see the letter was to spare his feelings, not to hide anything from him.

He squirmed uncomfortably in the seat as he read an account of his welcome to her. Seeing it written down in black and white embarrassed him even more than remembering his initial behavior.

Then he found himself leaning closely towards the screen, gazing at the words absolutely dumbfounded. He read them again. And again.

'There's been some misunderstanding Mum. He thinks Brad is marrying me, not you.'

Greg gave a guffaw of laughter, as he felt all the tension rush out of his body. He jumped out of the chair and hastily locked the door. He didn't want Manuela or Raven checking to see what the noise was all about. He needed time to assimilate all this.

Raven was not going to marry his father!

His body sagged as he threw himself back into the chair. There was an immediate feeling of euphoria, of elation.

She was free! And anything that he felt, or that might develop between them was not sordid or shameful. He did not have to suppress the desire he felt for her or feel guilty about it. It wasn't wrong!

He jumped up again. Feeling like a cat on hot

tiles, he couldn't stay still. He wanted to share this wonderful news with someone. Wanted to go and take Raven in his arms and whirl her round and round, share the joy of the growing awareness of each other with her. He hadn't felt so happy for a long time.

After some moments trying to calm himself down, Greg returned to the computer and read the rest of Raven's letter. As he read of her reason for portraying herself as a 'bride-to-be from hell', Greg felt an embarrassment so acute he groaned. This was all his fault!

Greg was sorry her letter ended so abruptly. He would have been interested to know what else she might have said, had he not interrupted her. However, he now knew the truth. Brad was intending to marry Raven's mother, a much more suitable match.

Greg found himself quite liking the idea, especially if she was anything like her daughter. Greg almost laughed aloud as he realized all his previous concerns over the impending marriage had disappeared. The house had been without a mistress long enough, and if Brad had found someone he wanted to spend his remaining years with—well good for him!

When did I decide Dad wasn't being taken for a ride? Perhaps it was Raven's declaration of love for Brad. He had had to believe she loved him. She'd been very convincing. And yet now he knew that love was not a romantic love, but a deep and meaningful friendship. If an affinity like that did exist, and he believed it did, he felt sure the relationship Brad must have with her mother would be equally meaningful. Somehow after spending yesterday with Raven, Greg had begun to trust her. It had been hard to believe that she, or anyone associated with her, could do anything that was less than honest and aboveboard.

Except try and fool him.

He grinned to himself as he replaced the letter in the recycle bin of the computer's memory and closed down the Internet. He'd give her a little time to come clean on her own. She'd be horribly embarrassed if he confronted her with knowing the truth, and rightfully annoyed at his tampering with her mail.

There wasn't any real hurry, not now that he knew the truth.

Chapter 7

Greg leaned over the swinging doors and asked Manuela, "Where's Raven?"

Looking up from the stove, the housekeeper glanced at the clock in surprise. She was always finished in the kitchen long before Greg put in an appearance after work. Greg merely grinned at Manuela's shocked expression.

"She said she had some postcards to write. Maybe she's in her room."

"Thanks." Greg turned to go, then paused. "What did she do today?"

Manuela continued with her dinner preparations. "Abby called this morning and picked her up. I think they went down to the old town." She looked piercingly at him. "She's not long back. She wanted to get her mail sent."

"Has she had a look around the house yet?"

"Not properly."

He knew Manuela was frowning as he turned to go. "I'll give her a tour."

Running up the stairs, he was pleased with himself. Showing her the house would give him plenty of apparently unplanned time in her company.

Knocking on her door, he waited impatiently for her to open it. Manuela had been right. She was writing up the postcards she'd bought yesterday in D.C., Greg could see some of them lying on the bed behind her as she opened the door.

She smiled slightly, but didn't say anything.

"Manuela says you haven't had a proper look at

the house yet. I could show you, if you'd like?"

Raven seemed to hesitate for a moment before answering, "Thanks, I'd like that."

Greg felt like rubbing his hands together. He wanted to pursue the smoldering intimacy he'd felt last night. He couldn't be too obvious, while she maintained her silly act. "Just give me a minute to get out of my work clothes." Dashing along the hall, throwing a smile back at her, he disappeared through his bedroom door.

He quickly changed into a pair of track pants and a bright yellow tee shirt. It had 'You want to do what with me?' emblazoned across the front. He knew she wouldn't see the back immediately where it said, "Play golf." One of his old girlfriends had given it to him. He only wore it to work out, but today, it might serve a purpose.

Raven had left her door open and jumped off the bed as he reappeared. He had difficulty keeping a straight face at the expression she wore as her eyes read the message on his chest. As they flashed up and met his, he sent her what he hoped was an intimate little smile. The blush rising in her cheeks made her look even more attractive, more desirable. He forced himself to go very slowly and keep his mind off his hormones, even as they were threatening to rage out of control.

"Let's start upstairs," he suggested, holding out his hand to her. He smiled as she moved past him, carefully avoiding any physical contact.

Greg was justifiably proud of the home Brad had built when Greg was in elementary school. He realized long ago that his parents had hoped for a larger family, but the four of them had managed to fill the big place.

He guessed from Raven's surprised expression when he opened the door at the end of the hallway that she had not even realized there was a third floor above the one they were on.

"No one comes up here much anymore," he explained, showing her two bedrooms and a full bathroom. The huge playroom with its moveable partition showed a neglected lack of use. He hadn't been up here for years. "This was our part of the house, mine and Abby's," he explained. "Dad built it so we could each have our own private play room, if we wanted it. Or we could pull back these doors and make one huge room. We usually kept it open, unless one of us had friends over. Abby would close off my side if she had a slumber party, and threaten all sorts of dire happenings if I so much as knocked on one of the doors." He smiled at the memories. "We had a lot of fun up here. It's a great space for kids." He turned to her. "Perhaps you and Dad might fill it up again."

Some imp had taken control and he hadn't been able to resist the little dig. Hastily he turned away as he spied the horrified expression she wore. Regaining control of his facial muscles, he turned to her again. "You shouldn't worry about Dad's age. He'll still be around for years yet. He'd be able to see a couple more kids through college." He made a point of acknowledging her expression. "Unless you don't want children, of course." He paused for a moment as if puzzled. "You did say at Abby's that you like children?" He paused again. Still she made no comment.

"I'm sorry, I didn't mean to intrude on something private between you and Dad. Just want you to know I really like the idea of having some little brothers and sisters." He patted her on the shoulder, ignoring her gasp, and led the way back to the second floor. There he showed her each room, including his own.

On the main floor walking her through the formal rooms she'd already seen, he led her towards his father's apartment.

"I don't think Dad was expecting to marry again when he designed it. It's a bit like a single man's dwelling. Dad always ate his meals with me, but there's also a full kitchen here." Showing her this part of the house in much more detail, he took delight in showing her the wardrobe spaces and cupboards. After all, her mother might like to hear Raven's impression of Brad's apartment, Greg tried to tell himself that's why he was going into such detail. "I'm sure Dad will have anything changed to suit you. In fact if you wanted to start making a list now, we could get some work underway, even before the wedding."

He watched something akin to panic run across her face. Her eyes darted everywhere—everywhere but at him. He warmed to her even more as he watched her agitation and heard the stumbled words that she would wait for Brad.

He had read her right. Lying and pretending didn't come easily to her. If his reaction to her arrival had been more friendly and welcoming, she'd never have ventured on this course of action. He guessed she would have corrected his misunderstanding immediately and they would have gone from there. This mess really was of his making.

She'd had some fun at his expense, and now it was his turn. Just for a little while, and then he'd give her an opening that would allow her to confess without any fear of retribution.

"Dad mentioned in his email that you might like to do some painting. I expect he was meaning for you to use this sunroom. It's very pleasant out here on a winter's day, and I guess artists like you need lots of natural light to create their masterpieces."

While he had noted obvious talent in the sketch she'd made for Vikki, he still wondered at her calling herself an artist. Not that he suspected her of lying, just exaggerating to create an image. She seemed so intelligent and her awareness of current affairs—even American current affairs—had really surprised him. She sounded more like a college professor than an artist. *Although I've never met an artist before,* he had to acknowledge to himself.

When they had seen Brad's entire apartment, Greg headed for the basement. She admitted surprise, saying she hadn't realized it even existed. "Most houses around here have basements," he explained, hoping he wasn't sounding too patronizing, "unless there's an underground water problem, of course."

"This place is huge." Raven seemed to be in a stupor. "It's at least three or four times the size of our place at home."

Greg watched as her gaze took in the extensive open space that was the basement. His eyes followed hers. Mostly he took all this very much for granted, rarely stopping to realize how fortunate he was. Seeing his home through someone else's eyes, someone who obviously wasn't used to so much space made him appreciate just how lucky he really was. He walked through this room almost every day and, like the rest of the house, paid little attention to it. He hardly noticed the beautifully laid out family room, the extensive bar unit in the corner, the Persian rugs on the floor. He felt a sudden flash of guilt; all these material things—did he really enjoy them? Their presence was a sign of his family's success, their wealth, and little else...

Greg shook himself mentally and joined Raven beside a water fountain in the corner of the room. She was allowing the water to run through her fingers.

"This is so beautiful, so peaceful..." he heard her whisper as she traced the edge of an imitation rock with her index finger. Greg found the movement oddly erotic, and was thankful that Raven seemed to have slipped into her own world for a moment. Teasing her was one thing, but he didn't need her to guess that he was not as controlled as he pretended.

Clearing his throat to catch her attention, he led the way across to another door. "Feel free to come down here any time you want."

He watched her puzzled expression change to one of excitement as she passed him into the next room. It was his gym—a very extensive gym. He spent some time here most evenings, and guessed that Raven would enjoy using the equipment—it took only seconds to see she was indeed familiar with most of the machines. He watched as she flitted from one to the other, quickly checking them out.

"You really don't mind?" she asked, looking at him openly for the first time since he'd teased her in the attic. He could tell that any sexual awareness she might have been conscious of was now gone. Her mind was firmly fixed on the gym and, he guessed, her plans for future workouts.

"Of course I don't mind." He dropped any attempt to hassle her. This was important to her. He could see that.

"Thank you." Her gratitude was obvious, even with just those two simple words.

"You haven't been able to work out for a while?" Greg guessed as he led the way out of the room.

"Seems like months," Raven replied. "It's been driving me crazy." She seemed to be almost talking to herself. "Now I'll be able to pace myself a little easier, see how I'm feeling before I hit the road."

She turned to Greg and gave him such a beautiful smile he felt his stomach knot. "Thank you so much," she added. "You don't know what this means to me."

Greg knew what it meant to him. Seeing that joyful look on her face, knowing that such a simple thing could get such a reaction—and it was something he'd offered so casually. It left him wondering what she might do if he offered her the beautiful clothes and jewels he wanted to drape her in.

Sucking in a deep breath, he imagined how she would look in a sleek black gown molded tightly to her curvy body. He saw himself placing a sparkling necklace around her neck, the low cut of the dress allowing him to see the swell of her creamy breasts as he leaned over her shoulder.

He shook his head to dispel the vision. He already knew what she would do if he offered such things—refuse them.

After her open expression of gratefulness, Greg regretted his earlier behavior. Raven seemed vulnerable, defenseless, and he felt the primitive male urge to protect his mate. Teasing her wouldn't make it easier for her to admit she wasn't going to marry his father.

Manuela was still in the kitchen, putting the finishing touches to the evening meal.

"How about something to drink?" Greg offered, going to the fridge. "Then I'll show you around outside before it gets any colder." They sat and chatted with the housekeeper for a few minutes before Greg excused himself and grabbed two jackets from the foyer closet. He smiled as he returned to the kitchen.

"Here," he said, carefully placing the other jacket around Raven's shoulders, "slip this on." He thought he noticed her nose twitch and hoped she had picked up the smell of his cologne on the jacket.

He led the way out the back of the kitchen and watched as he guessed Raven saw the extent of the house for the first time. He could not keep the smile from his face as he watched her growing amazement.

"This is a mansion." She gazed up at the huge

brick structure in awe. "I can't see all this from my window, or the roadside. I had no idea the place was so big." She twirled around. "And this garden, it just goes on forever."

Greg again felt a swell of pride. This was his home, the place where he'd grown up and spent so many happy years. Now, seeing Raven's reaction, he again counted his good fortune. He was indeed blessed.

His smile grew as he led her around the south side of the house, to where the large enclosed pool was visible; behind it, the tennis court. He didn't give a thought to the fact that he rarely used either anymore. While Brad had included this expanse of landscaping for the enjoyment of his family, it had been years since Greg had even been out in this garden. He glanced around, knowing Jorge would have every blade of grass, every shrub, every tree displayed to its best.

Greg found himself looking around again, suddenly feeling lost. He had a beautiful home, a thriving business, more money than he could ever spend, and the pick of any woman in his social circle. Yet he felt so empty, so alone.

He sighed deeply. Was this all that life intended to deal him? There had to be more. He remembered his childhood. The house had been full of love and laughter. Not silent and empty, like now.

His eyes fastened onto Raven as she moved across the garden away from him. His jacket, which she held tightly around herself to ward off the chilling wind, obscured most of her curves, leaving only her long legs visible in their tight jeans.

Man, but she is beautiful. And funny, he added.

She'd know how to fill a home with love and laughter.

****

Raven was surprised how quickly the days

passed. She had been in Ellicott City a week and was feeling almost like her old self. Her daily workouts in Greg's gym, always done during his working hours, had slowly increased until she felt ready to push her body to almost the same level as prior to her illness. Yesterday she'd gone for her first run, taking it very gently to start with, but increasing the pressure as she felt her old euphoria returning. Today she was heading towards a track in Patapsco Park that Jorge had shown her. She knew her strength was gradually returning; but she was careful to tell Manuela and Jorge which track she intended to take and when to expect her back. No point in being too optimistic.

Initially walking, Raven found the cool, crisp air a pleasure to breathe once her lungs got over the initial shock. Even in winter Auckland's temperatures did not sink anywhere near this low, and she was not used to such a nip in the air. She jumped over a gate and proceeded into the Park, surprised to see such a wide and seemingly well-used road.

She let her mind wander as her running shoes pounded out their tattoo on the gravel. Raven was enjoying her holiday. Abby, a perfect hostess, was visiting or taking her places. She guessed that Raven would enjoy a trip to the supermarket as much as some tourist area, and she seemed to enjoy Raven's company. Raven was surprised that the subject of the forthcoming wedding was never raised. Abby never asked personal questions. Raven felt terribly guilty about her deception, as a budding friendship appeared to be growing. Sometimes she would catch Abby looking at her with a strange expression on her face, but she had not yet found the courage to confess.

The day after she sent her interrupted email, Raven received a terse message from her mother, followed by an even more agitated phone call. Joy had been calmed by Raven's promise to sort things out. Since then her daily letters had been full of what she was seeing and doing in America. Raven carefully refrained from mentioning whether or not she had told all, filling her notes with questions about the boys and ignoring her mother's inquiries on the subject. Raven felt a continuing pang of guilt whenever she allowed her mind to dwell on the fact that she hadn't yet fulfilled her promise to fix things.

She hadn't seen Greg since Wednesday. There had been an accident on one of his building sites in Hagerstown and he'd had to spend long days trying to rectify the problem. Raven didn't really understand when Abby explained to her; after all, she had no knowledge of the fundamentals of the construction business. She was just thankful that no one had been injured—and that apparently, Hagerstown was far away enough to involve staying overnight. It had kept Greg out of her way.

The couple of evenings he'd been home had been spent companionably enough. They'd shared the meals Manuela left for them. After tidying the kitchen, they'd adjourned to the living room where they sat in front of a roaring fire, talking.

He was such an enigma! His behaviour toward her seemed to have changed again. He was no longer sarcastic, in fact quite the opposite. Their discussions were on the whole, very sociable, with some interesting clashes as they debated a wide range of topics.

Raven was surprised how much he seemed to like to talk, to argue varying points as if he welcomed the company. Previously he'd struck her as being introverted. More likely, he just didn't want to be bothered with such frivolity as quiet conversation.

She sometimes wondered if he was surprised

too. At times she would see a strange expression on his face, but it was only momentary and she was never able to analyse it. She'd become wary of his almost ingratiating manner. It scared her. He was so polite and seemed to watch her more closely than necessary. At other times she was very much aware of his aversion to her company. He was so changeable, she never knew what his mood might be. Sometimes when they were alone, his often intimate little smiles left her heart pounding—and wondering what he was up to.

He was being devious. She knew that. He was the type of guy who if he wanted something he'd get it, no matter what means he might have to use.

How could she stop her heart from quickening whenever he entered a room? How could she deny that she felt more alive when she was with him? This was so ridiculous. How could a man she had only just met make her feel like her life was completely upside down. It was crazy, irrational. She had to get a grip on herself.

Slowing her pace as the road narrowed to a dirt track, she paid more attention to the ground as she moved. It was still pretty smooth and not at all wet or muddy. Much different than the tracks at home, even in mid-summer there were likely to be slippery areas. Glancing up at the tall trees, she saw their bare branches just starting to bud. Even here in the forest, where the trees were very plentiful the sun still filtered through onto the ground. That was the difference, of course. With the evergreen bush at home the sun was blocked out high above the ground.

It was so peaceful here. She couldn't believe a busy highway was just a couple of hundred metres away, traffic sounds were so faint in the background. Slowing her pace to a walk, Raven looked more closely into the trees hoping to catch sight of some birds. It was disappointing that she'd seen hardly any. Brad told her of the abundance of bird life that fed in the garden: cardinals, orioles, robins, doves, to mention but a few. So far she'd seen nor heard nothing but crows. Somehow she couldn't imagine herself painting a crow, not when there were so many other beautiful birds in the world. Perhaps she would see some others before it was time to go home.

She stopped as the trees opened out to a small clearing, sinking down onto the grass to rest. Although she was short of breath and her legs felt tight, she was content with her physical progress. Taking a short rest until her breathing steadied, Raven did a couple of stretches before lying back on the long grass under the huge power lines that ran the length of the clearing. The humming was so hypnotic, she'd have to be careful not to fall asleep. She didn't want Jorge to have to come looking for her.

Tonight Greg was taking her out to dinner. He had called last night to say he'd be home tonight and invited her to a dinner dance at his country club. Raven felt nervous, although he'd made it sound so casual. He explained that Manuela and Jorge had planned to be away this weekend and that they would eat out to save the housekeeper worrying about preparing meals in advance.

Raven was trying to be nonchalant, but it didn't seem to have worked. Manuela's knowing little smile, as she confirmed this morning that Turf Valley was quite a swanky place and Raven would need to dress for dinner, did nothing to help Raven's state of mind. If the housekeeper thought there was more here than met the eye, what chance did Raven have to assume it was all so innocent?

Why did his image pop into her mind all the time? Couldn't she think of anything else but him?

She smiled as two laughing faces came to mind.

She'd been surprised she wasn't missing her boys more, but it sounded like they were being spoiled rotten by their new granddad. They'd arranged a phone call for tonight. Joy would be ringing soon after breakfast on their Saturday. Apparently both boys had exciting news that couldn't be relayed over the Internet. Looking forward to hearing what it was, she guessed it would be the results from their swim club. She knew they had performed well all season, and hoped that each of them might have been rewarded. She checked her watch, not knowing why. It was hours before she would hear their voices.

Alerted by a sound close by, she looked toward the trees. It was a deer. Raven lay very still, having never seen a deer in the wild before. There were two of them now. She watched as they skittishly sniffed the air and advanced into the clearing a few paces, only to return to the safety of the trees. What graceful creatures. Even if they are so destructive, they're beautiful, she thought. Perhaps one day she'd paint one if she ever tired of birds. She almost laughed. She would never tire of painting birds. Her eyes remained on the deer as they again ventured out into the clearing, finally deciding to make a break for the other side after much sniffing and prancing around. She felt disappointed when they disappeared this time, knowing she was unlikely to see them again.

Everything looks so dead, when will spring really arrive? Greg had mentioned that the landscape often seemed to change from bare and dormant to lush and green almost overnight.

There she was, thinking about Greg again. Couldn't he stay out of her head for even an hour? She viciously threw away a piece of grass she had been playing with. If only she had met him at a party, at the supermarket, on a bus. Anywhere else—so she could have gotten to know him without this pretence—where it would have been simple.

She shivered, knowing she was attracted to Greg, far too attracted for her own good. She wanted him to hold her, to feel his body close to hers, to be able to touch him and feel those muscles rippling under her hands.

While trying to convince herself that her feelings for Greg were totally under control, she knew that she felt more alive now than she had in a long, long time. She had to acknowledge the doubts and fears she was wrestling with now. It meant that she was ready to leave her memories where they belonged, in the past. But could she?

Rolling over onto her stomach, Raven rested her head on her arms. *I can't go on like this.* She felt a mass of emotions beyond her control. Right now she felt like crying with the frustration of all the nervous energy that she was not managing to run off. Running had always helped her clear her head and put things into prospective before. *Why isn't it working now?*

Because I feel so guilty, answered the little voice in her head. Once she came clean and confessed Brad was marrying her mother, all this playacting could stop, and she could relax and enjoy Greg's company. They could become friends. Perhaps even more...

She jerked herself to her feet. What was the point in fantasizing? Even if Greg did forgive her duplicity, nothing would ever come of it. Sure, maybe it could develop into a holiday fling, but what about afterwards? She would return to her home half a world away knowing she could never forget him. She didn't have the moral character for a holiday fling. She would have to love him to get involved and how did one get over a fling when love was involved?

Very painfully!

Raven started to jog, her mind made up. She had to tell him the truth tonight, as soon as he arrived home. Her anger and determination to smooth Joy's path had waned as she'd got to know Greg and Abby. Neither were the arrogant snobs she'd believed them to be. They were nice people and Joy would like them too. There had been no need to continue this pretence past the first couple of days. She'd been lying to herself when she'd justified her behaviour with concerns about her mother. She'd been a coward, with her concern for herself, not for Joy. While Greg believed the story of her engagement, she'd used it as a smokescreen, to help protect her from herself. She should have known she wasn't emotionally equipped to deal with all this lying.

Tomorrow she would tell Abby. She needed to confess to Greg first though. He was the one who'd borne the brunt of her anger. She hoped they could forgive her, understand her reasons and accept her apologies.

She did not regret the subterfuge completely. Actually it had been fun, to start with. Concern for Joy had been paramount and she would never apologise for that. But she would be sorry if this remained a barrier between them and her. She hoped to visit Brad and her mother in the future, and wouldn't want her visits to be overshadowed by bad feelings.

But now she had to subdue any growing feelings she might have for Greg. He could not be part of her future, so the only part he was going to play in her present had to be as Brad's son, her step-brother.

Her step faltered and she almost fell. She could never look on Greg as a brother. Her feelings ran much too deep, and, she grimaced, would be scandalous if attributed to one's brother. She sucked in a deep breath. She had to keep away from him.

Stay aloof. Ignore those little smiles that made her toes curl.

Oh hell! She was going back to the house to prepare for an evening of dining and dancing with him. It would be a struggle to remain aloof if he held her in his arms, but she had to do it—for her own sanity.

Chapter 8

Raven turned Brad's car out of the driveway and into the street, remembering to check the traffic on her left hand side first. She'd forgotten how much concentration was necessary to drive a car. At home it was just second nature, but here, where they drove on the right side of the road, where even the car was back to front, she found she needed to concentrate very carefully.

With his own experience of driving in New Zealand, Brad had been able to give Raven the necessary advice to survive on the roads in Maryland. Right turns on a red light were legal unless otherwise sign-posted, don't ever pass a school bus with its lights flashing and, of course, keep right.

Driving on the opposite side of the road, now that was an experience! Raven had been so grateful for Abby's company that first day as she not only tried to remember to stay in the proper lane, she also had to get used to the steering wheel being on the opposite side of the car. But she'd now been out in Brad's car a couple of times on her own and felt like she might be getting the hang of it. So many of the roads where actually divided by wide median strips that generally she found she could not make an error anyway.

As long as she kept her wits about her at an intersection—they were the fun places, intersections. She smiled as she remembered some berk impatiently tooting his horn at her yesterday when she was trying to figure out who had the right of way. What she needed was a big sign up in the windscreen above the dashboard telling everyone that she was a foreigner—and then they might steer clear of her. She laughed out loud at the very thought.

The school bus rule was different from at home and truly amazed her. When the buses stopped in the middle of the road, everything else stopped too. She was very thankful to Brad for warning her. While the rule was obviously there to protect the children, Raven couldn't help but wonder if they grew up thinking that when they were on the road all traffic would stop for them, when would they ever learn any road sense?

She slowed the car, trying to make out numbers on the houses. Wouldn't it be easier to have the mailboxes numbered? Thank goodness this was a quiet road, otherwise she was sure horns would have been tooting at her impatiently as she continued to inch the car along. Finally she spied the number she'd been looking for and pulled into the driveway of an imposing two-story house a few miles from Greg's.

She was thankful it was today she'd arranged to meet with Brad's best friends. Her churning thoughts of Greg, and the situation she was finding harder and harder to deal with had stayed with her all morning. She knew she needed to clear her mind and concentrate on something else, or she'd be in no state to go out with him tonight. Not if there was going to be soft music and candlelight—she had to settle down if she intended to pretend that being near him meant nothing to her. What could be a better distraction than a visit to an elderly couple? Especially when she knew that, as Brad's lawyer, Neal Zimmerman had been involved with the paperwork necessary to arrange for Joy's impending arrival as the fiancée of an American citizen. She did not need to pretend today. She could be herself, plain old Raven Titirangi. Not Brad Collins' wife-to-be.

The front door flung open as Raven reached the top step. The warmth of the welcome did not surprise her. Conversation on the phone with Jeannie Zimmerman had been full of friendly curiosity. Raven was sorry she'd not been able to visit sooner, but their short trip out of state made this their first chance to actually meet.

"Welcome, honey. We've been dying to meet you!" A tall, slight woman, with sparkling blue eyes quickly emerged to wrap Raven in a warm hug. "We're so sorry we had to go away."

"Let go of the poor girl, Jeannie. You'll smother her." Raven heard the teasing note in the voice, but was as yet unable to see a face.

"Don't be silly, Neal." Her arm still firmly around Raven, Jeannie led her into a beautifully furnished living room dominated by a huge stone fireplace. The burning logs emitted a warm glow as Jeannie showed Raven to a seat. She found herself craning her neck to look up at Neal before he settled on the sofa beside her.

"It's nice to finally meet you." He clasped her hands in his. Raven noticed that the knuckles were a little swollen with arthritis but the face she looked into belied his sixty-plus years.

What is it about these American men? Don't they age like other people? Thick white hair fell down over his forehead as he spoke. "We've heard quite a lot about you."

Raven felt her eyebrows rise.

"Brad's talked of you frequently," Neal continued, "but seems to be a little reticent about his new lady." His teasing grin caused his moustache to wriggle slightly. "We want to know everything that sly old dog has been up to."

Within moments, the Zimmermans had put Raven completely at ease, and she enjoyed sharing tales of Brad's adventures in New Zealand. She even found herself embellishing them a little, much to her hosts' delight. Joy would find no hostility or opposition to her marriage here.

Two hours passed like twenty minutes as they chatted over coffee, juice and cake. Finally, the marriage ceremony itself came up.

"Brad wanted me to organise things so they'd be as Mum would want, but to tell you the truth I don't really know where to start. If they'd been married at home it would have been easy, but Brad wanted Mum to meet his family and friends first." She found herself watching Jeannie. "I'm so grateful for those contacts you suggested. I've arranged a caterer, and the church, but I wonder if it would be too much to ask—" She hesitated. "Would you consider helping with everything else as well?"

Raven had to smile at Jeannie's response, the blue eyes sparkled and she almost clapped her hands with delight.

"Oh that's a bad move, honey," Neal warned Raven in a very droll voice.

"Now you hush up, you old grouch." Jeannie turned her back on her husband but not before Raven caught the wink he sent her way.

"You mark my words, Raven, Jeannie will organize you so much you won't know whether you're coming or going."

"Don't you take any notice of him. He'd be the first to complain if a function wasn't perfect." Suddenly serious, Jeannie looked at Raven. "I'm surprised Abby isn't helping. I would have thought this would be right up her alley."

For a moment Raven felt as if the breath had been sucked out of her. How could she answer? "Brad did say that Abby and Greg could help, but they're both so busy." She watched as Jeannie and Neal's expressions registered surprise.

"Aren't the two of you getting along?"

Raven found herself on her feet. She couldn't allow Jeannie to distress herself about this. "Abby's been wonderful. She couldn't be nicer." She moved over to the window and stared blankly at the garden. "But I can't ask her to help with the wedding."

"And why not?" Jeannie had moved behind Raven. She laid a gentle hand on Raven's taut arm. "I'm sure none of us would want anything to upset Brad and Joy's special day. Can't you tell us what's wrong?"

Raven wasn't sure whether it was the soft, coaxing voice or the possibility of ruining her mother's big day that caused the words to fall from her lips. "Because they think I'm the bride."

"Pardon? What did you say?" Jeannie turned Raven around until they were face to face.

"Greg and Abby think I'm going to marry their father." Raven tried to keep her voice steady and calm but knew she wasn't succeeding. It was a very wobbly statement that caused bursts of laughter to fill the quiet room. Raven hadn't known what to expect from her confession, but it definitely hadn't been that!

"How did they get such a harebrained idea?" Neal asked.

"I don't know really. I guess Brad didn't explain very well. Then when I arrived, Greg said some things that I kind of took exception to, so I thought I'd show him a thing or two, and—"

"Oh, this is incredible." Jeannie was actually wiping her eyes and trying to contain her amusement. "And have you showed him a thing or two?"

"No. That's the worst of it. All I've managed is to dig myself into a big hole and now I have to climb out of it."

She suddenly wondered what these people must be thinking of her. "Believe me," she beseeched, "I don't normally go around pretending to be someone else. I've hated the lies—but he was so arrogant and obnoxious."

Remembering her initial anger at Greg helped her take hold of herself. She still felt piped they could think the situation funny though. There didn't seem to be anything remotely amusing to her.

"So what did Greg say to get you this wound up?"

Neal seemed to see Raven's uncomfortable squirm and cut in on his wife's question. "I don't think that concerns us, Jean. What we have to do is help this girl out of her dilemma." He patted Raven's arm and gestured for her to return to her seat. "How about if we come with you to tell Greg and Abby? Lend some moral support. I assume you do want to confess this terrible secret?"

While he was trying to be constructive, Raven was very conscious of the twinkle in his eye. But she still felt a tremendous weight lift from her shoulders. "You'd do that for me?"

"Of course. You're going to be Brad's daughter. He'd expect us to keep an eye on you since he isn't here to do it."

Raven felt her eyes fill. "I guess this must be what it feels like to have a dad." She couldn't resist hugging Neal. "Even when he's not here, there's someone else to stand in for him. Thank you both so much for your offer but I'd already decided. I'm going to tell Greg tonight. It would look a bit strange once Mum and Brad get here and move into Brad's apartment." The attempted joke fell short but made Raven feel better. She hated being emotional in front of others, and until today these two had been strangers.

"Don't you worry. I don't imagine Abby will be too put out. And Greg—well Neal can sort him out if he causes any trouble, can't you darling?"

Raven watched as Neal rubbed his hands together, a look of pure glee on his face. "Just lead me to him."

Raven had to smile at the thought of Neal sorting Greg out. While Neal might be as tall as Greg, he was very slight and so much older; and yet Neal seemed eager for a showdown. Had Raven missed something? There seemed to be something underlying here that she did not understand.

"Might as well strike while the iron is hot," Neal said. "What time shall we come over? How about eight-thirty? And we'll talk to Greg with you."

"No!"

They both looked at her, surprised at her sharp response to Neal's suggestion.

"I can manage." *I've got to think about what to say, how to explain to him. I need time to rehearse, not an audience.* "Anyway, Greg and I are going out to dinner tonight."

What Raven had intended to be an added reason why she didn't need their support caused an unexpected reaction. She watched as Neal's eyebrows rose and his moustache twitched, and then followed his gaze as he turned to his wife and the two shared a knowing look.

"Ah," sighed from his lips, but his smiling face said much more.

"How wonderful," Jeannie breathed.

"No! No. You don't understand. Manuela and Jorge are going away for the weekend, so there won't be a meal." Of course, she could cook...

"Where are you going?" Jeannie's question sounded so innocent that Raven saw no reason to fabricate an answer.

"He said the country club."

"You'll love it—candlelit with soft, romantic music to dance to. Just the place to take a guest on the housekeeper's day off." Jeannie shared a smile with her husband. "Now Neal and I, we'd have taken a guest to a steakhouse, or a diner maybe."

"Of course Greg may just want to have a quiet dinner after a hard day at work." But Neal's snort of laughter suggested something much more.

"I think I need to explain—there's nothing—Greg and I barely know each other."

"But he managed to make such an impression on you that you've spent the week pretending to be his father's fiancée?" Jeannie's supposition that Raven had needed the pretence to protect herself was too near the truth for comfort.

"You don't understand." Raven spread her hands helplessly. "It's just a dinner invitation, nothing more."

Raven was aghast to hear Neal's murmur, "Me thinks the lady doth protest too much."

And then she swung around to see Jeannie smiling happily into space.

"Oh Neal, this is wonderful," she said. "I've prayed that Greg would come to his senses and realize that there was more to life than that construction company." She clutched Raven's arm. "I can't begin to tell you how relieved we are that he's found someone else. You know, he used to be such a happy boy, full of fun, loved to tease and share a joke. Losing his little boy just sucked the life right out of him."

Little boy? What little boy? No one had ever mentioned Greg having a son—or a wife for that matter. Raven sat perfectly still, willing Jeannie to continue, to give her some insight into Greg's character. Had he lost a custody battle? She found herself holding her breath.

"He became a hollow shadow of the man he had

been. And then, when that bitch of a wife of his took off with that guy from New York..."

Go on, go on, Raven begged silently.

"I tried to help—after the funeral. But he shut himself off from us all. If only Mary had still been alive, perhaps she could have helped. Perhaps he would have listened to his mother but he wouldn't listen to me."

No, it hadn't been a custody battle. Greg had had a son who'd died. But when? Recently?

"You did everything you could, honey," Neal said. This was obviously something that had caused Jeannie much heartache. Raven was desperate for Jeannie to continue with her musing. To lose one's child. Raven thought there could be nothing more devastating. If anything ever happened to one of my boys... She felt a tightness around her heart at the very thought. And Greg had had to deal with that, and apparently had pushed everyone who cared for him away, by the sounds of things.

Raven's heart swelled with pity. Death was not something to be faced alone. You needed love and support all around you to help you adapt. Maybe that explained his jaundiced outlook on life. Raven willed Jeannie to continue—*tell me what happened. Tell me about his wife. What was she like? Why did she leave him?* Raven stared at her clenched fingers. Finally, Neal's hand patting his wife's shoulder seemed to bring her back from the past.

"But now he has you." The bright blue eyes were swimming with tears. "I'm so glad." Jeannie's hands clutched at Raven's and she looked deeply into Raven's eyes. "He deserves another chance. He's a fine man. You take care of him and he'll make you a first-rate husband too."

Raven knew she had to correct the assumption they were making. "Jeannie, I'm afraid you've got it all wrong." She tried to be gentle. "There's nothing between us."

Raven was subjected to a very direct look. "You care about him. No point denying it."

She found herself unable to look away. She opened her mouth to refute Jeannie's claim, but found no words. Then she shrugged helplessly and said, "It doesn't really matter how I feel. Nothing could come of it, anyway."

"But why not? If you love each other—"

Raven was having trouble keeping hold of her temper. And she knew these lovely people didn't deserve to be on the receiving end of her sharp tongue. She looked at them apologetically and asked, "Could we just change the subject?"

****

True to their word, the Zimmermans did not mention Greg again. The conversation centred instead on arrangements for the wedding. Raven soon realized that Jeannie was a born organizer, and as her husband had warned could easily take over the arranging of any function at any level of society.

While Raven had happily told Brad she'd sort out all the details, since arriving here she had found that so many things were different. America was a different world and she felt completely out of her depth.

"Okay. We have everything covered I think. Now have Brad and your mother a date in mind? Once we've decided on that, then I can start making some phone calls."

"I've tentatively booked the twenty-second, but I wasn't sure what the regulations are over here. Don't they have to do blood tests or something?"

"Not in Maryland. There's no residency requirement either. So all they need to do is go see the county clerk and pay for the license. There's a two-day wait." Neal's statement reassured Raven.

"They arrive from L.A. on the seventeenth, I

think you said?" Jeannie was checking her calendar. At Raven's nod, she confirmed, "Then the twenty-second sounds fine to me."

"Do we have time to organise everything else though?" Raven was very doubtful. There seemed to be so many things they had come up with that needed to be done in less than two weeks.

Jeannie smiled confidently. "Don't you worry yourself. I'll see to it that everything gets done."

Somehow Raven didn't doubt it. She laid her head against the back of the sofa. What truly lovely people these are. Within hours they'd made her feel so much at home that she felt she'd known them all her life. They had also lightened her feelings of guilt. Their response to her confession had given her hope that maybe Abby would forgive her. She didn't think Greg would be quite so malleable. If only he would understand her reasons he might be a little charitable.

She sighed wearily. It had been a very tiring day, and she still had tonight to face. She had her phone call from home to look forward to before she had to prepare for the evening. She felt a small smile touch her lips; she was treating this evening as a condemned man might treat a meeting with his executioner.

Or was she?

****

Raven was pacing around the confines of her bedroom. She had showered, styled her hair, as much as it would allow her to style it, and applied a subtle amount of makeup. Her dress was hanging on the outside of the wardrobe door, waiting. For probably the millionth time, she consulted the watch on her wrist. It was too early, much too early to consider getting dressed. She hadn't heard Greg come home yet. Even allowing for the time she would be talking to her family, she still had time to kill before their date.

Date! Don't be stupid, she berated herself. It's not a date; it's simply a meal out.

Oh yeah, then why am I spending so long preparing? And she wasn't even dressed yet. She took another nervous turn beside the window and headed across the room to the door. *This is so silly.* She couldn't keep pacing around her room. Perhaps if she did some stretches, that might calm her down. She bent down to grip her ankles, only to discover a lock of previously well-placed hair falling down over her face. This wasn't going to work, unless she intended spending ages in front of the mirror again trying to force the wavy tresses back into some semblance of order.

She moved toward the window again, and then a sudden thought caused her to turn and inspect the carpet. *I'm not wearing a track on it, am I?* She had paced across this room many times in the last couple days. She bent to run her fingers through the plush pile. *I guess quality carpet like this is made to withstand neurotic women abusing it,* she mused.

She checked her watch again. Still more than an hour before Greg's note had asked her to be ready. Asked? No, told her to be ready. His behaviour might have improved but he was still too fond of issuing orders.

She continued her pacing, chewing on the edge of her thumb. She had to be so careful. Things could get out of hand if she didn't keep her head tonight. Raven knew what Greg's little smiles indicated. There was tension between them always just bubbling under the surface. As long as she kept her head it would be okay. And if things did get a bit dicey, she could always play on her relationship with Brad as a smokescreen. Even after she admitted the truth, she could still stress that Brad and she were very close.

Despite her early accusations Raven knew that Greg cared deeply for his father. He would never do anything to hurt him—but would he consider that attempting to seduce Raven might cause Brad grief? She hoped so, because that assumption could be her saviour if things got out of hand.

They could—get out of hand.

She finally acknowledged this attraction she felt for Greg was much more. A man did not occupy your every waking thought, and many sleeping ones too, unless you cared deeply for him. Unless you loved him.

There, she had finally admitted it. *I love him— selfish, arrogant, obnoxious man that he is.*

Not entirely true, Raven thought. He'd seemed so at the start, but not anymore. Now Greg was kind and gentle, interested in many of the things that she was. Now she'd learned something of the pain in his life and understood the fleeting expressions she'd sometimes caught on his face, and why he'd been so quick to assume the worst about her. If his wife had betrayed him, he probably thought all women had been tarred with the same brush. He was a man who had learned to mistrust women. Did he now use them for his own needs and then discard them? Raven didn't for a moment imagine Greg had remained celibate since his wife left him, but something told her he felt no attachment to the women he knew. He'd developed into a solitary man who filled his empty life with work. Raven had witnessed the love his family felt for him and knew they must have tried to ease his burden. Yet he remained alone—seemed to prefer it. Maybe all he needed was someone to love him unconditionally, to show him he could pick up his life and live it to the fullest. He was still a young man. Surely he'd have to find someone to share his future with, or he'd live a cold, barren old age.

That someone isn't going to be me. Can't be me. Pacing, Raven gnawed harder on her thumb. Greg wasn't ready to acknowledge he needed someone permanent in his life any more than she was. Anyway, she couldn't imagine giving up her world. She accepted Joy's choice to follow Brad to America but Raven never wanted to live anywhere but New Zealand. It was home. She and the boys were happy there.

Yes, they were. Even if sometimes she knew life was slipping by, she was happy!

She started when a door slammed downstairs. She'd been alone in the house so it meant Greg had arrived. A new taste registered and she looked down at her thumb. She'd been chewing so hard on the edge of her thumb that it was bleeding. She barely registered the footsteps or the knock on her door.

Her eyes flew up as the door burst open. She grasped her dressing gown tightly at the throat with her other hand, but it was Abby who stormed into her room.

"Well, soon-to-be Mommy dearest, I think we have some talking to do." The anger on Abby's face faded a little as she faced Raven.

Why is Abby here? What does she want? Raven's heart stopped as her eyes fell to her bleeding thumb. *Does Abby know the truth? Oh no.* It was important that she be able to confess, to explain her reasons, to try and make them both understand. If Abby had found out...

Raven stood there, watching the blood accumulating and starting to run down into her palm.

"What on earth have you done?" Abby hurried through to the bathroom and came back with some tissues.

"Sit down." She pushed Raven into the armchair near the window, knelt down beside her and gently

139

wiped the blood away. Her eyes shot up to Raven's face. "Don't we feed you enough?"

Abby's attempt to lighten the atmosphere didn't work. In fact, it had the opposite effect. Raven's eyes filled with tears as Abby sighed deeply. "Do you have any band aids?" Raven was confused just for a second, until she realised Abby meant plasters, and she directed Abby to her toilet bag in the bathroom.

"Thank you." Abby seemed surprised at Raven's wobbly tone and teary eyes. They hadn't known each other for very long, and Raven had never shown her any weakness. She hadn't dared. For Abby to find her half dressed, pacing her bedroom, and chewing on her thumb to the extent that she had made it bleed was not a situation Raven expected to find herself in.

"Something wrong? Anything I can help with?" Abby asked, throwing herself down onto the bed.

Perhaps she didn't know...

For a moment Raven hesitated, but then she shook her head. Turning her head away, she felt Abby's eyes as they moved the length of her body.

"Are you sure you're all right? You're not having a relapse or anything, are you? You look pale."

Raven forced her lips to move, but she doubted it was a smile Abby saw. "No. No, I'm fine. In fact today I finished the last of my medication." She rose from the chair and looked out the window.

"So what have you been doing today?" Abby asked.

Raven wished she'd go away. She didn't feel like talking right now. She hadn't given much thought about talking to Abby. There would be time enough to figure out how to tell her tomorrow, right now she was worried about telling Greg. So that he might understand and forgive her.

Why is Abby here anyway? Surely she should have been busy with the children's homework, or preparing tea, whoops, dinner, about now. And yet here she was lying across Raven's bed, apparently without a worry in the world.

"Oh, I did a workout, then went for a run in the park. It's very nice up there."

"Yeah it is, isn't it? You just laze around the rest of the day?"

Raven didn't realise her thumb had travelled back up to her mouth, until the bandage got in the way. She dropped it quickly, not looking at Abby, not wanting to lie but not yet able to confess.

"I went and visited the Zimmermans. It was the first chance I'd had, although we've spoken on the phone a couple of times."

Raven found herself pacing between the window and the door, feeling Abby's eyes on her all the time.

"They're lovely, aren't they? We spent heaps of time together when we were young, but since their kids moved out of state we don't see so much of them anymore. They were so great when Mom was ill. I don't know what we would have done without them. They'll do anything to help anybody."

"Yes, I guessed that." Still, the pacing; back and forth. But Raven couldn't say more.

Abby's patience seemed to run out. She swung her legs off Raven's bed and sat up. "Raven, Jeannie came and saw me a little while ago."

Chapter 9

She'd been right. Abby did know the truth.

Raven should be grateful to Jeannie, who had tried to ease the burden of her confession. But what had she said? Had she explained so Abby would understand? Raven remembered the anger visible on Abby's face as she burst into the bedroom, and doubted it. The guilt lay heavy upon her and tears gathered, slowly spilling down her cheeks.

"I'm so sorry." Raven was standing at the window again but facing Abby. "I never meant to lie to you." Abby watched her closely as she brushed the tears from her cheeks. She needed to make Abby understand what had led her to behave like this. She'd liked Abby from the first, but the lies would always stand between them unless they could clear this up now.

"I don't understand. Why did you pretend you were going to marry Dad? I knew something was screwy but I couldn't figure it out—not while you were telling us how much you loved him."

"I do love him." Raven's voice strengthened as she refuted any thought that Brad was not important to her. "I've never had a dad—at least not one that I remember. Can you imagine what it was like getting to know Brad? He's the most wonderful man I've ever met. He's the kindest, gentlest person.

"And when he met my mother, I saw the change in her. She didn't deserve to live alone all these years, devoting herself to me; and then after Chris died, to my boys and me. She deserved someone good and kind that could look after her and make her happy. Brad's that person—of course I love him!"

"Okay, okay, I believe you. I guess I agree with you. He is a pretty neat guy, isn't he? I never really thought about it much."

"That's because he was always there for you."

Abby nodded agreement. Brad had always been there for his family. He was that sort of man. People always came first with him.

"I still don't understand how this all happened? I know Dad's email confused us. We were expecting his fiancée. But why didn't you tell us we'd made a mistake?"

"I was going to." Abby face softened as Raven begged for understanding. "That first night I was so tired and groggy I didn't realise what had happened. The next day when I came downstairs, I heard Greg talking to you on the phone. I knew then that you'd somehow been expecting my mother, but before I could interrupt..." Raven's voice trailed off. She broke eye contact with Abby and fidgeted with the back of the chair.

"Go on," Abby ordered in a stern voice. "If we are ever to get this mess sorted out we have to be straight with each other. No more pussyfooting about. I want to know exactly what happened. No more fabricating."

"I'm not sure if you remember the conversation..." Abby shrugged. Raven started again, "Greg was talking about me, what I looked like, discussing my clothes, and he was guessing whether or not they were from some Goodwill shop."

She watched the blood drain from Abby's face. She apparently did remember now.

"Then he decided that I was a gold digger, after your father's money. We didn't know Brad had money. He told us that he had a small construction company, and that he'd been waiting all his life to retire so he could travel a bit. We assumed he's been saving for years and was now able to afford it. We didn't know that you were loaded to the gills." Abby smiled faintly at the expression but she still looked dismayed. "Mum might have known, but I sure didn't. Not until I got looking around the house and the neighbourhood.

"Greg said there was no way he was going to let his father marry me. No way! What the hell did it have to do with him anyway? Who did he think he was? Deciding who his father could marry." Raven was in full flow, reliving the anger she'd felt on her arrival.

"No one's going to treat my mother like that. She loves Brad dearly, and I won't let either you or Greg do anything to upset her. I thought that when she arrived you'd see how wonderful she is—and be so relieved that Brad is marrying her and not me, that you'd gladly welcome her into the family."

Raven glared at Abby. "She deserves to be treated with respect, at the very least. Not contempt."

Abby grabbed Raven's hands and drew her to sit down on the bed beside her. "You're so right, Raven. She does deserve our respect. When we get to know her, I'm sure we'll grow to love her. If she truly loves Dad, of course we'll welcome her with love. Please don't worry about your mother anymore. She'll be welcomed into our family, I promise." She lifted a hand to Raven's cheek. "And so will you and your sons, if you can ever forgive us."

Raven squirmed, looking everywhere but at Abby. She felt embarrassed that Abby had accepted her explanation so readily. It showed even more clearly that this should never have continued. Why hadn't she just come out with the truth immediately?

"Raven, I do remember that conversation now. How arrogant of us." Clutching Raven's arm, she continued, "Please believe me when I tell you that I am so ashamed. I cannot believe we behaved like that. A stranger coming into our homes and being treated in such a manner is completely inexcusable."

"I can only ask for your forgiveness and promise you that you and your family will never see any sign of such arrogant snobbery again, Raven. I hope no one will ever see us behave in such a deplorable manner again."

They were holding hands. Who had made the first move, Raven wasn't sure, but they seemed to have reached some plateau of understanding.

"You know, I came rushing over here as soon as Jeannie left. I was so angry. Caleb must be wondering what had happened. I just yelled at him to look after Vikki as I tore out the door. Not once did I think we might have done something to cause all this. I was all set to rip you to shreds. And then when I arrive, you're standing there with such a woebegone expression. Jeannie was right, wasn't she? You have been worrying yourself sick about it all."

Raven shrugged and remained silent.

"I often wondered what it would be like to have a sister. It might be fun. What do you think?" Abby asked.

"I'm an only child. I've always wished I could have had a sister too."

Abby drew Raven towards her into a quick hug. "Well, you have one now. Guess we'll have to take some time to get to know each other better." She got up from the bed and moved over to the window. "Hey, don't forget you'll have a brother too."

Raven prayed that Abby had not seen her face as for the second time today she was faced with the thought of Greg being her brother. The feelings Raven harboured for Greg were not brotherly, not in the slightest.

"I just hope he'll be as understanding as you've been," breathed Raven.

"I don't see how he could be anything else. After all, it was his assumptions that started all this mess."

"I'm going to tell him tonight, before we go to dinner." She glanced up from her clenched fingers and caught the sympathetic expression on Abby's face. "So, do you have a spare bed? In case he throws me out." She tried to make a joke of it, but Abby must have seen through her.

Raven found herself clasped in Abby's arms. "You're not going to need a bed. But you'll always have one at our place." There was a ring of confidence in her voice as she continued. "Greg's a pretty cool guy. If you could forget those things he said, I'm sure you'd get to like him."

Like? If only Raven's feelings were lukewarm, she could have handled that. Instead they were raging like a summer bush fire, intensely hot and totally out of control.

****

Raven had one last check in the mirror before she headed downstairs. She hoped she wasn't overdressed, but Manuela had approved her choice before they'd departed this morning. She needed to feel confident when she faced Greg. Looking good and feeling self-assured goes hand in hand, doesn't it?

Perhaps I'm worrying too much. The Zimmermans had thought her escapade humorous. Abby had been angry initially, but had quickly forgiven her when everything had been explained. Perhaps Greg would accept her confession equally as charitably.

Yeah, and perhaps the sun will forget to rise tomorrow.

Raven tried to push her troubles to the back of

her mind as she moved downstairs, checking the large clock in the foyer as she approached. The boys should be ringing any minute now. She'd heard Greg arrive home just moments before so knew her time would be limited, but she'd still get to talk to them for a few minutes.

"Hello." She picked up the phone at the first ring.

"Kia Ora, Mummy." She heard two dear wee voices speak in unison, so knew one must be on the extension in her bedroom.

"Kia Ora, tamariki ma," Raven greeted her sons, blinking rapidly to stop tears forming at the sound of them. She missed them desperately. "How are you, guys?" She forced herself to speak lightly.

"We're good." Tane spoke hurriedly. "Mum, we've got the neatest surprise—"

"You said I could tell first." Raven heard the petulance in Scott's voice, before it became stronger. "I'm telling first," he yelled.

"Are not. I am."

Raven smiled as she listened to the exchange. Now she relaxed, they hadn't changed in the whole week she'd been away. Opening her mouth to sort out the growing conflict between the two boys, she heard her mother's voice in the background, laying down some ground rules for the expensive phone call.

"Acshally we have two cool things, Mum." Scott must have been given permission to start first.

"Mine's the coolest," broke in Tane.

"Is not." Scott was not as self controlled as his elder brother, and had been sidetracked again.

"Look here, you two." Raven tried but knew she could not speak sternly to them, not over the phone. "Who gets to go first?"

"Scott does."

"Well, let him speak then," Raven said, "and

next time you call me, Tane, you get to talk first. Is that a deal?"

Raven was pleased they could not see her smile as they mumbled their agreement. "So what's been happening, Scotty."

"It was swimming on Thursday night. Nana said we couldn't ring until this morning to tell you. I winded the biggest trophy."

"Wow, Scotty, that's marvellous. What was it for?" Her hand tightened on the receiver. She should have been there to see this, not hear about it over the phone.

"Cos I'm the best improved. Out of the whole club, I'm the bestest swimmer."

"The most improved, darling, not the best. That means you've worked very hard this season to get better. I'm so proud of you." Raven was a little hesitant when asking, "How did you get on, Tane?"

"Bet you'll never guess, Mum." Raven felt the smile grow as he never allowed her a chance to try but hurried on, "I got the under-nine boys cup. Can you believe that? Can you?"

Raven laughed aloud at the excitement in her son's voice.

"I only won cos Barry Tisdale broke his arm. I could never beat him."

Raven felt a little compassion for the boy who had missed much of this year's swim season, but after a moment she knew Tane's pride in his achievement outweighed any feeling but extreme delight.

"Well done, Tane. And hey, maybe you would have beaten Barry this year. You're turning into a great little swimmer."

Why had she missed this event? It was a milestone in her sons' lives and she hadn't been there to share it with them. "I'm so sorry I wasn't there, guys, I wish I had been." Now the guilt was setting in.

"That's okay, Mum. Nana and Granddad took us." Raven could detect nothing in Scott's voice that suggested he was upset by her absence.

"Did you know that Granddad makes so much noise?" Raven guessed Tane was whispering into the phone. "He clapped and cheered louder than anyone else."

She bit her lip to stop the humour entering her voice. "Did he embarrass you?" Tane was reaching an age where peer respect was of utmost importance. To have an adult make a fuss, in public—nothing could be worse.

"Nah, not really. He was cool, actually. Temuera Roberts is so jealous that we have a granddad who lives in America. I told him we're going to Disneyland next week."

It sounded like Tane might be enjoying his new grandfather a little too much but there would be time enough to put a stop to any bragging he might be indulging in.

"Scotty's got some other news, Mum. Go on, Scott, hurry up and tell her."

"Guess what, Mum. My rugby team might have a new coach this year." Raven recognized the awe in her son's voice and already had an inkling what he was about to say. "Cameron Richards' dad said he might help us."

This was a major news flash in the life of a five - year-old. Cameron Richards' dad was none other than John Richards, the recently retired All Black rugby fullback. The prestige of having an ex-All Black as coach was tremendous for any team, the Takapuna Under Sevens must be ecstatic.

"Wow. You're joking." Raven made sure she sounded suitably impressed. "That's terrific, Scott. I bet all the boys are really excited."

Again Raven heard her mother's voice in the

background and knew it was time to say farewell to the boys. "So how many sleeps now?"

"Six!" She shifted the phone from her ear at the scream.

"Remember to mind your Nana. Don't forget, I love you, guys." She blinked furiously. "Take good care of Nana and Brad, won't you?"

"We will."

"See you soon."

"Off you go and play now, while I talk to your mum," Raven heard her mother saying to the boys as she obviously took the phone from one of them.

"Hello, darling. How are you?" Joy asked.

"I'm fine, Mum. In fact I'm almost back to normal now I think," Raven answered. "I went for my first run yesterday and there's no ill effects."

"I'm so pleased. But you won't start overdoing it, will you?"

"No, Mum," Raven smiled. She had missed her mother too and was looking forward to her arriving. Right now she could use some of her mother's good common-sense advice.

They chatted for a few moments, catching up on each other's news, and then the inevitable question came from Joy. "You have cleared up that silly misunderstanding."

"Not exactly—"

"What do you mean?" her mother cut in. "Raven Anne, you are not to let this go on a moment longer, do you understand?"

Raven grimaced at the tone of her mother's voice and the use of both her names. Joy was really ticked off.

"I know, Mum," she hastily agreed. "Greg has been away for the last couple of days so I haven't had the opportunity. I'm going to confess as soon as I see him and that should be any minute now." She tacked on, "Abby knows and wasn't too angry." No need to admit that it hadn't been she who told Abby.

She heard a heavy sigh at the other end of the phone and quickly promised, "Mum, I've been trying to figure out all day how I'm going to do this, how I will approach him, so you can relax. I'm not going to throw away a day's worrying by not following through. Stop worrying, I'll sort it out. I promise."

"I do appreciate what you were trying to do, sweetie; you know that, don't you?" Now Joy's voice took on a more consolatory tone. "But I don't expect you to fight my battles for me. If there's a problem there, well, Brad and I will have to work it out. There's no reason for you to get involved. I wanted you to have a pleasant holiday and relax until you were fit again, not get embroiled in some family feud."

Raven laughed. "Hardly a family feud, Mum, just a little misunderstanding which will be all sorted out before you set foot here. And don't think I'm not having a good time. I'm loving it."

That might have been a bit of an exaggeration, but she didn't want her mother to think otherwise. She was loving it, except for the emotional turmoil she was finding herself in.

"Did you manage to track Justin down?" Joy asked.

Someone had mentioned to Joy that Chris's cousin, Justin, was supposed to be working somewhere in Washington. They'd almost lost touch over the last few years, and Raven had been delighted to track him down so easily.

"Yeah, he actually works at the Embassy and he's coming to take me out for the day tomorrow." She laughed. "He was pretty surprised to hear my voice, I think. I can't wait to see him again, find out what he's been up to."

"Make sure you give him my love and invite him to the wedding. That'll make four on my side of the church." Joy's laugh assured Raven that she was not concerned about the lopsided guest list.

Raven could hear movement above her and knew Greg had left his room. "Mum, I have to go, Greg's coming. Ring me again the same time on Thursday. Love you, bye."

****

Greg hurried downstairs just before the arranged time. He knew Raven would be ready, but there was a possibility she would have waited in her room. He couldn't quite analyze why he was so eager to see her. He also wanted to watch her, just for a moment, without her being aware. He adjusted the dimmer on the massive chandelier. If he stood in a certain area of the foyer, he would be in shadow, and he could watch her as she came out of her room and floated down the stairs. She wouldn't be aware of him and he could enjoy the sight of her.

He couldn't wait any longer for her to admit the truth. He'd missed her, missed the companionable evenings they had spent together. These last few days had proved one thing to him. He wanted more from her than hesitant little looks and the occasional sign of smoldering desire that she quickly suppressed.

He sucked in his breath sharply as a door opened, not upstairs but right beside him. She came from the living room and stood in the doorway, watching him. His heart raced as he stared. She looked stunning in a long black dress that accentuated her height. He was glad it was plain; she didn't need any fancy designed gimmicks to make her more beautiful. He thought she'd look wonderful in anything she wore—or didn't wear...

Her fair hair didn't have the windswept look tonight. Maybe later, if he got the chance to run his fingers through those tresses... He'd always favored women with long hair. He couldn't immediately think of anyone he'd dated who wore her hair short, yet somehow, on Raven—Greg loved her curls, which seemed to have a mind of their own.

He sighed. Those ears—he was developing a fetish about those ears. She was wearing a small stud in each tonight, and each stone sparkled as it caught the light. How he would love to strip her of everything except those twinkling earrings. Could he control his impatience?

"You're looking very beautiful tonight." He spoke gallantly, holding out his hand to her as she approached him. While she placed her hand in his for a moment and smiled graciously at the compliment, she all-too-soon pulled her fingers from his grasp.

"Manuela did say it's a swanky place we're going to. I hope I'm not overdressed?" His wolfish grin caused her to stumble over those last words.

"Personally, I would much prefer you under-dressed." He took her hand again and drew the unwilling limb through his arm, holding it tightly in place. "You look just fine," he assured, starting them towards the garage. "Everyone will want to meet you."

He knew she couldn't see his grin as he moved her in front of him toward door, but her stiffening back told him all he needed before she halted.

"Greg," she began uncertainly. Raven had hoped for some time—thought perhaps he'd offer her a pre-dinner drink before they left but he seemed intent on going straight away. "There's something I need to talk to you about."

"Sure thing. Let's just get on our way, though. We don't have that far to go but the traffic was pretty snarled when I came through."

She seemed uneasy, nervous. Good, the two days apart had not lessened her awareness of him. He hated to imagine he might be alone in his feelings.

No, he wasn't imagining anything.

As he climbed into the car he saw her fingers clenched together in her lap. His breath caught at the hastily suppressed expression on her face. She was apparently very aware of him as she pressed tight against the seat, making sure he didn't touch her as he turned to reverse the car out of the garage.

This was going to be an interesting evening. It might even develop into a fascinating night—if he played his cards right. She had to admit the truth; she'd never allow him to make love to her believing she was Brad's. But even more he needed her to admit that she wanted him as much as he wanted her. Well, tonight all this subterfuge would end; hopefully in bed.

He was glad the dress trousers he wore were looser than his normal jeans. He doubted if he would have been very comfortable driving otherwise.

Trying to get his mind above his belt, Greg sent her a small smile, holding eye contact just a little longer than necessary before he inquired politely how she had spent the last couple of days.

****

"You don't mind coming tonight, do you?" he asked. "I normally just eat out whenever Manuela goes away. It's so much easier."

"No, of course not," Raven lied. She was more nervous than she could ever remember. "But there's no need for you to worry about me. I could have easily whipped up something simple."

"No way. While you're my guest, you're not going to be working in the kitchen."

In other words, 'know your place, lady, and it's not in my kitchen,' Raven thought he meant.

I have to do this. Now!

"Greg—" she began, only to be interrupted by a phone ringing. She couldn't believe it, just like in a cheap novel.

Greg's curse as he reached over to the glove compartment did nothing to ease her frustration.

"Sorry," he apologized as he flicked it open and up to his ear. "I thought I'd turned it off."

Raven was left in no doubt that something else had happened on the site in Hagerstown. Greg listened for a moment before barking instructions into the phone. Raven was at a loss to understand exactly what had happened, but Greg's anger was very apparent. He swung the car into a side road off Baltimore National Pike before he finished the call, and Raven realized they had reached their destination.

Now his mood was no longer convivial—definitely not a favourable time for her confession, not if she expected understanding.

He jumped out of the car and hurried around to open her door. "I apologise for the interruption, Raven..." he began.

"That's all right," she murmured. What else could she add? "I hope everything is okay?"

"It's fine. Just a minor obstacle that my foreman wasn't happy about committing to, without checking first." He smiled down at her but she felt his mind was still in Hagerstown sorting out whatever problem there was.

"Will there be a lot of your friends here tonight?"

"Sure to be, it's a pretty popular club. They have these functions every month or so. Most of the members attend."

"Will a lot of them know Brad?"

"Of course," Greg replied absently, "He's a member too. He hasn't been very involved in the social side of the club since Mom died, but he plays golf here so almost everyone knows him."

They were nearly at the steps. She'd run out of time! She couldn't tell him the truth inside, where others might overhear. She grabbed his arm jerking him around to face her—just as she heard his name called and two other men, who noisily slapped Greg on the back and shook his hand, joined them. Their smiles were open and friendly as Greg introduced her, using only her first name.

After just moments Greg motioned Raven up the steps, leaving his friends to finish their cigarettes. As he held open the glass door for her he turned with an apologetic look on his face. "I'm sorry, you were trying to tell me something?"

Raven looked around helplessly. There were people everywhere, perhaps not in large numbers, but she knew there was unlikely to be anywhere quiet or private she could talk to Greg. Not here, anyway.

Shrugging her shoulders, Raven let the matter drop. *What's a few more hours? I'll tell him when we get home, or if it is very late, tomorrow.*

Despite the phone call that had interrupted her attempt to talk to Greg, Raven had been aware of the heightened sexual tension inside the car. It was as if any time they were together emotions took over and threatened to run out of control. They had managed to spend a couple of quiet evenings in the living room without any strain, why was tonight any different? Because she was different.

She had accepted the depth of her feelings, and the new insight into his character made her rethink her initial impression. *Am I brave enough to let my heart take control?* Why not? It was what she wanted. Her eyes fastened on his face. Her heart started to thump. She wanted to be in Greg's arms, to feel his body close, intimately close. Why shouldn't she allow herself to enjoy his company? She guessed if she could forget everything else, her evening with him would be wonderful—could last until breakfast...

She sighed. More likely she'd be full of remorse

and painful memories that might never leave her. And disgust that Greg would care so little for his father that he'd bed his 'fiancée'. Raven tore her eyes from Greg and looked around the room. She must not allow Greg to get too close; even now that she knew him better, knew why he was often withdrawn and cynical. Even though she loved him, she mustn't indulge in dreams of any future. Even if he did desire her he wasn't looking for a mate, just a temporary relief from boredom.

Raven could not fault Greg's behaviour during the early part of the evening. He was the perfect gentleman. He had introduced her to a few people, simply using her Christian name, before guiding her to a small table at the back of a large room. Raven had rashly ordered wine, aware of Greg's surprise. Oh no! Had she mentioned at some time that she didn't drink alcohol?

She didn't think she'd touched anything alcoholic since Chris's death. And yet, here she was, supping on a glass of wine with the bottle prominently placed between them on the table. Greg mustn't think she needed fortifying, even if that was precisely the truth.

Just have one glass, to give her the courage to face whatever was to come...

Chapter 10

Raven was surprised as conversation during the soup course remained light and convivial. Greg seemed to have forgotten his work problems and had reverted to a friendly, if slightly impersonal, escort. She felt herself relaxing and letting down her guard. They'd discovered many shared interests during previous evenings and could converse easily when there was no sexual tension in the air. Greg seemed very interested in New Zealand and she enjoyed sharing her love of her birthplace with him. For the first time she admitted to him that her living came from teaching at a local high school, rather than from art, as she had previously hinted.

"Do you wish you could paint full time?"

Years ago there would have been no hesitation in her answer, and yet now she wasn't so sure. "I love to paint. I always dreamed of doing it professionally, but I love teaching too. I don't know if I'd want to give that up. It's so rewarding." She warmed to the subject as he listened attentively. "To actually see the light go on in some child's eye, I doubt if anything could replace the joy that brings." She shrugged. "But really the question doesn't arise. I can't see me ever being able to make enough painting, especially in New Zealand, to pay all the bills, so I should never have to make that decision."

She leaned forward. "What about you? Have you ever thought of doing anything besides building?"

"To be perfectly honest? No, there was never any pressure to join the company and Dad made sure I started at the bottom. In fact Tony and I were apprenticed to the same guy. We thought we were going to run rings around him, have a pretty good time, learn a bit on the side, but not take things too seriously for a year or so."

Greg's tone and woebegone expression told Raven that the two young men had received a mighty surprise. "But?" Raven prompted.

"His name was Jorge." Greg waited for the penny to drop.

"Manuela's husband?"

"The very same. What a con job he pulled on us. Led us around by the nose, then he'd let us loose with enough rope to hang ourselves with, and when we screwed up, he'd reel us in like a couple of stunned mackerel and start all over again. At the time it felt like we were working twenty hours a day. Man, did we hate that guy. We figured we were no better than slaves. Dad wouldn't listen to our complaints. Just told us to grow up and stop whining—or give up. Now that really annoyed the hell out of us. Tony had his eye on Abby and was willing to do anything to impress upon Dad that he was a suitable guy for her. Me, well I wasn't going to let some broken down old man get the better of me." He laughed at the memories. "I tell you, it took us quite a few years to realise just how much a student of human nature Jorge was. He had us figured from the start; knew the way to make us appreciate how good it feels to build, to actually make things with your own two hands."

Raven looked down at the hands he held out in front of him. He caught her eye and grinned a little self-consciously. "It may not be art, but it is creative."

Hearing him talking like this made him seem so much more human, more approachable. She was pleased that the job he used to fill the emptiness in his life was so satisfying and rewarding to him.

159

"Would you like to dance?"

Raven unreservedly placed her hand in his and headed for the dance floor. Their conversation had been so friendly and comfortable; dancing surely wasn't going to jeopardize the camaraderie.

Raven wasn't surprised to find him moving rhythmically with the fast-paced music. Somehow she knew he'd be a good dancer, light on his feet and not afraid to let the music dictate to him. Raven loved to dance but hadn't been on a dance floor since before Chris had died. They'd loved dancing. Now she found herself enjoying the music, the noise, the frantic movements to keep pace—and the watching.

Watching his body as he moved effortlessly with the music, watching the muscles ripple under his shirt, the hair that fell down over his forehead. There was but one word to describe him: sexy. He knew it, and unfortunately, so did she.

They returned to their table during a break in the music and enjoyed, what Greg explained was a local delicacy, crab cakes.

Raven was aware of Greg's intense gaze, but he neither said nor did anything that she could take exception to. Even so, she felt her heart rate increasing ever so slightly, and it was with a trembling hand that she lifted her glass to her lips and took a long swallow of wine.

Somehow the tone of their evening had subtly changed. She didn't feel threatened, but his lowered voice and the way he leaned across the table to talk heightened her awareness of him dramatically. Again her hand reached for the glass. She'd all but emptied it when he suggested another dance.

Raven was already on her feet and preceding him onto the dance floor before she realised the music's tempo had changed. She halted so suddenly he bumped into her back.

This wasn't wise. She was asking for trouble.

They couldn't dance like those other couples on the floor, glued together, hardly moving. That wasn't dancing; it was a courting ritual, a prelude to something much more.

She tried to move past him back toward their table but he fastened his arm quickly around her waist. She caught the gleam of amusement in his eye before she was clasped tightly in his arms.

He knows, damn him! He knew she didn't want to be this close, to feel his every move, every line of his body. To feel his hand slipping toward her bottom, pressing her body closer.

She felt the heat rush into her face as she became intimately conscious of him moving his body against hers. She pulled his arm up to a more decorous position, but that didn't help much; now her breasts were pressed against his chest and she could feel his breath on her neck.

He held her hand very tightly and she couldn't push him away. Did she want to?

There was a hypnotic feel to the music, the rhythm was romantic and sensuous. She found herself moving to the slow beat, forgetting her embarrassment at the blatant way she was wrapped in this man's arms. She wanted to enjoy the feel of his body pressed so closely to hers, to inhale the scents that were his alone, to run her fingers through hair that hung long at the back of his neck. She watched her arm sneaking up his shoulder, her eyes intent on that hair. What would it feel like to touch?

The shiver that seared down her back was almost her undoing. He had his mouth on her ear, lightly at first, but as she felt the lobe being drawn into the moistness of his mouth, she couldn't stop the shudder that pulsed through her. His tongue circled the tiny stud earring with erotic little movements that were turning her legs to jelly. She was thankful for the hold he had on her, or she might have fallen.

Now his hands caressed her back, up and down, up and down, holding her tightly against him, letting her feel the affect she was having on him.

Now he was teasing the other ear. She hadn't been aware of him moving his head, nor of her hands moving, and yet they were now entwined in his hair.

They were virtually making love, right here on the dance floor. She took a deep breath as she felt his teeth softly nip at her ear.

This had to stop, now! "Greg..." Was that her voice? That slumberous sexy whisper? She tried again, valiantly attempting to ignore the lips that swept across her neck, the arms that held her firmly, and the sensation she was getting in her lower body as he moved himself against her.

"Greg..." It sounded like she'd screamed his name, but no one else on the dance floor paid them any attention, so she guessed she hadn't. Greg pulled back his head a little and looked into her eyes. The smile on his lips would have melted any woman's heart.

But not hers! Her head was finally in control here, not her heart. "I think we should sit down now." She pushed against his chest.

"No, not yet." He pulled her close. "You're beautiful, so beautiful tonight."

He murmured the words close to her ear; she could feel his breath again, sending shivers through her body.

"Feel what you're doing to me." He ground his hardness against her. "I want you in my arms tonight."

She heard a heavy sigh escape him. "I want to find out how beautiful you really are." His lips moved against her neck, kissing her in between his words. "I want to peel that sexy black dress off you

162

and run my tongue over every inch of you."

"Greg!" Raven pushed against him. "Stop it. We need to go back to our table, right now."

She was infuriated at the way he smiled at her—desire alive in his eyes. He allowed her to move out of his arms but kept hold of her hand as they moved off the dance floor.

"Let's go home. Forget the meal. It's not food I'm hungry for right now." His arm snaked around her as they neared the table.

She hastily sat down. She was safer here than anywhere else right now. Her hand reached out for her glass, glad the waiter had appeared to refill it. She needed something to steady her nerves. To calm her. She gulped the wine down, not considering any possible effects it might have on her teetotaller's body.

Greg did not look happy to be sitting there, to have had his suggestion thwarted so quickly. *I should say something. Something to break this tension.* But she didn't have a clue what. Greg must have more experience with these types of encounters, so she sat silently sipping wine, waiting for him to break the silence.

"I'm not giving up, you know." He leaned over and grasped one of her hands. "Tonight, I want us to be together. I want to make love with you. In fact, I'm having the greatest difficulty not stripping that damn dress off you right now."

Raven was aghast, hastily looking around in case anyone might have heard. "No, I don't think so." She shook her head, knowing that her voice was weak and wavering. She hated that look of smugness on his face. As if he only had to crook his little finger and she would fall into his bed. She had to stop him somehow, because if she didn't, she might easily end up exactly where he wanted her. And that would lead to nothing but heartache.

"I have no intention of sleeping with you, Greg." Thank heavens her voice was almost back to normal. She sounded in control, even if she didn't feel like it. Perhaps another sip of wine might help.

"Is that right?" Greg's voice quizzed as his eyebrows rose. He lifted her hand to his lips. His teeth flashed as she hastily pulled her fingers from his grasp.

He doesn't believe me! The arrogant sod! He really thinks I'm going to fall into his bed tonight. How could she convince him to back off? She had to think of something. Although she knew he would never force her, she also knew in her heart that she could withstand only so much persuasion.

"I think you've forgotten Brad." That was it. She sighed very quietly. *He'll never hurt his father.*

"Oh no, I haven't forgotten him, although sometimes I wonder if you have. I'm sure he wouldn't approve of his 'fiancée' dancing with another man like you were dancing with me..." There was an angry glint in Greg's eyes for a moment before he veiled them.

Raven felt the blood rush into her face. She didn't need reminding that their dancing was hardly that. It was not the way an engaged woman would behave with another man.

"Nor the way a gentleman should behave either," she quickly quipped back.

Greg's eyes hardened. "Make no mistake, Raven," he warned. "I'm no gentleman."

A tense silence followed. Raven could think of nothing to say. She hadn't discouraged Greg's behaviour. Her own body had betrayed her as it melted into his arms. She couldn't deny that. She shifted uneasily in her chair, wishing the evening could return to the companionable experience it had been. She was sure it couldn't, and yet she didn't want it to end. Again she reached for her glass, giving herself a moment to think. Greg's body language told her in no uncertain terms that he was not about to ease the atmosphere.

"Greg?" At the sound of her tentative voice, Greg's eyes ceased wandering over the other patrons and swung back to her face. She felt as if his angry gaze was piercing into her very soul. "Greg..." She began again, trying to put more strength into her voice, "There's something—"

"Well, well, well!" Raven's head flew around as a tall brunette approached their table. A pale blue gown clung to her perfect figure and offset the beauty of the perfectly made up face. "So you've been busy at work, have you, Greg?"

Raven noticed that Greg showed no signs of awkwardness, merely looking up at the woman, a cynical smile touching his lips. She held her breath, suspecting that this could easily become an ugly scene.

"Actually, yes I have, Sue, thanks for asking. We've had a couple of problems lately."

"Oh, yeah?"

Raven kept her eyes firmly on the glittering candle, wishing she could sink under the table.

"Do you think I'm that stupid? I saw you on the dance floor. The least you could have done is broken up with me before you started bedding someone else."

Although Raven cringed at that assumption, she could hear the tears in the woman's voice. This woman was hurting. Raven could almost feel her pain and humiliation.

"I never suggested there would be anything permanent in our relationship, Sue."

Raven's eyes followed Greg's face as he stood and confronted the woman. She was horrified to notice that he appeared to have no compassion, no consideration at all for how this woman was feeling.

He had obviously just brushed her aside, without so much as a word.

How long they might have been lovers, who knew? But knowing now that he could shrug off one of his women with not so much as a glimmer of compunction strengthened Raven's resolve. She was never going to allow herself to be treated in such an off-hand manner.

Raven watched as the blue eyes filled with tears, and trembling fingers pressed against the quivering lips. Her own face must have registered some sign of sympathy, or womanly solidarity; for instead of a spiel of abuse that she felt Greg so richly deserved, Sue turned to her with a warning. "Don't trust him. He'll eat you alive and spit you out in little pieces. And when he's finished with you, he'll toss you out without so much as a goodbye." Her voice broke for a moment, but she quickly controlled it to turn a subtle attack on Greg. "I hope she can keep you happy in bed, Greg. That's the only place you could satisfy a woman. You're not man enough for anything else."

Raven watched Sue stalk away, silently applauding her final punch line. It had definitely got under Greg's skin. She pretended not to notice the way he angrily returned to his seat and grabbed at his wine glass. She glanced around at the nearby tables, embarrassed to see how people hastily looked away. They must have heard every word.

Raven blushed, mortified to be at the center of such a display.

Greg downed his wine. He glanced at Raven, but she refused to meet his eyes. How could he be so uncaring about someone's feelings? The uncomfortable silence lengthened.

"Let's go." He reached into his wallet and threw a wad of bills onto the table. The waiter was going to appreciate his tip tonight.

Greg all but dragged Raven out of her seat and headed toward the door, his hand firmly attached to her arm. He slowed his pace and she saw his lips twist into what some might mistake for a smile as he became aware of the looks from some of the other patrons. She knew the frozen expression was far from a smile, and watched warily as he signed the check the maitre d' presented to him. He grabbed at the door handle and yanked it open, ushering Raven through in front of him.

She shuddered as the cold air hit them, stumbled and would have fallen had he not grabbed her quickly. She sucked in a great gulp of air. "Would you mind if we walked for a moment? I feel a bit funny."

Greg looked down at her closely in the light from the glass doorway. Her face felt flushed and hot. Despite his black mood, she now recognized a genuine smile that came to his lips.

He thinks I'm tipsy! She might have been supping on that glass quite often, and the waiter had kept it topped, but she was not drunk. However much she'd had wouldn't have been enough to make her feel like this. His expression lightened as he shrugged out of his suit jacket and placed it around her shoulders.

"Sure, let's walk for a bit." He kept an arm firmly around her as they moved down the steps onto the sidewalk. *Wow! Maybe I am a little tipsy,* she wondered, as she staggered along beside him.

Raven tried to shrug out of Greg's coat. She remembered she wasn't in the mood to accept pleasantries from him. Trying to stalk ahead of him, she found her legs did not want to follow her instructions. They felt rubbery and were acting like they had minds of their own. Her head felt light. *What's wrong with me?* She'd never felt like this before. Her mind was perfectly clear, but her body was refusing to obey the instructions it was receiving. A few sips of wine couldn't cause this sort of euphoria, surely? Even to a teetotal body. Could it?

She tripped again and would have fallen without Greg's quick arm circling her body. She glanced up and felt her blood begin to boil at the smirk on his face. He was enjoying seeing her like this, defenceless. He had better think again. She was not about to give in to the lust that had reared its head on the dance floor. She wasn't that stupid, or that drunk.

"I'm perfectly capable of walking by myself, thank you." She was shocked by the slurred voice that sounded nothing like her own, and matched her words by pulling away from his arm.

"Whatever you say."

Was he laughing at her? She turned back to glare at him, and in doing so managed to run into a tree that suddenly appeared in the middle of the footpath.

"There is nothing humorous about this evening at all. That poor girl. How could you be so cruel?"

"Sue has nothing to do with you."

Raven eased herself around the tree, keeping her hand firmly on the trunk to steady herself. "She made it my business when she assumed I was leaping in and out of your bed."

She shivered, but not from the cold. Even in her fuddled state, her body still responded to the image. She tried to hold her head high as she stumbled on, throwing over her shoulder, "I'm not going to bed with you. I'm marrying Brad!"

****

Greg felt his mood darken again. She was such a fraud, trying to hoodwink him. "I think it's time you forgot about my father for a while." He grabbed her and effortlessly swung her around to face him. "You

168

forgot about him on the dance floor. I think we can manage to forget him a while longer." He ground his mouth against hers, all his annoyance at the outcome of the evening expressed in that one kiss.

He ignored Raven's tentative struggles, forcing his tongue into the warmth of her mouth, feeling the immediate response of her body. He knew this was the end of what could have been, should have been, the most intriguing night of his life. He dragged his lips from hers and pulled her tightly into his arms, burying her face against his shoulder. He didn't need her sudden hiccup to remind him that any plans or hopes he might have had about tonight had gone down the drain. He wanted Raven as a willing participant, not a drunken one.

He needed something he could hit, very hard. His feelings were such a jumbled mess. After watching Raven and gradually getting to know her, his fantasies had often got out of control. His heightened libido was encroaching on his life right now—what a time to run into an old girlfriend.

He hadn't thought of Sue for weeks. She'd gone to Florida with her parents before Christmas and as far as he knew, stayed there. There had been a couple of nondescript messages from her on his voicemail he remembered guiltily, but they hadn't inspired him to return her calls. Theirs hadn't been an impassioned relationship that would survive such a lengthy separation. Surely Sue had realized that? Justifying his lack of responsibility for what had just happened inside wasn't working. He drew in a deep breath. He'd unintentionally hurt Sue. But for him the relationship had ended when she'd left. He thought he'd made that perfectly clear at the time. Obviously not, because Sue wasn't the vindictive type. She would never have made that scene just to annoy him. If he'd known she was back in Ellicott City he could have called, but contacting her would have re-established a link he hadn't sought. His mind had been firmly involved with work before Raven arrived on the scene, after which he had become totally absorbed with this woman.

He had to do something for Sue though, had to apologize in some way. Tomorrow he'd arrange for some flowers, and a huge box of chocolates—he remembered she loved those soft-centered ones—to be delivered. That was the best he could do. His feelings had changed. The thought of a casual liaison didn't appeal anymore.

He was looking for something else, something perfect. Maybe even something permanent.

Raven had looked at him as if he was the lowest life on earth. He clenched his fists even as he held her close to him. He'd seen where her sympathy lay. Somehow he had to show Raven he wasn't the unfeeling brute she now thought him to be. He wanted Raven, wanted her desperately. And yet he wanted it to be perfect with her. Wanted more than a roll in the hay, a quick fix—because he was beginning to imagine there could be another woman in his life, permanently.

He only had to close his eyes now and imagine the two of them in ten years, in twenty years, still together, still perfect. He knew there were obstacles to overcome; she had to admit the truth about Brad, for starters.

That was beginning to really annoy him. He'd given her plenty of opportunity to tell him the truth. Although having to go to Hagerstown had messed up his plans. Still, he had hoped by now that she would trust him—that she would know that if she explained to him, he'd understand.

And of course, she'd have to give up her life in New Zealand. That might take a bit of persuading, but Greg was confident he could offer her far more than she would have back there.

Another hiccup jerked the body that had suddenly slumped against him. He moved her away, but kept a tight hold on her arms. All the fight seemed to have gone out of her and she hung in his arms.

A sudden crack of lightning illuminated her pale face. Her eyes flew open at the noise and he registered the fear that leaped into them. It wasn't so much the huge raindrops that accompanied the rolling thunder that made him tuck her under his arm again, as the vulnerability he had seen on her face. Whether it was the suddenness of the impending storm, or just storms in general, he wasn't sure, but he did know she was frightened. All his long-forgotten urges to guard and protect the female of the species came rushing to the fore.

Even the coat around her shoulders did little to keep rain from drenching her as they struggled back to the car. Greg hadn't realized how far they'd managed to walk in what seemed like only a few moments. The journey back was not without mishap. He had to all but drag Raven along the flowing sidewalk as the rain pelted down on their crouched-over bodies. She continued to stumble and trip over every imaginable obstacle, making their journey so much longer than necessary. By the time he had got himself into the car, they were both totally drenched.

He quickly turned the heater on and headed the car for home as fast as the atrocious conditions would allow. He noticed Raven's body shaking every now and then from a hiccup, but she said nothing. Turning to study her as they waited for a green light, he thought she might have passed out.

He knew she was going to hate this tomorrow. She was always so sure of herself, so much in control; she would deplore this evening as a complete lack of restraint. Her dignity would take a dive, that was for sure. He wondered just how much she would actually remember. He doubted if he would be lucky enough for her to have forgotten Sue arriving at their table. That would be hoping for too much.

While Raven made some noises when Greg tried to waken her, he realized she was not capable of getting herself upstairs and out of her wet clothes. He quickly opened the internal garage door before he returned to the car and awkwardly lifted her out. His coat fell forgotten on the floor as he struggled to maneuver her around the car and into the house. He was thankful for the heat he felt as they entered. His clothing was sticking to him, and he was beginning to shiver. As he hoisted Raven higher in his arms and headed towards the staircase, her eyelids sluggishly lifted and he found himself staring into her eyes. For a moment he halted, mesmerized by the glow. But her shivers quickly bought him back down to earth.

"Put your arms around my neck," he instructed as he started up the stairs. She willingly obliged and he found his hold was lightened. He tried valiantly to keep his mind occupied and to ignore the lips moving seductively across his neck.

"Stop that," he ordered as he felt her teeth nibbling at his ear.

A giggle and tightened arms were the only response. His head reared sideways as he felt her tongue entering his ear. He dumped her unceremoniously onto her feet at the top of the stairs.

"Quit it, Raven. You don't know what you're doing!"

"Don't I?" Raven's hands slid up over his chest until they were encircling his neck. Her black dress had accentuated her figure wonderfully before, but now the wet material clung, highlighting every curve.

He gasped in oxygen as she continued to press

those curves against him. Ignoring her blatant invitation, he tried to keep his cool. He held himself stiff, his hands fisted against his sides, talking to himself, thinking of other things, trying desperately to ignore what her body was doing to his. His good intentions almost came to grief as she pressed her lips against his and he felt the tip of her tongue invading his mouth.

Think of something else, anything. Anything but the feel of this woman, the taste of her. Anything that'll keep my mind above my waist. His libido was almost rearing out of control.

It was an unconscious hiccup from Raven that broke the seal of their lips and allowed Greg to take charge of his slipping ethics. As he drew another great breath into his screaming lungs, his eyes fell on an old family portrait on the wall. He found himself staring at his father's image. His gaze went from his father to the head of the woman lying against his chest. Her arms were clinging to him, while her lips tried to seduce him. She was inviting him to do things he'd recently fantasized about.

He sighed raggedly. The disappointment and frustration this evening was causing would stay with him for some time. But he was in control now, definitely. If the idea germinating in his mind worked, he'd be in the control seat for some time. Hopefully, until she admitted the truth to him.

Just because she was drunk didn't mean she couldn't suffer a little bit too.

Chapter 11

Greg swung Raven back up into his arms and set off along the hallway. He quickly passed the door of her room and went on to his own. Her arms clinging around his neck allowed him to partially free one hand to open the door without dropping her, and he used his sodden boot to kick it wide open.

"Raven..." He needed to get her warm and dry. "Raven, you need to get out of those clothes. I'll run the shower. Get into it and warm up while I find you a night gown." He shook her slightly. "Raven, get into the shower and warm up, okay?"

He couldn't help smiling at the expression on her face.

"Yessir." She almost fell over attempting to salute. Greg steered her into his bathroom, and sat her on the commode. He turned and adjusted the shower until the water was steaming hot.

"Can you manage?"

"Of coursh I man canage," she slurred, "I'm not an imb...imb... I'm not an idiot, you know. Anyone can take a shower. It doesn't take too much effort."

"I'll be back in a few moments with your night things." As he closed the bathroom door, she'd already kicked off her shoes and was standing up. He figured she just might be able to manage after all.

Quickly stripping down to his briefs, he threw his drenched clothes into a corner. Slipping on the robe he'd grabbed from the bathroom door, he headed for Raven's room to find something for her to wear.

He'd not been into her room since her arrival. He drew a deep breath, distinguishing her perfume, very subtly at first, but as he entered her bathroom, the scent grew stronger. He looked around hoping to find some nightwear, but settled for the robe on the back of the door. As he moved back towards the bedroom, his eye caught sight of a bottle on the counter. He quickly picked it up and read the label. It was a prescription drug. Not one that he recognized, but obviously part of her journey back to good health. He turned the small bottle over and read the instructions on the back.

Do not take with alcohol. He quickly opened the bottle and saw it was empty. Had she just finished her prescribed course? Perhaps she hadn't considered the drug would still be in her body? Greg was sure that she would never jeopardize her health by drinking in association with taking drugs. She must have finished her medication and thought alcohol would no longer cause any complications.

How wrong she was! Greg smiled. He almost wished he could have videotaped her performance at the top of the stairs. She'd be mortified if she had any memories of her behavior tonight.

He put the bottle back down on the counter and moved toward her bed, understanding now why her actions were so different from what he'd come to expect from her. Having a bit of fun was one thing but he knew the wantonness she'd displayed was totally out of character. He flicked through the drawers until he found a very sensible cotton nightgown and stuffed it under his arm. As he straightened, he noticed a small gold photo frame propped up on the nightstand. Intrigued, he moved around the bed to have a closer look.

The air felt like it had all left his body in an enormous rush as he stared. He'd expected to see an image of her husband. He'd craved to put a face on the ghostly figure that so often interrupted his dreams.

Instead he found himself starring down at two individual photos. School prints he guessed, two little boys. They could only be her sons. Who else's photos would she have at to her bedside? He swore loudly and crudely as he threw the frame down onto her bed. All the times they had talked, she'd never mentioned having children; never said a word.

Lying bitch. Even as the words took form in his mind, he hurriedly dismissed them. *What gives me the right to be judgmental?* They'd been making a habit of lying to each other since they met; or pretending. *I haven't lied,* he assured himself. Parts of his life belonged to him and him alone. He wasn't about to share them with anyone. His past was just that—past. Not like hers. *Why hasn't she mentioned her family? What else is there about her that I don't know? Almost everything,* he acknowledged. He knew absolutely nothing about her except that he wanted to be with her. She drove him crazy, invading his life, his mind, until he thought of little else.

He sank down onto the bed and watched his hand snake out to clasp the photo frame again. Now that the initial shock was gone, he found himself looking more closely at the faces that grinned back at him. He tried to guess their ages. The bigger one looked younger than his nephew Caleb, and yet there was something in his eyes that suggested sadness, or maybe maturity beyond his years. The younger one made Greg's heart pound. He was so like Raven. His hair though darker then hers, flopped down across his forehead just as hers liked to. His eyes sparkled as if with some hidden joke that he couldn't wait to share. They were very handsome boys and Greg guessed Raven must be proud of them.

He scrubbed a hand across his face. He

remembered her saying her husband had been twenty-five when he'd been killed. Oh, my God! These boys must have just been babies. She had to bring them up alone—all that responsibility, and on such young shoulders. He mentally added a few years to the age he'd guessed her to be. She definitely wasn't in her mid-twenties.

He wondered how often she'd worried, concerned about doing the right thing, having to make all the decisions by herself. His heart swelled with a sense of ill-placed pride. She really was some kind of woman.

He gently replaced the photos next to her bed and smiled down at her sons. He guessed he would get to meet them soon.

A loud thump sent him racing back to his bathroom. Throwing open the shower door, he found Raven in a heap on the floor; giggling as the steaming water pounded down on her upturned face. Once again the thought crossed his mind, where's a camera when you need one? She didn't seem to have deemed it necessary to take off her clothes.

"I guess I shipped over," she said, giggling.

"Are you hurt?" Greg doubted if her shaking head meant much. She probably couldn't feel any pain even if she had hurt herself.

"Do you normally shower with all your clothes on?"

"Only if I'm showering alone." She held up a hand so he could help her up. "Diya wanna join me?" she asked saucily.

"I really don't think that would be a good idea." Greg tried to sound stern as he reached in and turned off the water. He lifted her out of the shower stall. Gently he unzipped her dress, slipped the straps from her shoulders, and eased it down over her hips until it fell to the floor. He grabbed a towel and shoved it at her before unclipping her bra and pushing her panties down over her thighs. Reaching for another towel he turned her around and rubbed it across her shoulders, hastily turning his back on the mirror and the sight he caught in its reflection.

"Come on! Dry yourself off." He had no intention of drying the more intimate parts of her body. He was already having enough trouble just being this close to her.

Before he could retrieve her nightgown from the counter, she suddenly turned around to face him and dropped her towel. He sucked in a huge gasp of air. She was beautiful, even more beautiful than in his wildest fantasies.

Without any apparent awareness of her nakedness she slipped her hands inside the lapels of his robe and pushed it off his shoulders.

"Are we gonna make love now?"

Thank God for her slurred speech. Without it he might have been lost—he might have forgotten that she didn't know what she was doing.

"No!" he snapped, trying to untangle her arms and move her towards the bedroom.

"Don't be sush an old grump. Make love to me."

God! Give me strength, he prayed as his body responded to the feel of naked flesh against naked flesh. Luscious lips traveled over his chest, his neck, his face.

"You are going to bed—"

"Ohh, goodie." She squirmed her body against his.

"Alone."

"Oh no, you don't." She seemed to have developed the strength of ten women as she pushed him towards the bed. With a well-placed heave she brought them both down in a tangle of arms and legs. Before he could avoid her lips, they fastened on his and he felt the resistance draining from him. Somehow one of his hands had fastened onto her breast and he found himself gently massaging the soft flesh and erect nipple. His mouth left hers and moved downwards towards its heightened peak.

He was only human. He had a beautiful naked woman in his arms; a woman he had been fantasizing about all week. She was begging him—begging for his possession.

Would it be so wrong?

Yes! Damn it! Of course it would be wrong.

How could he even allow himself to consider differently, even for a second? He wasn't exactly a gentleman; nor was he a scumbag. He shifted his weight so he could lever himself away from her. He paused for a moment, savoring the feel of her body, the sight of her nakedness—knowing he might not get this close to her again, might never see her in his bed, feel her wantonness. He reached up a finger and gently traced the outline of her beautiful face. He leaned over and lightly touched his lips to hers. He watched a frown gather and her forehead crease as if she was trying to concentrate.

"Chris?" There was doubt in her voice, but not fear. She seemed to realize that he wasn't her dead husband...now. But what about before? Had she thought she was inviting a ghost to share her bed?

"Go to sleep, Raven." Greg slid off the bed, his emotions a tangled mess. He didn't know how he felt now. Had she thought she'd been kissing her husband all along?

He looked down at her, eyes already closed. The evenness of her breathing suggested she was asleep. It gnawed at his gut, not knowing whether it was him she was trying to entice or her long-dead husband.

He bent down and grasped his robe, slipping it back onto his shoulders. A drink, that's what he needed. It was going to be a long night.

Well, that's what he'd planned and hoped for—a long night with Raven in his bed. He hadn't expected he'd be spending it sitting beside her, ensuring that the mix of drugs and alcohol wouldn't cause any harm, assuring himself that she was okay.

****

It was well into the early hours of the morning when Greg's own befuddled brain came up with another idea.

Not only would Raven awaken in his bed, she would be shocked with what she'd find.

He'd been in and out of his room checking on her. He'd even lain down on her bed for a while trying to get a few moments sleep. But sleep was eluding him. His mind was in overdrive and he could not calm himself down. He forced himself to consider what direction he wanted a relationship with Raven to take. He wasn't sure, but he doubted if he would ever get her out of his blood. Sleeping with her was not going to fix this craving eating at him. He didn't spend all his time thinking about bedding her. He wanted more, wanted her beside him as a part of his life.

He turned over and looked at the photo of her grinning sons.

Was he ready to consider them as well?

He didn't know. He'd never been able to get close to children. He tolerated his nephew and niece, but had never done anything to allow them, or himself, to develop any sort of relationship. Since Ethan...

Any time marriage had come to mind, he'd axed the idea, because with marriage came children, and he didn't think he could risk going through...

Raven's youngest son would probably be about the same age as Ethan, he mused, wondering what his name might be. *Did he play baseball, basketball? Who served as their male role model? Perhaps she has a 'friend'*—the very idea made his stomach knot.

No. She didn't. He was sure of that. At least no one permanent, no one intimately associated with her or the boys. She would protect her sons from anything that might seem unsavory. That's probably why she'd been so adamant earlier, before the alcohol had taken effect, when he'd intimated his desire to make love.

Raven had responsibilities that he could only imagine. Responsibilities that no doubt colored everything she did—especially the more intimate side of her life. He now knew she would never indulge in a 'fling' knowing her sons and mother would be arriving any day now. She would continue to hold him at arm's length—unless he forced the situation.

He sprang up from the bed. He would never get anywhere near her. She would always hold herself aloof from him, certain that he was only looking for a passing fling. And meeting Sue last night at the club did nothing to help his cause. It only reinforced her erroneous impression that he used and discarded women at his own whim.

He rushed back into his room to check she was still sleeping. He stared down at her for some time, watching the way her eyelids kept flickering. *What are you dreaming?* Her hair fell down across her face, framing it against the dark pillow. Her breast moved with each breath—he hastily pulled the sheet up and tucked it under her chin. Smiling down at her, his hand gently moved her hair aside so he could place a soft kiss onto her cheek.

He took a deep breath.

This is a hell of a risk, but hopefully, it'll make her open up to me; tell me the truth about her and Dad at least. And that will be a start. She won't be able to freeze me out. Not after this night we'll spend together.

He went into the bathroom and picked up her discarded clothing. After wringing it out in the basin, he moved back into the bedroom and looked around. He very carefully placed the items across the room, scattered on the floor. One shoe he put close to the door, the other further into the room. Next the dress, as if it had slid from her hips. The underwear he tossed. The bra landed, one strap hooked over the arm of a chair, the lacy panties dangling from the seat. Greg then retrieved his own clothing and strategically placed them near Raven's. For good measure he fastened his shirt, then ripped it open, causing a couple of buttons to pop and land just beside the bed. They stood out quite clearly against the solid blue carpet. She was hardly likely to miss them when she jumped out of bed.

The bed—it was much too tidy; hardly the scene of a night of passion. Very carefully he rumpled the bedclothes until they lay in apparent disarray. Pausing, he looked down at her. What would she be like, he wondered, what would it be like, if she didn't have to pull back? If she loved him?

He sighed deeply. He prayed he might soon find out that she could believe in his love and return it without reserve.

At last he stood back to survey his handiwork. Yes. Anyone looking at this room would assume exactly what he hoped Raven would assume—that they'd spent a large part of the night wreathed in passion, wrapped in each other, oblivious to the outside world.

She wouldn't be able to hold him at arm's length after that. She'd have to talk to him—come clean. Only then could they discuss their true feelings.

He looked down at her again, contemplating his next move.

Would it be too much?

No. He didn't think so. He was counting on this

working. He put everything he could think of into it, because if it didn't work...

He reached into the bathroom cabinet and opened a packet. He contemplated the foil packets inside and tipped them out into his palm. He grinned as he ripped open the first one and threw the contents into the toilet. He then followed with three more. He grinned at himself in the mirror—might as well boost his ego at the same time. He carefully placed the empty wrappers where she could hardly fail to see them, on the table beside her, by his 'side' of the bed, another on the bathroom counter. He was careful to ensure they looked as if they'd been carelessly thrown aside. He returned to the bathroom, getting rid of the condoms, and then decided to add to the scene by dampening a few more towels and throwing them next to the spa bath.

Bubbles...that would add to the scene. He ran the water for a moment to froth some shower gel, making sure all the bubbles didn't entirely drain away.

He stood back and surveyed his handiwork, first in the bathroom, then the bedroom. Perfect, he thought. If he awoke from an inebriated night to see this sight, he would have no doubt how the night had been spent. Even if she didn't wake up with him beside her—he'd decided he couldn't trust himself that far—she couldn't help but assume they'd become much closer.

He'd top it off by taking her breakfast in his bed. He'd noticed some crocuses flowering in the garden yesterday. He'd pick some and add them to the tray. Maybe they weren't red roses, but they'd still express some of his feelings. He'd use the day to gently show her she could trust him, open up to him, and share her thoughts and feelings with him. It would be uncomfortable at first, but with no Manuela or Jorge around to interrupt or cramp his style, he was confident he could make her realize that sexual tension like the kind between them wasn't supposed to be suppressed.

He'd have all day to convince her that she could believe in him, rely on him. He would make her see that they were two kindred spirits who could never be whole again, unless they were together. He'd take his time and persuade her that they belonged together, that no issue was too big for them to overcome. By working together, in unison, they could find a future.

****

Raven felt consciousness creeping up on her gradually. Immediately she knew that something was different. She normally moved from heavy sleep to wide awake in split seconds, but now she could feel the wakefulness rolling over her like gentle waves on a tropical beach. Each ripple encouraged her to open her eyes, but they remained glued together ignoring the messages. She felt totally unable to move even one muscle.

She wasn't sure how much time passed as she lay there, strangely at peace and unaware of her surroundings. She was aware of a passing car, a slammed door, and footsteps, followed by the ringing of the doorbell. She hadn't noticed being able to hear noise from the driveway before. Raven continued to snuggle into the comforter, dismissing the early morning visitor as of no interest to her, content to savour a few more moments before she would have to move.

Early morning visitor? Justin! He was coming to take her out this morning, at half past nine. Her eyes flew open and she reached over to the bedside table to check her watch. The sudden movement caused her head to spin so severely that she had to lie back slowly onto the pillow. Her eyes felt gritty, but this time when she moved her head, Raven found the spinning wasn't quite so bad. She reached out for her watch, blindly groping the nightstand. Her brain registered surprise as her fingers found scraps of paper where she normally kept only the boys' photo, and at night, her watch. What might she have thrown there last night?

As she struggled to remember, she recalled that embarrassing display on the dance floor. She buried her head deeper into the pillow, feeling the blood rise into her face as she remembered the way she had melted into his arms. She squirmed with embarrassment. For the first time since awakening, she felt her skin against the sheets—her bare skin.

Very slowly Raven lifted up the edge of the comforter and peeked under. Naked, completely naked! She never slept in the buff! At least not since Chris had died; too often she'd be up during the night to tend the boys, or one of them would slip into bed alongside her.

Slowly Raven dropped the comforter, and for the first time looked around the room. A sense of dread assailed her. She ignored the dizziness as her eyes took in a different colour scheme. She recognised it immediately. She had been in this room. Not for long, but she remembered from the day Greg showed her around the house.

Oh no! How could I?

Her desperate mind searched for another possible explanation. She remembered a storm, getting wet. Perhaps Greg had only helped her out of her wet clothes?

Ha, fat chance! Raven remembered the expression he wore as he held her, the desire in his eyes as he invited her to share his bed. She swung her legs over the side of the bed. Sitting up slowly, Raven's horrified eyes fastened on the white circles lying close to her toes. Shirt buttons lying near to a man's shirt, its sleeve tucked under a pile of black material Raven recognised as her once beautiful dress. She clutched at the vague possibility the evening had not ended as Greg quite openly had wanted it to.

All semblance of doubt was washed away when her eyes lighted on the nightstand. She pressed her fingers tight against her lips, trying to stem the nausea that threatened to engulf her.

Flashes of the night came back to her, flashes she would rather have not remembered. Like, being on this bed...

She jumped from the mattress and faced it as if it were a monster about to attack, arms wrapped tight around her. She remembered lying with Greg naked on this bed. She remembered his hands, roaming her body, his lips on her breast. Horrified, her cool nipples hardened at the memory. This time the threatening nausea could not be controlled and Raven rushed into his bathroom.

Afterward, she leaned weakly against the shower wall. What was she going to do? How would she face him? The tears that had welled up now threatened to overflow. She didn't remember most of what had happened. She had acquaintances that laughed away nights of memory loss, but it had never happened to her. She'd never allowed herself to get out of control, especially at the whim of her treacherous body.

She couldn't blame Greg. What good would that do, anyway? It had happened, and she had to live with the consequences, period. She moved over to the hand basin and turned on the cold tap to splash water on her heated face. Her stomach heaved again as she noticed yet another ripped foil packet and evidence of the huge spa bath having been used. She groaned. *Not here as well! Had we been at it all night? How many times...?*

She refused to contemplate any further.

Somehow she had to figure out what she was going to do now; how she would react when they next met. Thank God Justin was coming today. His visit would give her a respite, a time to think, to plan...

Justin! He was downstairs. That was he she'd heard arriving. She leapt out of the bathroom wrapping a large towel around her nakedness, hastily grabbed up the clothes she found scattered all over the bedroom, and headed for the door. Hopefully she would be able to avoid Greg this morning and have time to consider her very few options.

Unfortunately not. She swung the door open just in time to collide with his hand reaching out for the handle.

She felt the blood drain from her face, her stomach muscles clenched. *I can't look at him.* Her heart was pounding as she tried to push around his anchored body. She jerked away from the hands that came out to grip her shoulders. She couldn't bear the thought of those hands on her bare skin again.

She wasn't sure what her body might want to do and she was not taking any risks. Her brain was in control again. No more signs of weakness, or indulging the flesh.

"Good morning." He spoke softly, intimately, his voice husky and inviting. "Did you sleep well?"

Her eyes flew to his for a split second.

Did she sleep well?

Is that what he wanted to know? How obtuse.

No, I didn't sleep well. At least she assumed she hadn't, if she was to believe the state of the bed, the room, the bathroom. It looked like they hadn't had much time for sleeping.

She shied away from the hand that tried to cup her face, and the lips that moved towards hers landed harmlessly in midair.

"I was looking forward to us spending the day

together," he murmured. "I didn't realise you had plans."

"It's my cousin. Well, Chris's cousin, actually. I haven't seen him for years. He works at the New Zealand Embassy. My mother sent me an email telling me..." She would have prattled on inanely until she could slip around him and escape; but as if he realized her intentions, Greg pulled her into his arms. She struggled against him but felt the towel begin to loosen so was forced to stay rigidly still. He ran his hands up and down her back, dipping them lower and lower with each stroke, until the pressure on her buttocks had her standing tightly against him. She tried to ignore his chin leaning on her forehead, but the scratchiness of his morning's growth was somehow soothing.

"I don't suppose you could put him off? I thought we could spend the day really getting to know each other." His hands were causing havoc. "I was just fixing your breakfast. I'd even been out to pick some flowers from the garden."

Was that disappointment in his voice? Had he really intended that they should share the day together, get to know each other better? Perhaps she should...

Raven shuddered as his lips found her ear lobes again. What was it about her ears that seem to fascinate him—and turned her on so much?

"We could spend the whole day here, never get out of bed." His voice was muffled but the intention was clear as he began edging them both back into the bedroom. "I'll tell your friend you're not feeling very well and want to postpone." One hand deftly pulled at the towel and Raven felt it begin to slip down. She hastily grabbed it but not before his eyes had fastened on her erect nipples.

"No." Then more forcibly, "I can't do that."

"Come on," he coaxed, "you know you want to."

Now his lips were trailing over her face. "Come back to bed with me. We'll see if we can go even higher than last night. Although I doubt that's possible. This time I'll do the seducing."

As her horrified mind took in that comment, it gave her strength. She had to get away from him— had to think without her body melting under his expert caresses.

She struggled out of his arms, no longer concerned about the clothes she'd haphazardly clutched under one arm or the state of her towel. She just had to put distance between them, now.

****

He watched as she pulled the towel up to cover her breasts again. His disappointment was so acute he could physically feel it. Still, maybe a day of thought would improve his chances of being able to convince her that he wasn't a womanizer out for a quick lay. He wanted so much more. He wanted a physical relationship of course, but that could wait. First he had to build up her trust, show her nothing was more important in his life than her. She was shocked and upset now, tonight would be soon enough to talk. Besides he could use a couple of hours sleep before embarking on the most important discussion of his life.

She couldn't hide behind anything now. She was obviously quite convinced they'd spent the night together and her body was still betraying her. Even though he knew she was horrified at what had happened, her body still melted against his. He only had to touch her and she was his. No more could she pretend.

"Raven?" he called softly.

Did she realize that while she might have the towel draped chastely in front of her, her whole back was exposed as she ran to her room? He sure knew it, as his body reared to attention at the sight.

She paused for a moment at her doorway, as if suddenly aware of coolness against her back. His teasing smile grew into a full-blown grin, and he saw the color flame into her face. Again he called her name to halt her escape.

"You were magnificent." He paused to allow his words to sink in. "Last night was beyond description."

He could hardly read the expression on her face, it was so quickly covered by the towel which exposed more than just those beautiful long legs. But her gasp was quite audible as she disappeared into her room and the door closed. He guessed it might have slammed but for the fallen clothes that blocked it. Smiling, he moved toward the stairs.

It was time for him to play the polite host with this man and find out a few more things about Raven.

****

Why did I have to run into him? Raven groaned. She'd hoped for time. Time to decide how to approach this situation. But oh no, there he was, gloating. His smugness was so infuriating. She'd felt like slapping his face. How dare he be so open, illustrating the effect of their embrace on his hormones?

She didn't want to know. She didn't care. She really didn't care.

She threw the remaining clothes in her arms onto her bed with a force that surprised even her, suggesting they might never be suitable for wear again. Ignoring her nakedness, Raven stormed into the bathroom and turned the shower taps on full. She stared into the mirror while the water heated up.

Do I look any different? She studied her body. Had he found her attractive? After all, she had borne two children, and wasn't as young as some of the dolly birds she suspected he normally dated. Despite her exercise regime, she detected a sag here, a droop there. Had he noticed?

She quickly quelled her thoughts. What was the matter with her? She'd just spent the night with Greg—obviously with no reluctance. Shuddering, Raven stepped under the shower. The hot water did nothing to warm the chill as she remembered portions of the night. He wouldn't have forced her; she knew that. Raven succumbed to an inescapable sense of guilt and betrayal as she remembered all that she'd shared with Chris—love and laughter, hopes and dreams, absolute enjoyment of each other's bodies.

She dropped her face into her hands and let the water beat against her head. How could she have allowed this to happen? She loved Greg, but any relationship with him was doomed from the start. He was not the type to want permanence and she couldn't settle for anything less. A somewhat hysterical laugh rose in her throat, but quickly died as she recalled her immediate predicament. Did he expect that they'd continue what they started last night until she returned to New Zealand? And then, a casual farewell? Such a possibility brought tears to her eyes. She'd never forget Greg, and didn't want to even think about goodbye.

Raven remembered the woman at the club last night, the hurt in her eyes. Greg's callous attitude towards her obvious pain merely reinforced Raven's stance. His ability to effortlessly shrug off relationships scared her; if sharing the ultimate intimacies meant so little to him...

Raven gasped, suddenly feeling like a sledgehammer had hit her. The shower water couldn't penetrate the cold that washed over her. Greg had made love to her believing she was marrying his father!

Her stomach heaved. Scorching bile rose in her throat but slowly subsided, leaving its bitter taste burning her mouth. Cringing against the shower wall, she accepted there could be no excuse for the shallowness of Greg's feelings. To knowingly hurt Brad... Groaning, Raven knew she had to get away from him.

Then she remembered, Justin was downstairs now, waiting to take her out for the day. Maybe he could help. He could at least be her buffer for today. Maybe he could even put her up for a few days. Mum and the boys would be here soon, so if she could keep away from Greg until then she'd be safe.

She couldn't deny her attraction to him. But this flaw in his character devastated her. Greg cared so little for his father, he'd seduced his fiancée. One thing was certain—she couldn't give him the satisfaction of knowing she was in love with him.

Slowly turning off the shower Raven stepped out of the cubicle. Was it possible to love a man that she couldn't respect? She wasn't sure, but didn't know another name to call this all-consuming passion she had for him.

Greg was downstairs with Justin, questioning him, no doubt, digging into her past, trying to find out about her. Things he had no right to know.

Raven hastily threw on some clothes, not even caring whether or not they were suitable for a day out. She had to get downstairs as quickly as possible and rescue Justin from Greg's probing. On the way out the door, she paused, went back to her dresser and grabbed a spare pair of briefs from the drawer and stuffed them into her bag in case Justin okayed her staying a few nights at his place.

Chapter 12

Greg was struggling to hide his annoyance. While this New Zealander seemed pleasant enough, happily talking about the up-and-coming baseball season, he'd been very reticent when Raven's name came up. Several times Greg tried to angle the conversation around to her but each time found himself sidetracked. He felt his temper beginning to rise as he eyed the other man warily. Obviously Justin Titirangi was no man's fool. He was not about to discuss Raven with anyone, not without her approval anyway. *Who does he imagine he is anyway? Some kind of knight in shining armor?* Raven didn't need this pretty boy to protect her. That was his job now.

Greg studied him. He wasn't actually related to Raven, so perhaps he had designs on her. He supposed women might consider Justin good looking. Though Greg knew with a woman like Raven it'd take more than good looks. And Justin was a New Zealander, not a foreigner. During his sleepless night Greg had gone over every conversation they'd had. He realized that convincing her to leave New Zealand and live with him in America might not be easy. Glaring at this interloper who'd ruined all his plans for the day Greg admitted the jealousy that raged within him.

Silently they waited for Raven. *Damned if I'm going to entertain him if he's not going to tell me anything I want to know.* Even as he was cursing this man's discretion, he was secretly glad that Justin shared the belief that Raven's welfare was not something to be bandied about.

"Kia Ora, Justin."

"Aroha."

Greg grimaced as he watched Justin jump out of his chair and rush across the room to take Raven into his arms.

Aroha. Is that some sort of pet name? And is it really necessary to swing her around like that? Greg felt his fingers clench into fists. That was definitely not a kiss between friends! They were acting like a couple of teenagers. Raven smiling broadly while enjoying Justin putting his hands all over her.

Greg felt the knots in his stomach tighten.

"Ah, Aroha," Justin repeated. "It's been too long."

"Kuia's tangi, wasn't it?"

Were they deliberately trying to exclude him by using another language? Greg's fists cracked as he realized that they were totally ignoring his presence. Although his annoyance was growing by the second, he recognized their conversation hadn't been manufactured for his benefit. It deepened his realization that in Raven's eyes he was definitely a foreigner.

"I know. I'm sorry I took off, but I couldn't stand another funeral. Not so soon after Chris."

Raven reached up and gently touched Justin's cheek. "I know. It was pretty rugged."

Again they hugged. What was it about these two?

"Time seems to have run away on us since then, hasn't it?"

"How are the mokupunas?" Justin asked.

"Growing like weeds."

Greg noticed how Raven's expression softened as she answered him.

"I always meant to be around to help with them. I'm sorry." Greg couldn't remember seeing a grown man look so discomfited before.

"That's okay, buddy. We managed fine. And now we're able to catch up on lost time."

"You could have knocked me down with a feather the day you rang the Embassy. I never expected to hear your voice. What ever happened to you saying you'd never leave Godzone?"

Greg ground his teeth at the teasing tone in Justin's voice fueling the twisting turns of jealousy deep in his stomach. Then he felt as if the wind had been knocked out of him at Raven's reply to Justin.

"A short holiday away from New Zealand is okay."

"Not enough inspiration for your painting anywhere else, aye?"

Again the teasing note in Justin's voice grated on Greg's nerves.

This time Raven merely shrugged then bent down to pick up her bag where it had fallen. "Let's go, shall we?" She looked in Greg's direction, but would not make eye contact. "I'm sure Greg has plans for the day, right?"

He knew his forced smile didn't fool her. "I had plans but they seem to have fallen through," he murmured.

"Teach you not to count your chickens," she muttered back as she moved past him into the foyer. "Good thing you gave me a key because we'll probably be late. So don't wait up!"

She pulled Justin out the door and down the steps. Not waiting for his assistance, Raven jumped into the waiting car and slammed the door.

Greg's stomach dropped at the expression in Raven's eyes as they caught his for just a second through the car window. They'd been full of disgust and loathing.

This had been a mistake. He couldn't allow her to spend a whole day berating herself for something that never happened. He rushed down the steps calling her name, aware of her frenzied gestures at Justin to leave. He saw the relief in a furtive glance she threw back over her shoulder as Justin sped away with a squeal of tires.

Oh, Hell! He had no way of contacting her, to tell her she had no reason to feel as she did. Greg slammed a fist against the doorpost as he moved inside. Why had he done such a stupid thing? He'd rather cut off his right arm than cause the pain she was feeling right now.

****

"Are you going to tell me what's going on, or should I just leave it to my imagination?"

Raven hadn't expected Justin to question her so soon but she wasn't surprised that he'd been aware of the tension in the room they'd just left.

"Do you think we could just drive somewhere? Get away from here?"

"Sure thing. Whatever you want. Shall we find somewhere and go for a quiet walk?"

Raven smiled thankfully.

There was silence in the car for a little while and then Raven broke it by asking Justin what he'd been doing since last she'd seen him. Soon the flow of conversation was as fast and furious as one would expect from two good friends who hadn't seen each other for years. Having grown up next door to each other, and gone through school together, they had many friends and acquaintances in common. For a while Raven was able to forget about Greg and their predicament.

Although both Chris and Justin had been her lifelong friends, it had been Justin she'd met first. They were all well into their teens before she and Chris realised that beneath the constant antagonism between them hid quite different emotions. Justin's role in her life had quickly slipped into the background. But they'd shared heartaches and triumphs from kindergarten all through school, so that even after five years, they found it easy to pick up the threads.

"You know until now," Raven said, smiling across at Justin, "I never realised just how much I've missed you."

She was rewarded with a quick hug before he exited the car and came around to help her out.

"Come on, let's walk." He took her hand firmly in his and led her down a narrow walkway to the edge of a small lake.

They hadn't gone very far before she felt his eyes on her. "Now tell me what's going on."

Raven shrugged, but he persisted. "Come on. I could have cut the atmosphere with a knife back there. And the way that guy was trying to pump me for information... Don't try and pretend there's nothing going on between the two of you. Only thing I'm trying to figure out is why neither of you seem very happy about it."

She pulled her hand from Justin's, stuffed both hands tightly in the pockets of her jacket, and stalked ahead.

He caught her up. "Come on, babe. You can trust ole Just," he urged. "I know you well enough to know when you're hurting." He walked quietly beside her for a moment, then stopped, turning her to face him. "Did I arrive at an awkward time?"

The flush of colour that invaded her face meant no answer was needed.

Justin's arm went around her shoulders. "You wanna talk about it?"

"No. Yes. Oh, I don't know." She flung her head down onto his chest grasping his arms tightly.

"Hey, steady on." He feigned a stumble. "You nearly knocked me over. Let's just walk for a while. You can talk if you feel like it later."

"When did you suddenly become so understanding, Justin Titirangi?" she queried teasingly. "Have you been working at getting closer to your feminine side?"

Raven felt a rush of remorse as she saw his sparkling dark eyes suddenly cloud.

"Maybe," he muttered. Taking her hand in his again, he added, "Maybe we could both use some advice right now."

****

The day was full of emotional turmoil. Amongst the enjoyment they found in each other's company were the ups and downs of their romantic lives. She found out Justin was almost as much an emotional wreck as she was. Two troubled souls consoling each other, or trying to—that's what they were.

Justin showed just the right amount of common sense and humour to help her understand the feelings Greg might be suffering from. He queried more than once Raven's insistence that Greg was not the type to want any permanence from a relationship.

"How can you be so sure, Rae?" They were munching huge juicy hamburgers in a small diner. "You've not given him a chance."

"I don't want to give him a chance. Can't you understand?" Raven was becoming agitated. "What if..." She looked helplessly at him, one thumb travelling up to her mouth.

Justin reached out and grasped the hand before she could inflict any more damage. "Crikey! You've been giving these a good going over, haven't you?" he murmured, as he rubbed his thumb over her torn skin. "How long has it been since you tried to chew your thumbs off? I bet it's been years. And yet you're doing it again now."

Raven pulled her hands away and clenched them in her lap. "Mind your own damn business."

Justin threw back his head and laughed. "Same old Raven, jumping down my throat every time I'm right about something. You could never stand me being right, could you?"

"I never had to think about it very often," she parried back.

"Ah, but I'm all grown up now. And I'm right about this. You're in love with the guy."

"So what if I am?"

"What do you intend to do about it?"

"What can I do? There's nothing in it for me but heartache."

"How can you be so sure, Rae? That guy seemed pretty edgy this morning. He didn't like me being there. Perhaps—"

"He was just worried about having his plans foiled, that's all."

"Can't say I blame him." Justin smiled.

"Just because I slept with him, doesn't mean..." Raven's voice faltered, feeling the blood rush into her face as she realised that in her agitation her voice had risen. Other customers in the diner were watching their table. "It doesn't mean I was ready to spend the day in bed with him!" she finished in a fierce whisper.

"Don't you think you're being a little unfair, expecting him to know that?"

"No," she snapped. Watching his eyebrows rise again caused her to take a deep breath and try to calm down. "Oh Justin, I don't even remember." She buried her head in her hands. "I slept with someone and I don't even remember it. What does that make me?"

"Considering you're in love with the guy," he teased, "a pretty unlucky lady. Until next time, that is."

"What's the matter with you? Are you really that dumb? There isn't going to be any next time.

Get that through your thick skull."

"For your sake, I hope you're wrong."

Were men all the same? "I can't handle a few quick rolls in the hay. I'm not made like that. I couldn't be satisfied without some semblance of permanence. It would just tear me apart."

She leaned over and grasped his hand. "I have the boys to think of too." She couldn't risk their getting hurt. If they sensed the attraction between Greg and her—they might like him too—what would happen when he dropped them all?

More than once during the day she'd thought of her sons. Any time that her heart appeared to be getting the better of her, she reminded herself of her responsibilities and firmly pushed aside any surfacing temptation. She would not subject her sons to any unnecessary emotional turmoil.

"So what are you going to do now? I don't imagine it's going to be easy keeping him at bay. He didn't seem the type to allow you to call the shots."

Raven was so upset that she felt physically sick. "Could I stay with you?"

"I share an apartment, Raven. We don't have any spare beds."

"I could curl up on the floor for a day or two. Just to sort myself out?"

"Okay, okay, relax." Justin spoke calmly, clutching her hands. "The guys are having a bit of a party tonight. You can come to that, and just not go home. But you can't avoid Greg forever, Rae. You can't use me as a shield. You're going to have to face him, sort all this out—and soon." His voice was firm and persuasive. "When did you say Joy arrives?"

"On Friday."

"It's Sunday tomorrow, that only gives you a couple of days to deal with the situation—before the wedding—" There was no mistaking the warning in his cool tone.

Feelings of selfishness crept in on her. This was all her own fault. Why hadn't she just marched straight into Greg's office that day and corrected his misunderstanding? She wouldn't have felt the need to tease him, to goad him, to get back at him for what she'd thought was snobbery. Within a couple of days she'd come to realise concern for his father was paramount in his early dealings with her. There was no excuse for not clearing up the mistake before this, except a lack of courage.

What had emerged from those first few encounters had set the pace for a very intense relationship, which she should have recognised sooner as bound to end up with a physical reaction. *Why wasn't I prepared?* Despite the mutual attraction, nothing like this should have happened while he remained in the dark about her relationship with Brad.

Now she had to deal with Greg's betrayal of his father too. It hurt, knowing she loved someone who could do such a thing, and strengthened her newfound determination to clear this up once and for all.

"Thank you, Justin," she said quietly, coming out of her reprieve. "I'll go back tomorrow and sort things out."

"Just trust in yourself. And give Greg a chance to put in his two pennies worth too, Rae. You might just be surprised."

Justin paused. She waited while he studied her. Finally he spoke. "Widowhood doesn't suit you, Raven. You're too young to be alone."

Raven felt her hackles rise as she prepared the same old arguments. "I am not alone," she stressed, gritting her teeth. "I have the boys, remember?"

"You know as well as I do what I meant," Justin spoke gently. "And, I suspect the boys are fast approaching a time when they need a father."

Raven refused to comment. What argument could she use? She knew he was right.

"All I'm saying, Rae, there's nothing wrong with you finding another man attractive. No reason why you shouldn't fall in love and find happiness again. You're not betraying Chris's memory or anything." He looked at her solemnly, allowing the words time to sink in. "We both know that Chris would never have wanted you to make a martyr of yourself, devoting your whole existence to bringing up his sons."

"I have not made a martyr of myself."

"Haven't you?" Justin's voice was kind.

"I love my boys. They're my life."

"Exactly, Raven. Have you ever wondered what will happen, when they don't want to be 'your life' anymore?" Justin continued to press his point, guessing that Raven had never considered that her sons could someday sacrifice their own happiness because of her. "How would you feel if they never attempt an OE? Every bloke needs to gain experience from overseas travel and employment."

"Or what if they spurn a girlfriend who might not be willing to have Mum move in with them? They could grow up feeling that you forfeited a chance of happiness because of them, so they owe you the same devotion." He could see the shock in her eyes. "Okay, so that might seem pretty unlikely, but it could happen, Raven. You and Chris had a wonderful thing going for you. I can only assume you produced pretty wonderful kids as well."

Raven felt the blood drain from her face. That could never happen. Could it? "But I would explain. I'd tell them how travel broadens the mind, how much there is to learn out there—how much they'd miss out on if they didn't take their big Overseas Experience."

Raven was very perturbed at the points Justin

had forced her to consider. "They'd listen to me, I'm sure they would. And I would never want to live with either of them once they marry."

"You're missing the point, Rae. They might just take it upon themselves to assume you should live with them. Just like you're assuming they won't feel the burden you're placing on them."

"What burden?"

"Do they think they're stifling your dreams of being a professional painter?" Her expression must have given away the fact the boys did know of her dreams. "See? Already you're saddling them with the idea that they're keeping you from your dreams. They're going to feel the weight of that burden more and more as they get older."

"I won't let—"

"You won't be able to stop them, Rae. Not if you throw away a chance of finding another mate for yourself." He leaned forward earnestly and clasped her wringing hands.

"Look, you're in love with this guy. Maybe, just maybe...Don't you think he could be in love with you too? No, don't shake your head. Think about it. Think about things he's said. Think about the way he looks you, the way he touches you. Forget his past. You don't know anything about it really. Only hearsay, and that's often sour grapes. Consider the possibility of him actually being in love with you."

He grinned at the look on her face. "You never know, babe. You're pretty cute," he teased. "I could fall for you in a big way—if I didn't know all your dark secrets."

Tears flooded her eyes. She might be feeling a bit battered and woozy at the moment, but she knew now that Justin had been trying to make her see that this was a crossroad. If she had the courage, she might have an option not to continue to travel along a long and lonely path. Whatever might happen within the next few days, she had to ensure the boys understood that this loving and nurturing was to be from parent to child, not the other way around—at least not for the next forty or fifty years anyway.

"Thank you, Justin." She gave him a watery-eyed smile. "I understand. Thank you for making me consider things that had not crossed my mind before."

"Hey, what are best friends for?"

The hug they shared had a sense of desperation about it. She was grateful that Justin cared enough about her happiness to force her to listen to some home truths.

****

Raven found it impossible not to join in with the party atmosphere at Justin's flat. There were only about a dozen people there and she found their warm American friendship a balm to her battered soul. They accepted her without question and treated her as a welcome addition to their group.

It was well into the early hours of the morning before she crawled into Justin's bed, which he'd insisting on vacating for her, and fell into a deep dreamless sleep.

She woke suddenly, sunlight streaming through the window.

Justin sat up quickly from his makeshift bed on the floor. "What's wrong?"

"I meant to ring Greg last night, tell him I wouldn't be home."

She felt awful. She might still be unsure how she was going to approach Greg but she didn't want him to worry. And knowing him, he'd probably waited up all night.

"He knew you were with me." Justin lay back down, and then he grinned up at her. "Probably won't have done him much harm. A sleepless night raging with jealousy might work in your favour."

She threw a pillow at him. "Get me a phone," she ordered in her sternest school ma'am voice.

Trying to think what she could say to Greg, Raven sat cross-legged on the bed waiting for the phone.

"So, what're you gonna say?"

"I have no idea. He's going to be angry."

"Stuff him. He's not your keeper. You're a free agent. Just tell him you'll be back sometime tonight."

Raven looked across at him. Yesterday he had been championing Greg's cause, yet this morning...

"Sorry, guess I had a lousy night. Don't mind me."

"What time can you take me back? Anytime?"

Justin nodded. "I am at your beck and call for the day, m'lady."

She flashed him a smile before taking a deep breath and punching in the numbers.

****

Greg grabbed the phone lying beside him on the bed. The sun was shining, so obviously he'd finally fallen asleep. "You've been out all night."

"I'm sorry I never phoned last night, but—"

"You're sorry?" he tried to stop his voice from rising. He'd spent the long night worrying about her being in an accident, dead on the freeway—or wrapped in that guy's arms.

"Where are you? Do you need a ride? I'll come and pick you up right away."

"I'm at Justin's, Greg, and I don't need picking up, thank you." Greg picked up the chilly warning tone of her voice.

"I've been worried sick about you. I expected you home," he explained. "You never mentioned you might stay overnight."

"I'm sorry. I did mean to ring, but I forgot."

Forgot! How could she have forgotten? He'd

205

spent a miserable day thinking of little else but her, and here she was telling him that she had forgotten to call him!

"When are you coming home? Are you sure you don't need me to come and get you?" Greg tried to keep his voice even although he felt far from relaxed.

"Thank you, but Justin will bring me back."

"And when might that be?" Greg snapped.

"Later on today, I'm not sure when." Her voice was stilted, as if talking to a stranger.

"Raven, we have to talk. There's something I have to tell you, but not over the phone..."

"I'll be back tonight, I promise. Then we can talk. There are some things I need to tell you too." He caught a sigh in her voice.

His anger deserted him. She sounded about as happy as he was right now. Tonight they would sort this whole mess out.

"Come home as soon as you can," he whispered. "I'll be waiting."

While Raven made no reply, he waited some seconds before he heard the connection being severed.

Chapter 13

"I think we've put this off as long as we can, Raven." It was late in the afternoon and Justin had pulled into the circular drive and stopped his car. His face mirrored his concern as he turned towards her. "Will you be all right?"

"I'm scared out of my wits," Raven whispered, fingers clenched in her lap.

"Scared?" Justin's voice changed as he clutched her shoulder. "Raven..."

"No, silly. Not that sort of scared. Greg would never hurt me."

"Right now he looks like he'd like to kill me."

Raven saw Greg at the open front door. He must have heard Justin's car approaching although he made no further move towards them. The setting sun highlighted the cold expression on his face and his whole demeanour had a menacing aura about it. A shiver of fear ran through her. Justin must have felt it.

"Raven? Are you sure? We can go back to Washington right now if you want." His arm slid around her shoulders and he gently forced her to face him. Shifting her eyes from the angry stiff figure in the doorway had been an effort, and she had to force herself to concentrate on Justin's words. "I'll come in and help you pack if you want."

Raven found her hand going up to touch Justin's face, not even considering that her movement might further infuriate the watching Greg.

"It's no good trying to hide, Just. You've shown me that. Thank you for your concern but I'm really quite safe." She leaned over and pecked his cheek, then muttered to herself as she reached for the door handle, "Not too sure about my heart though."

Justin was around and at her door before she had a chance to get out. "You're sure?" He was frowning up at the silent figure. "Suddenly I don't like this at all. Shall I stay?"

"You most definitely won't." The steely words from the doorway were spoken quietly, but the message was quite apparent; Justin was not likely to get a chance to put a foot inside that door.

Raven felt a flood of warmth as she watched Justin turn and straighten under the intense stare. He was willing to be her champion, to take on any odds to protect her, just like in the old days. She didn't realise how gentle and loving her expression was as she reached up and grasped his shoulders. "Thank you, Just. You'll always be my hero." She kissed him quickly before moving toward the bottom step. "Go home now. Thanks for all you've done. I'll ring in a couple of days."

He was still eyeballing Greg, his stance anything but defensive. "Promise?"

"Sure thing."

"Aroha?" She smiled up at him. "I love you." He leaned over her. "He's so jealous he can hardly stop himself from hurtling down those steps and wringing my neck," he whispered just before his lips lightly touched hers. "Good luck."

"I love you too." Then, "Just...?" He turned to Raven before getting into his car. "I'll hold two seats for the wedding."

He smiled and shrugged. "Who can tell?" he returned, raising a hand.

And he was gone.

Raven felt so alone. Did she have the strength to go up those steps? All the confidence she'd felt suddenly disappeared, leaving her weak and frightened. The speeches she had composed were gone. What now? What, what, what?

He was waiting silently. She could feel his eyes, could imagine their blazing fire without needing to look. Despite the heat, a shiver ran through her. Raven could only hope Greg hadn't seen it.

****

She slowly started up, carefully avoiding his eyes or getting too close to him as he stood back to allow her access into the house.

"Are Manuela and Jorge back yet?"

"No." The icy monosyllabic answer sounded harsher than he had intended. "We're alone." Greg grasped her arm. "And we'll be alone all night." He glared down at her. "You're not going to run out on me again."

Raven exhibited confidence he hadn't expected. Her chin lifted as she turned. "I'll do exactly what I want to do."

Her threat found its mark. "Is that right?" he snapped, holding her forearm in a vice-like grip.

"I'm not afraid of you." She stared defiantly up at him.

He was horrified at the turn of the conversation. He'd wanted to remain calm, talk this out sensibly, quietly; try and find some common ground that they could build something on. Yet here he was, threatening her. His hand leapt from her arm as if burnt.

"I would never do anything to physically hurt you, Raven."

"I know that."

He swung back to her. "You're sure? You're not acting like it."

"You were angry. R-really angry." Her words stumbled over each other. "You looked like you wanted to kill poor Justin."

"Poor Justin!" He couldn't stop the anger from

rising again. "You spent the night with him," he accused.

"Greg, I've known Justin practically all my life." Color rose in Raven's cheeks. "Anyway, my relationship with Justin has nothing to do with you." Her voice was cool and controlled. "Keep your snide insinuations to yourself, and mind your own damn business."

She turned toward the stairs. "No, Raven, don't go. Please." He quickly released her arm. "I'm sorry. Can we please just talk quietly?" He gestured toward the living room. Noticing her hesitation, he pressed his advantage. "Come and sit down, Raven, please."

Careful not to sit beside her, he moved one of the chairs to face her. He felt like he was walking on eggshells, not sure what he could or shouldn't say to her right now. But somehow he had to make this work.

He took a deep breath. "I'm as jealous as hell of him. I can't bear to think of you two together. Seeing him touch you made me want to strangle him. I don't know if I've ever felt like that before." He had her attention. She was listening to him, and he might as well go for broke.

"Raven." He reached out a hand, but again was careful not to touch her. "I don't want anyone to touch you. I don't want to have to imagine you being close to anyone ever again." He held up his hands—before she could voice the words he was sure had formed in her mind. "I know that sounds chauvinistic and selfish. It is. But I want you for myself. I really care about you Raven. I want us to be together."

Finally I've said it out loud.

But the lengthening silence and the shocked expression on Raven's face were not the response he had hoped for.

He rushed on, alarmed at her reaction. "I want...want a relationship with you." In his agitation he edged his chair closer, tentatively reaching out. "I wouldn't try to rush you, Raven..."

She jumped up and darted to the window. "It's a bit late for that, don't you think?" she mumbled, staring out into the gathering darkness.

He watched as her arms encircled her body and she started to rock slowly back and forth. For a moment he'd forgotten his set-up two nights before. She thought their relationship had already been consummated.

He couldn't stand watching the distress his backfired idea was causing. He needed to hold her in his arms, to assure her he hadn't meant to hurt her and would never hurt her again. He approached carefully, fearful of overstepping the imaginary fence she'd erected between them.

Lightly he placed his hands on her shoulders. When she did not pull away, he gently slid his arms around her. Encouraged, he moved closer until his body was resting against her back. He didn't attempt to speak for a moment. He just savored the knowledge that she was allowing him to hold her.

Although the very thought of her being this close was working on his libido, he was very careful to keep his hold comforting and non-sexual. He allowed himself to be content just to hold her, to enjoy the smell of that wonderful perfume, to gently rock back and forth with her. After a moment he was conscious of her body relaxing a little but he was very aware that a great tension still held her.

Finally she tried to speak.

"Greg. There's something I have to tell you."

"Shhh. In a moment." Just for a few more seconds he wanted to thaw the coldness that seemed to surround her—before he made his confession. He rested his cheek against her hair, breathing in the scent of her.

He wished he could keep her in his arms, but gently eased away, turning her to face him. "Raven, I'm so sorry. I've done something that's hurt you terribly." He gently touched her cheek. "I don't know how to tell you except admitting it up front and say that I thought I had a good reason for doing it." He took a ragged breath, closed his eyes for a moment, and then let the words jump out. "We never made love. I set it all up to seem like we had."

"We never—but I remember..." Raven was shaking her head, confusion written all over her face.

"I promise, we never." He reassured her. "You were completely zonked out on those damned pills. I spent most of the night sitting with you to make sure you were all right. We never ended up in bed together." Much to his regret; but now was not the time to mention that.

"You lied to me?" Raven's voice was faint, disbelieving.

He nodded.

"How could you be so cruel?" He hated the expression she wore, it made him feel like crawling away under some rock. He wished she'd get angry—her pain was cutting into his very soul.

"I don't sleep around. I've never been with anyone but Chris. Can you imagine how I felt? Thinking that—thinking that..." Her voice broke and he watched tears gathering in her eyes.

He saw her take a deep shuddering breath as she pulled away from the hands holding her forearms, turning her back on him.

He allowed the silence to lengthen, giving her time. Although Raven was clearly agitated, he was encouraged that she did not put any real distance between them.

Finally she spoke. "For two days—I've been a

nervous wreck for two days because I couldn't remember." She swung to face him, her voice much stronger now. "Why?" She pleaded. "I don't understand why you'd do such a thing."

"I'm sorry. I was desperate. I had to find a way to make you talk to me—really talk to me. I felt you were never going to let me get close to you. I figured that you couldn't deny what's going on between us if you thought we'd already made love." He scrubbed a hand across his face.

Will she understand why I did it?

He reached for her, lifting her tense hands and holding them gently in his, rubbing his thumbs across their backs. "Raven, I love you." He watched her eyes widen with shock. "I needed you to trust me, talk to me, share your troubles and fears with me. I'm sorry that you worried," he implored her to believe him, "but I never intended it to go past breakfast. I didn't know you were going to disappear for two days. I would have told you yesterday morning. I actually tried to catch you but you were very keen to get away."

Raven's eyes dropped from his as he saw her register the truth. His desperation must have been apparent as he chased Justin's car, but she had misunderstand its reason.

Greg watched her carefully, unsure what more he could say—except, "Is what I did any worse than the games you've been playing with me?" he asked quietly.

He saw Raven's face become even more ashen as his words slowly sunk in. She remained silent, refusing to meet his eyes. Greg watched as first one band-aided thumb, then the other, traveled to her mouth, only to be discarded, as she seemed to be trying to find some way to explain. Greg saw her drag a deep breath into her lungs before she whispered. "You know I'm not going to marry Brad?"

Her troubled eyes finally rose to meet his.

Greg nodded silently.

"Abby told you."

"Abby?" Greg shook his head in disbelief. *Abby knows and hasn't told me. What game is she playing?* It seemed there had been slyer conniving than he'd realized.

"I thought she'd give me a chance to explain to you."

Greg heard the disappointment in her voice and hastened to correct her. "Abby didn't say anything to me."

"Then how? How did you find out? I thought I was pretty convincing."

"I'm ashamed to admit I sneaked a look at that email I saw you sending." At her confused frown, he continued. "You were very nervous and scared I might see what you were writing. I decided I wanted to know why?" He held up a hand, "I know it wasn't a very nice thing to do, but it explained so many things I couldn't understand. I'm not sorry; I'm not going to pretend I am. But I am embarrassed that you felt the need to protect your mother that way. I can't believe I created such an impression."

He must have looked suitably regretful, because she seemed to accept his explanation. He was encouraged enough to move with her to the sofa and sit beside her, sliding an arm lightly around her shoulder.

"I thought you'd betrayed Brad—on Friday—I hated that you could do that to him."

His heart leapt as he realized much of her pain had been because of the imagined slight against his father, not because of their 'actual' making love. His arm tightened.

"I would never have done that."

"I wasn't really sure," Raven murmured. "I mean, you have women hanging around you, relationships don't seem to be very important—I wasn't sure if your dad was any more important..."

Surprised, Greg turned her to face him. "Raven, where on earth have you gotten the impression that I'm a womanizer? That's what you think, isn't it?" He tried to keep his voice calm, but the accusation still rang out.

"We-l-l-l." Raven hesitated.

"Go on," Greg ordered. "I want to know. We're going to get everything out in the open."

"Well..." Raven was literally squirming on her seat. "You're very attractive—" He watched the thumbs moving up and down to her mouth. "—and—sexy." Greg's chest expanded upon hearing her admit she found him attractive.

"Go on." His lips twitched as he attempted to gather her closer.

"I've seen the way women look at you—and there was that woman at your club." She did not resist his arms although her hands were pressed firmly against his chest, ensuring eye contact could be maintained. "Don't try to pretend you live a solitary existence. I wouldn't believe you."

His confidence was growing, he even felt able to bend and brush his lips ever so lightly against hers. He knew he was smiling broadly. "I wouldn't do that. But, Raven, I am far from the womanizer you take me for, I promise."

"Why didn't you stop me—pretending about Brad, I mean?"

"To start with because it was fun. I enjoyed watching you, never knowing what you might come up with next. I liked teasing you too. You blush beautifully, by the way." He grinned, running his lips across her cheek. She didn't try to avoid him; in fact he thought she leaned into his embrace. "Then after the first few days—well, I wanted you to tell me. I thought we were getting to know each other well enough to trust, but you wouldn't..." He tried to glare down at her, but thought the love was probably blazing from his eyes far too brightly.

"So you set me up?"

"Yep."

"I guess that might have worked."

She looked up at him earnestly. "But I did try to tell you, Greg. Two or three times I decided it'd been a really stupid thing to do, and tried to come clean—but something always stopped me."

"That's okay. I always knew you could never marry Dad anyway."

"Oh yes. And how did you come up with that mighty deduction? I'll have you know that I think your father is a very attractive man."

"Why, because you're going to marry me, of course." Greg wondered if he'd overstepped the mark, made his play too early, but her question had allowed for the perfect opportunity. He wanted to let her know that this was no short-term relationship that he was suggesting. He knew he had done the right thing when he noticed the sudden blaze of happiness that sprang into her eyes before she quickly dropped her gaze away.

His elation at the ease of his remark quickly disappeared as she lifted her eyes back to his. The shine had gone, and she was shaking her head.

He thought quickly, *Perhaps I sounded too arrogant, too sure of myself.* He carefully picked up one of her hands and looked deeply into her eyes.

"Please, will you do me the honor of becoming my wife?"

****

Raven could not still her racing heart.

Never, never had she expected this. She'd been ready for enticements, gentle coercion even to get her back into his bed. She'd been composing reasons and excuses all day. And yes, she had to be honest to herself, she'd also given a lot of thought to accepting those offers. She'd even found herself wondering if an affair with him might have been a choice. But marriage?

Never in her wildest dreams had she considered Greg might ask her to marry him. He wasn't interested in marriage, he liked to play fast and loose. She'd seen that.

Have I been wrong?

He sounded sincere, and he was just standing there quietly waiting for her answer. What was she going to say?

Yes, yes!

"I can't marry you, Greg."

She hated the way his face tightened. She could tell his teeth were firmly clenched, and for just a moment his eyes closed, as if he was trying to find an inner strength to cope with the rejection. But to her surprise, when he opened them, there was no sign of sadness or disillusionment. On the contrary, those eyes actually twinkled across at her as he lifted the hand he was holding and slowly caressed it with his lips. His hold tightened as she tried to pull it from his grasp. A smile deepened into a grin as she renewed her efforts, he knew how much his lips could affect her, the blighter.

"Is that so?" he queried softly.

"I'm serious, Greg. I can't marry you." She tried desperately to keep her voice steady.

"Why not?"

She was astonished that her rejection had caused this type of reaction. He didn't appear to be taking her seriously. What is the matter with him? Can't he understand plain ordinary English? She couldn't stand too much more of this conversation. She had to get away from him—but first he must accept her decision. She had to make him realise it was impossible.

"We hardly know each other."

"I know all I need to know."

"Greg. You know nothing about me." Raven tried to reason, tried to stay calm, while her heart was pounding painfully in her chest.

"I know you well enough."

"No, you don't." Raven felt her voice rising. "I've lied to you." Even that bald statement didn't seem to crack his air of confidence.

"I know."

"Well, maybe there are other things you don't know about me."

"Raven, there are a million things I don't know about you, but what I do know is that I love you, and want to spend the rest of my life with you. You're proud and passionate. You care deeply. The extent you went to, to ensure your mother's happiness shows me the type of commitment you're willing to make to someone you love. You have the wickedest sense of humor, the most gorgeous body; I love just being with you. Don't worry about what we don't know, let's concentrate on what we do know about each other. I figure by the time we're in our eighties, we'll have worked out most of the important things."

"For goodness sake, stop talking like that." She finally pulled away from him. "You're driving me crazy." His attitude was confusing her so much she'd started to wonder which way was up. "How can you take it so lightly? I lied to you. Perhaps I've lied to you about other things too."

"I prefer to call it pretending. And I know you had a perfectly good reason for doing what you did."

"But having a good reason doesn't excuse being dishonest. I might be a generally dishonest person." What was she saying? Her mind was in turmoil, he would soon think she was losing it completely.

But he just smiled at her. "You could never be dishonest," he told her, confidence ringing in his voice. "And after tonight, I hope you won't ever feel the need to pretend again." She tried to evade his touch, but felt his lips run faintly across her jawbone. She couldn't prevent the shiver that coursed through her body. *I've got to calm down, for goodness sake, he's barely touching me.*

"I wish you'd stop pretending now."

She tried to move away from him, but he seemed to be anticipating the move and pulled her firmly against himself.

"I'm not pretending."

He was ignoring her message completely. "You're pretending that you don't want to marry me."

"I am not. I'm telling you straight. I can't marry you." She said it slowly, clearly, one word at a time. He had to listen to her.

"And you're pretending you don't care for me. We both know that's not true."

His hold on her tightened as she struggled.

"I am not pretending—"

"Good." His lips hovered closer as he whispered, "Then you won't mind proving how wrong I am, will you?"

The touch of his lips on hers was Raven's undoing. Much as her head tried to tell her to ignore the flash of longing that sped through her body, she could not heed the message. She was not aware of her hands sneaking up Greg's chest until she felt the curls at the back of his neck under her fingers. She pressed herself closer to his lean body, savouring the feel of him. Did it matter? She needed something to cling to in the empty time ahead. She would have so little to remember him by—except the feel and smell of him now. The way he could make her feel. She clung to him, trading kiss for hungry kiss. The invasion of his tongue into her mouth conjured up such erotic thoughts that she felt her knees go weak.

This had to be goodbye.

"Come upstairs," he mumbled against her lips.

"This is crazy," Raven gulped. "We have to stop." She strained back, her hands pushing against his chest but he would not let her go.

"Why?" Desire blazed in his eyes as he looked down at her wriggling in his arms. As she watched his eyes closed for a moment, and she was able to drink in every nuance of his face without him being aware. This was the expression she would hold in her heart. Suddenly his eyes opened and gazed so intently into hers.

"You really should stop wriggling," he teased. The pressure of his hips against her told her exactly the effect her struggles were having.

Raven stilled her body, hardly daring to breathe. Her delight at the feel of his manhood against her almost overrode her determination to take the path leading away from him.

"Greg," she beseeched, "I can't think straight. Please let me go."

She couldn't fail to recognise the satisfaction on his face as he slowly let her escape from his arms. "Maybe for a moment. But then we'll be all through thinking and talking." He leaned over and his lips seared a path across her cheek towards her ears.

Oh no! Not the ears!

If his tongue touched her ears again, she'd be lost. Almost as if he could read her thoughts, his lips bypassed her ear and were content to trail across her neck for a spellbinding moment.

Raven pushed hard against his chest. "We have to be sensible about all this."

"I agree, let's go to bed."

"Greg. Greg, stop talking like that, please," she begged. The bandaged thumbs were speeding up to her mouth regularly now. In her agitation, even the antiseptic taste of the band-aids did not register.

Keep cool, keep cool, she chanted to herself. "I have to keep cool." She didn't realize she had spoken the words aloud until she caught his teasing grin. Her nervousness continued to increase. How could she make him understand? Was he never going to accept her refusal?

"I can't marry you, don't you understand?" she all but yelled.

Greg immediately adopted a more serious expression, although she could still detect the teasing glint in his eyes. "I'm sorry, I'll stop being so pushy." She watched as he combed back his hair with nervous fingers.

They were shaking! She could see a tremor as he returned them to his knees. He was not mister cool, calm and collected after all.

"Let's just take this one step at a time, shall we?" he suggested. She noticed his fists clench for a quick moment before he reached out and took her wringing hands in his. "Let's clear something up to start with—" His eyes bored into hers. "—You can't marry me, or you don't want to marry me. Which is it?" He seemed to be holding his breath while he waited for her reply.

The silence lengthened as she battled with herself. Dare she admit the truth? Could there be a solution? Her eyes fell away from his.

"Can't," she whispered. She heard the whoosh of air escaping from his lungs and saw the tension leave his body. Despite his air of self-assurance, here was another sign he was not as confident as he wanted Raven to believe.

"Raven." He took a deep breath and held her hands tightly. "Look at me." Raven forced her eyes up. "I love you. I want you to marry me and for us to spend the rest of our lives together. I want you in my arms every night and every morning for as long as I live. But your happiness is the most important thing. Tell me right now that you don't love me, that you want me to get out of your life and I'll do it. That's how much I care about you. Tell me to go and I'm gone."

Raven's head began to shake of its own volition. The thought that he might match his words with actions scared the living daylights out of her.

"Can you tell me that you don't love me?"

Again the head shook, only more emphatically this time. She would never forget the smile that burst over his face, the relief that was there in his eyes.

"Thank God," he breathed. "Oh, Raven. You've been scaring the heebie-jeebies out of me. Do you know that?"

She managed a watery smile. Did he really love her enough to find a way to work through all the issues that she was sure separated them? Could she begin to hope? Or was she just laying herself open to more heartache.

"I know you have some issues, but we can work them out together."

He sounded so confident, so persuasive.

The sound of the ringing telephone had all the intensity of a fire alarm in the silent room. Its intrusive peal destroyed the ambiance that had started to settle around them.

Greg cursed under his breath as he strode over and grabbed the phone.

Chapter 14

"What?" he barked into the mouthpiece.

He felt his knuckles tighten as he recognized the accented voice. He resented anyone interrupting them now, and if Justin Titirangi thought he was going to speak to Raven... Well, he could think again.

"What do you want?"

"I wanted to tell you a couple of things." The static in Justin's voice alerted Greg that he was calling from a cell phone, probably from his car Greg guessed.

"I doubt I want to hear anything you might have to say." Especially now. Greg ground his teeth. He didn't need to be reminded that Raven had spent the night with this man.

"Oh, I think it would be worth your while to give me one minute of your time."

Greg's clenched fingers whitened still further on the receiver at the tone of the other man's voice, but he couldn't slam the phone down. He wanted to know exactly what this creep was going to say.

"Go on," he snarled.

"Is Raven with you now?"

"Yes."

"Is she all right?"

"Of course."

"She won't appreciate me ringing you. It might be wise to watch what you say."

"Don't you worry about what I say. Say your piece and then buzz off." That was greeted by a shout of laughter.

Laughter! Greg knew if Justin had been in the

room right then, he would have taken great delight in punching him in the face.

"I gave you the wrong impression today." He heard Justin clear his throat. "Answer me this: Do you care about Raven?"

"That's none of your damned business!"

"Just answer the bloody question. Believe it or not, I'm trying to help you."

Greg began to wonder at the reason for this call. Justin didn't sound resentful. *Why does he want to talk to me? I've made my feelings towards him perfectly obvious.*

"What d'you want?" he demanded.

"Are you in love with her?" He recognized the steel in Justin's tone. "Cause if you're just playing with her—"

Greg ignored the unspoken threat. "What's it to you?"

"It's just I'd hate to see Rae get hurt. She's had a rugged life. She deserves some happiness."

Greg could think of nothing to say. Could Justin really be prepared to champion Greg's cause? It seemed unlikely—and yet?

"She's one special lady."

Greg wasn't about to disagree with that.

"I got to thinking after I dropped her off—figured I should tell you. You have no reason to be jealous of me."

Greg swung around. He was afraid his expression might alert Raven to who he was talking. He felt his teeth grinding as he recalled the affection he'd witnessed between Raven and this man.

"I love her like a sister. Nothing more, nothing less."

Raven hadn't spent the night in Justin's arms!

"She's mixed up right now."

Greg could only murmur into the phone.

"You gonna ask her to marry you?"

Moments earlier, Greg would have taken great umbrage at such a question, but now he was willing to use anything he could to help smooth the rocky path between him and Raven.

"Already have."

He was watching Raven again. She had no idea it was Justin on the phone, Greg was sure of that. He watched her hands, never still, the thumbs traveling up to her mouth, in a move he now recognized as acute agitation. Her eyes stared down at the carpet, but thankfully she'd made no move to leave the room.

"Been given the cold shoulder?"

Greg could hear the amusement in Justin's voice, and knew there was more he could learn before he went back to Raven.

"Not exactly, but close."

Again he heard a burst of laughter from the phone. "She loves you, mate. Don't give up."

Give up? That option hadn't occurred to him, not even when he'd suggested the possibility to Raven earlier. But now, hearing Justin speaking like this, he was certain. He would never give up on Raven.

"I don't intend to, believe me."

"She has some things to tell you, to confess."

"I'm aware of that."

"Okay, so you're muddling through all right by yourself." Justin sounded resigned.

"No. No, I'm not," Greg yelled hurriedly, afraid the connection was about to be severed. "Anything you can suggest right now would be most appreciated."

"Don't try and rush her. She's a stubborn bint when she wants to be." Greg heard Justin chuckle. "Just remember, mate, she's in love with you. When the going gets tough, just think of that. What a life you'll have. It'll never be dull, I can promise you!"

Greg was at a loss for words. How did you thank

some stranger who had just given you the insight you needed to pursue your life's dream? So what if there was more she needed to share with him than the truth about Brad, and the existence of her sons? Justin obviously knew all the reasons for her hesitation, and was still willing to encourage Greg's pursuit. Nothing she could tell him would ever change the way he felt about her. And now he had the added confidence that someone close to her approved.

"I don't know what to say..." he began.

"Say you'll make her happy."

"I promise I'll do my damnedest."

"Good luck," Justin said with a carefree note in his voice. "Catch you." And the connection was cut.

Greg slowly replaced the phone, his mind slipping into overdrive. Be patient, those had been Justin's words of advice. Hell, he didn't feel like being patient. He wanted to bulldoze his way over any objections she might like to come up with, and get her promise to marry him.

He sighed, resigning himself to however many more cold showers it might take. What was a little bit of patience, if in return he could have Raven happy and contented to be his wife? It would take effort on his part, but he was going to step back and not rush things. He needed her to be part of his life, forever. He didn't care how long it might be before she was able to commit herself, as long as she didn't reject him completely. In fact, it might be fun to court her the old-fashioned way.

He didn't even sit down beside her, just held out a hand. "I really need a caffeine fix right now. Would you like a hot chocolate, or a soda or something?"

****

Raven's gaze flew to his face.

The interruption had only prolonged her agony of trying to explain her feelings to him. To make it clear why she had never mentioned her sons, why she couldn't marry him, no matter how much she loved him.

His face showed none of the intensity it had worn before the phone interrupted them. He appeared to be almost relaxed now.

How could he be relaxed? They were in the middle of the most important discussion of their lives, and he was talking about coffee.

Oh God, she prayed, *Give me the strength to understand what makes this man tick. One moment he's bombarding me with all sorts of arguments, and now he wants to make coffee! Please help me to cope with the cold after so much heat.*

But as she studied his face for some hint to understand this sudden change in attitude, Raven knew that there was no coldness about him. His eyes still blazed with the love he had pledged, his faint smile was warm and tender. She let her fingers join his and he gently pulled her to her feet.

"I'm trying to be sensible," he explained, slipping his arm around her shoulder. "Isn't that what you wanted?"

"Y-e-s-s-s," Raven answered uncertainly.

"Okay, then. Let's get a drink and we'll talk."

Raven wasn't sure if her legs would have carried her into the kitchen if he hadn't been there to guide her. She knew she'd never felt more confused in her life. She watched him, bemused, as he prepared a percolator, and then poured her a soft drink. Her hands were shaking so badly that she probably wouldn't have been able to pour the drink without messing up Manuela's pristine bench, or counter. "Whatever!" she muttered under her breath.

She watched him pour the liquid. His hands had no tremor, but then he had no dark secrets to confess, did he? He had no reason to doubt that her trust would remain intact.

She forced her fingers to remain around the glass. She hated the way she was feeling right now. Like a wimp, a jellyfish, a gutless wonder. She needed to be strong, confident, sure of herself, like she usually was. *What's happening to me?* She felt like she wanted to roll up into a little ball and let the world pass her by.

No! She wasn't going to allow that. She had to get some steel back into her backbone, some determination. *Do I love this man?* She watched him as he poured his coffee. Oh yes, almost more than life itself, she breathed to herself. Then if he's worth fighting for, start fighting. Stop being such a wimp and just tell him everything. Then you can start to work out all the problems.

Could she really do that? Throw caution to the wind, just jump right in and hope for the best. She took a shuddering breath.

"Greg?" She refused to look at him as he sat down on the other side of the bench. If she looked at him, she might lose what little courage she had managed to find. "There's something else I have to tell you. Something you have to know, before—"

"Okay." His voice was so calm, so soft, so encouraging. "But first you could tell me that you love me." His voice held a teasing note. As she finally allowed her eyes to meet his, she thought she detected a shimmer of uncertainty. "You haven't actually said it."

She didn't hesitate. "I do love you, Greg, but—"

He gripped her hand tightly for a moment before returning his to encircle the coffee mug. "I'm sorry," he apologised, "I just needed to hear you say it."

Raven winced.

Tonight, Greg had been so open about his feelings and his intentions, but she had not voiced hers. While he appeared to be very sure of himself, now she knew differently. This confidence had been a front. He'd felt the need to seek reassurance that she loved him, especially as he probably had no idea why she was refusing his offer of marriage. He was not as self-assured as she had initially thought.

"I love you so much, Greg, that it's cutting me in pieces. There's nothing more I could wish for than to marry you, but that's not possible." She stared into his face.

"I have two sons," she stated, waiting to see his expression change. To see the realisation that she was not alone, but a woman already part of a family. He had no time for or interest in children. Raven understood this mindset had stemmed from the loss of his son, but she could not allow her own boys to be subjected to his indifference.

The silence seemed never ending. There was no change in Greg's expression.

"What are their names?"

"Tane and Scott," Raven answered automatically.

"Tane's the oldest?"

Raven nodded.

"Then Scott's the scamp?"

Again Raven nodded. How could he guess such a thing as her baby's personality? His love of life and his constant tussles with mischief. Unless...

She watched as Greg replaced his cup on the bench and held up his hands, as if to ward off the expected assault.

"I saw the photo in your room on Friday night."

So he'd known about the boys prior to his proposal. He'd known she had children, yet still asked her to marry him! He was willing to take on a ready-made family, just because he loved her.

She felt tears well up as she reached across the bench. "You knew, and still you asked me to marry you?"

"Of course." He sounded oddly hurt that she

would have thought any different. "They're your children, part of you." His hold on her fingers tightened. His eyes bored into her. "I've told you, I don't want a life without you in it."

"Me—and my sons?"

His hesitant shrug was not the answer she was hoping for.

"I want you in my life, forever." His eyes wavered away from hers. "I don't know much about kids, but I'd never mistreat or abuse them. They'd have everything they want and need."

"What if they want a father, Greg?" Raven asked, gently laying a hand on his arm.

Raven was shocked at the desperate expression in his eyes as he swung to face her. "I don't know." He scrubbed a hand across his face. "I don't know if I could be a father."

"I heard about your son, Greg," Raven whispered. "Can't you tell me about him? What happened to him?" She moved around the bench and hugged him closely for a moment. "I think you'd be the most wonderful father. But you seem to have so much hurt inside that you can't allow a child to get close to you." She could tell that he was still not ready to share with her, so she continued earnestly. "If my sons lived with you, Greg, you couldn't keep them at arm's length. You would have to share yourself with them. It's not enough to provide for them. You'd have to be their father."

Raven was dismayed to see the tears in his eyes, to hear his voice cracking when he said, "I don't know how to be a father. I never had time to learn."

Raven had never had a man cry in her arms before. Even Tane was fast approaching the age where he would rather suppress his emotions than allow a woman to see him cry. She felt at a loss, but held him tight and whispered sweet nothings in his ear, just like she had always done with the boys. She tried to think quickly, how could she avoid his embarrassment? He needed to talk about this, but would he feel too humiliated? She hoped not. His release in front of her did nothing to lessen her love for him. In fact, she now felt much closer to him.

"Can you talk about him? His name was Ethan, wasn't it?"

"We called him Ethan Bradley." He pulled away from her and scrubbed his face. "Oh God, I'm sorry." He looked everywhere but at her.

"I'm not." She moved along the bench and refilled Greg's coffee mug, allowing him a moment to compose himself.

"You must think I'm such a wuss." He reached across the bench and ripped off a paper towel, blowing his nose loudly.

"Not at all," she replied emphatically. "Sharing grief is important. It's healing. Nothing wussful about it."

She was relieved to see him glance at her for a moment before he accepted the mug she offered. Then she decided to take the bull by the horns. "How did he die?"

"He was only five months old. He's a SIDS statistic, Sudden Infant Death Syndrome." He drew in a ragged breath. "We had such a short time with him. He was just starting to sit up by himself. We were so proud of him. Typical first-time parents, as if he was the first child who had ever smiled or sat up." His voice cracked again, but he continued. "I can't help but wonder what he'd have been like. When I see other boys who'd be about the same age, I wonder what Ethan might look like. It's just been less painful to keep away from children, not get attached."

"Yet you're willing to open your home to my sons?"

Again the shrug. But at least this time she was

a little more aware of his feelings. "How long is it since you lost him, Greg?"

"It was in the spring, five years ago." He seemed willing to answer her questions, but didn't offer anything without her prompting.

"Five years," Raven mused. "That's too long to grieve, Greg." She laid a hand over his as they clenched around his mug. "It's way past time to let him go. You have to forget the tragedy of his loss and start remembering all the wonderful things."

She looked deeply into his sad eyes. "Time does heal, Greg. I know—the pain goes away. But you have to be willing to let it. It can stay and fester inside, or you can open your heart and let it out."

She shared his pain as he silently clutched at her fingers, head bowed. His anguish brought back memories of her own heartache. She struggled to remember how she had initially dealt with the agony of losing Chris. Instead of wallowing in the enormous empty hole she felt, she'd had to quickly pull herself together for the sake of their sons. She'd had to keep Chris' memory alive for them.

Tenderly looking down at Greg's bent head she knew he hadn't had the impetus to focus on the happy memories to get him through the pain. Her heart ached as if a giant hand had tightened around it. There had been so little time for Greg and his baby to create memories.

Her minister's very wise words had shifted Raven's abject misery to appreciation and gratitude for what Chris' advent into her life had given her. The emptiness remained, but she'd agreed to celebrate her husband's life, not mourn his death.

Greg's situation was different. Unable to suggest he was lucky to have had his little boy, even for so short a time, she leaned her cheek against his bowed head, holding him close. Reminiscences of Chris had strengthened her but by comparison Greg's memories must be so sparse.

For a moment her eyes filled with tears. Blinking hurriedly she straightened, taking a determined breath. Somehow she would help Greg. She wasn't sure how yet but if he would allow, their empathy could begin to combat his sorrow.

Raven stayed quietly beside him, holding his hands, assuring him she was there, but not attempting to intrude on his thoughts. It was some moments before Greg moved.

"Thank you, Raven." He sighed raggedly. "I know you're right. I need to sort this out in my mind before I can even think of your boys. I don't want to make you any false promises. I don't know anything about being a father. I'm thirty-three years old, Raven." His voice was faint, hesitant. "I would like to try..."

Raven was aware of the sincerity in his voice, though it was almost completely covered by his self-doubts. But she would rather this honesty, than any show of bravado. Being a father was a never-ending job, far more time consuming and demanding than anything else a man might ever attempt. Raven could sense Greg's fear and uncertainty, but knew they were born of his own perceived shortcomings rather than an unwillingness to try.

"You could teach me how to be a father to your sons, Raven. I would do my very best," he pledged, putting his outburst into the past, where it belonged—along with all the memories of the pain of losing Ethan. They belonged in the past too.

"I think parenting comes naturally, Greg, along with love. I reckon you use your own parents as guides. If you had a good childhood with good role models, I think you can turn out to be a fine parent." She smiled at him. "You had a wonderful father. I think some of that is sure to have rubbed off on you."

"You think so?"

Raven nodded, surprised at the eagerness in Greg's voice.

"Let's just wait until the boys meet me," Greg suggested. "We can't expect them to be willing to share their mother with a stranger, can we?"

No, we most certainly can't, Raven thought as she watched Greg's whole demeanor change.

He seemed to be in a hurry to leave this discussion behind. Raven knew he was regretting his show of emotion, but she was glad he'd been able to tell her a little about his son. Perhaps one day he'd feel able to talk more freely.

What am I thinking of? There isn't going to be any one day for them. Is there?

"Now we've managed to discuss the existence of your sons, what's the next issue we have to face?"

Raven smiled wearily. He was definitely back in control of himself and appeared ready to steamroll over any further arguments she might come up with. While the outpouring of emotion seemed to have rejuvenated Greg, Raven suddenly felt psychologically drained.

"Would you mind if I went to bed now?" Raven asked quietly. On seeing the bereft look on his face, she quickly reached up a hand and gently touched his cheek. "So much has happened. I need some time."

Greg opened his mouth to protest, she suspected. But as if someone had tapped him on the shoulder, he quickly refrained.

"How about I call Tony and tell him I won't be coming in tomorrow." He hesitated. "That is if you'd like to spend the day together?"

Raven smiled tenderly at him. Greg, taking a day off work? She had a feeling that was an unheard of occurrence. "I'd like that very much."

She felt his eyes on her as she moved out of the kitchen and hoped she was doing the right thing.

234

Talking when her mind was not clear wouldn't solve anything. She needed to do some heavy thinking before tomorrow.

Greg loves me. He wants to marry me. She'd not considered either possibility.

She couldn't believe he actually wanted to marry her. She felt a little giddy just thinking of being his wife. She and the boys were being offered a new life, a new beginning. Her heart plummeted as she added the final part of the equation—in a new country. A foreign country, where they would be considered aliens. Was she willing to give up her home, everything she knew, for love?

Love didn't come with guarantees, she'd already learnt that. Love hadn't kept Chris beside her. Love was risky. Could she risk everything on an assumption that they could be happy here with Greg? What if the boys resented him—or he couldn't learn to love them? Raven stepped under the shower trying to straighten out her thoughts.

Brad was a wonderful person. Greg was his son. Surely some of that parenting expertise Brad obviously used—he had two children he was justifiably proud of—had rubbed off on Greg. He's a fine man and he'll be a fine father if he gives himself a chance, she mused as she prepared for bed.

Raven found herself drifting off to sleep, still undecided. Surprisingly, sleep came quickly, but not before a very important thought popped into her mind. Anyone who had grieved that hard, that long, for a child he knew that short a time, must have a huge capacity for love!

****

Greg watched Raven leave the kitchen. The creak of the swinging doors grated in the silence as they settled back into their closed position. He wasn't sure what to do. He balled his fists and thumped them uselessly against the counter.

Nothing had been resolved. She still hadn't changed her mind about marrying him.

What am I supposed to do now? His head sank into his hands. He couldn't lose her. Think man, think.

Be patient. That's what Justin had said. Don't rush her.

He heaved a sigh, his mind clear again. Okay, he'd be patient. He had the rest of this week to woo her as no woman had ever been wooed. He'd spend time with her, wine and dine her, romance her with anything and everything he could think of. *And if that doesn't convince her she couldn't live without me, then I'll enlist the support of Dad and, what was her name, Joan,* he mused. He suspected his father would be in favor of such a union. After all, he must be concerned that he was taking his new wife away from her family. If he could persuade Raven to live here too, that family would still be together.

Greg wasn't so arrogant that he didn't realize there were still more issues to face. She loved him! That was the most important hurdle. She was justifiably concerned about his attitude towards her sons, but he thought he had come through that ordeal with, well maybe not flying colors, but at least without a completely blackened character. He would try really hard with her sons. He'd get to know them very quickly, show them that he cared for their mother, and wanted them all to be a family. Maybe they were old enough to help teach him what he needed to know?

He strode up to his room, ready to plan the way ahead. But first, there was something he needed to do. Digging deep into the back of his closet, he came out with a shoebox. Sitting down on his bed, he slowly opened the lid. He was not surprised to see his hands shaking. He had not touched this box since the day Sybil put it away. He could never bring himself to look at what little he had left to remind him of his little boy. Raven had helped to burst the dam he'd been hiding behind. Now he thought he might be ready to go forward.

Sybil had taken so many photos of Ethan. Greg knew these were but a few, carefully sorted out and left by Sybil. She understood the need to accept Ethan's passing, grieve and carry on with living. *Unlike me!* Greg's shaking fingers grasped the first photo ever taken of their little boy, moments after he was born. The image blurred as he recalled the intense emotions that had overwhelmed him that day.

They'd been such proud parents. They had both seen Ethan's arrival as a true blessing, and they'd relished the task of parenting. As Greg slowly flicked through the photos he couldn't stop the tears from building up in his eyes, or the pain that gripped him. At least this time, he could express his grief alone. He didn't need to feel the embarrassment of breaking down in front of someone else. But he knew he shouldn't feel embarrassment. Raven had not given him any reason to suspect she thought he was less of a man because of his loss of control. That's what true love is, he decided, an acceptance of a person's weaknesses as well as his strengths.

He became lost in the memory of the joy Ethan had bought to this house. That's what Raven had suggested he remember—the joy and happiness that was theirs while Ethan was with them. He must stop dwelling on the horror of finding his cold, still baby that terrible spring morning. Stop thinking of what might have been.

He knew his inability to accept Ethan's death had been the catalyst to his marriage breaking up. He'd been unable to provide Sybil with the support she needed as she had openly grieved. Instead he had shut her out, forcing her to seek comfort elsewhere.

That was something else he'd kept hidden inside himself—the knowledge that Sybil hadn't been a terrible cheat who had deserted him for a richer man. She had found someone who was not an emotional wreck, someone who could love her as she deserved.

Could he really chuck off these chains that he had been carrying for years? The guilt he now recognized for allowing everyone to blame Sybil for their divorce. It had been he who had caused the rift, long before she had met her oilman.

And could he accept that Ethan's death was not something he could have prevented, that blame and guilt did not enter into it? It was not an indication about his ability to be a parent. It had been God's will, and no matter how hard that was to accept, to understand, he must not allow guilt to color the rest of his life. He had already thrown away too many years, lost in a sea of self-pity.

Tomorrow was going to be the first day of the rest of his life, and he was going to make every minute count.

****

Raven could not remember when she'd had such a wonderful time. Greg had rarely left her side during the past few days. Except at night, when he chastely kissed her goodnight at her door before heading down the passage to his own room. Every night.

While Raven was relieved he made no attempt to extend their relationship, she also acknowledged that she desperately wanted to welcome him into her bed. She was grateful that he had assumed such a role, because she knew she was fast losing her lifelong inhibitions. She wanted him. She yearned for him in her lonely bed each night. But it was more than that: She wanted him in her life, forever.

She was beginning to doubt her own argument that they were from two different worlds. She began to wonder if she could give up everything in New Zealand. Never had she imagined leaving her beautiful, uncomplicated country, and yet she found herself giving it so much serious consideration.

Greg hadn't said much when she voiced her concerns. She had expected vigorous arguments in favour of her shifting to Ellicott City, and had been more than a little surprised when he'd shown real understanding of her dilemma. He genuinely seemed to understand her reluctance. Except to point out that the world was getting to be such a small place now, and that he had enough money to ensure she could travel wherever or whenever she wanted, he had not sought to persuade her.

She wondered if she could love him more deeply. His awareness of what he was actually asking of her made him so much dearer to her. His clear intention to court her in such a real old-fashioned way endeared him even more. She felt in limbo. There was this huge decision to be made, and yet until Greg met the boys she wasn't going to be able to make it anyway. Even then, she didn't think an answer could be arrived at straight away.

She wouldn't marry Greg unless the boys approved. During her career, she'd seen more than once, the damage done if children's feelings weren't considered when parents remarried. She loved her sons too much to allow them to become welfare statistics. Greg had to win the boys' acceptance, at least, before she could commit to marriage.

She knew she was taking the easy way out, but just for the week, why shouldn't she forget all about worrying and decisions, and enjoy being carefree and in love? Greg was being so considerate and thoughtful. Her heart swelled with love for this wonderful man. She prayed the boys would fall for him as quickly as she had.

Greg's avoidance of work, except for a couple of flying visits to the office, each time with Raven sitting in the car, soon alerted Tony and therefore, Abby, to the fact that something was going on.

Last night the four of them had spent the most delightful evening together. Abby's attitude left Raven in no doubt as to her excitement at the possibility of another marriage in the offering. Greg, bless him, had quickly pointed out that nothing had been decided, and that they would not be committing to anything until he had a chance to get to know her sons.

Chapter 15

They were at the airport, waiting.

Raven stood back a little from the Collins family group. Although it was a late evening arrival, the whole family was here to welcome Brad and his new family home.

Abby had insisted to Raven that nothing would go wrong with this meeting. She was very nervously waiting, a huge bouquet of flowers clasped in her arms, almost constantly voicing her concern at her children's behaviour. Raven smiled. As far as she could see, Vicky and Caleb were behaving perfectly.

How different this was from when she had arrived. They were all eager to meet Joy, and Raven knew her mother was about to be welcomed with so much openness and warmth she would feel immediately at home. Joy would be happy here.

Raven's eyes returned to the arrival area for the umpteenth time. How much longer? The video screen said the plane had arrived on time. How long could it take for its doors to open? She knew there wasn't far to walk before passengers became visible on the other side of the security counters. It was the same gate she'd arrived at. But the corridor remained empty. Checking her watch again, she compared it with a large digital clock hanging above them. Surely some passengers should be starting to trickle out by now.

"Excited?" Greg's arm slid around her shoulders. He really didn't need to ask, did he? Her impatience must have been obvious to everyone.

"Oh yes," she breathed. "I've missed them so

much."

She'd spoken to them yesterday but phone calls could never hold a candle to actually holding them in her arms.

She glanced up at him, for a moment wondering how he was feeling. Is he very nervous about this meeting? He knew how much depended on a rapport developing between him and the boys. Does he have any reservations?

"I'm fine." He seemed to be able to read her mind. He hugged her close for a moment, allowing his lips to wander over her cheek, forgetting the fact his niece and nephew were an avid audience. Abruptly he dropped his arm and moved away from her.

Her eyes swung back to the arrival doors and sure enough, people were now dribbling through from the plane. And who should be leading the way but the two most wonderful boys in the world. She watched them break into a run as they sighted her. She could barely see through the tears by the time the two leapt at her, with what seemed like all the power of an All Black rugby scrum. She clasped their precious bodies tightly against hers.

****

Greg watched the reunion with mixed feelings. He had lied to Raven. He wasn't fine at all. He was more scared than he had ever been in his life. *What if I can't make friends with these young strangers? What if they hate me on sight? How do I even begin?* He had no idea at all.

What should I do? What should I say? One wrong word and I could ruin everything. Raven would never consent to marry him unless her sons approved. He felt panic rising up in him like bile. He thought he was about to hyperventilate. He could feel the sweat breaking out, imagined droplets running down his back.

Then he was aware of a hand gripping his arm, fingertips tightening through the thickness of leather between his skin and Abby's fingers. "Relax," she ordered harshly. "Here they come. You're not going to make a mess of this." She glared at him. "Forget your own worries for a moment."

Stepping forward, Abby welcomed her father and his companion. Greg took a sharp breath. She was right. First things first, they must make Joy feel relaxed and at home.

"Good to see you, Dad," he said as he gripped his father's hand. Then his eyes moved on to meet Raven's mother.

He'd stopped thinking of her as his father's wife-to-be. These past few days she'd assumed the role of mother-in-law, in his mind at least.

He found himself looking into the brightest blue eyes that he had ever seen. He thought they seemed to be studying him a little warily, so he pinned on what he hoped was his nicest smile, and bent to kiss her cheek ever so gently.

"I'm so pleased to meet you," he said sincerely. "I want to assure you that I am very happy to welcome you to our family. Anything else your daughter might have suggested is a lie." He hoped his smile sufficiently indicated the teasing quality of his words. "I'm afraid I just didn't think Raven was a suitable companion for my father."

"Neither would I." Her voice sounded exactly as it had when his father had introduced them over the phone, bright and cheerful, with that lovely accent he'd found he could listen to all day.

He felt a little of the tension ease from his body as they shared a smile across the bunch of flowers she now held. He found himself looking for similarities between her features and Raven's as his father drew her aside to continue with the introductions. He could see none, except that they were of a similar height and build; unlike he and his father, almost peas in a pod.

Greg found himself wondering, How alike will they be in personality? Would Joy accept him as a worthy suitor for her daughter? Would she encourage Raven to accept his proposal? Or would Joy back Raven's insistence that she could not leave her homeland? Oh God! His gut churned anew. Even if these boys could accept him, they weren't the only obstacle in his path.

He found himself watching openly as Raven rose from the huddle with her sons to greet her mother. Greg guessed how close they must be, and was not surprised at the delight they expressed at being together again. He was a little hurt when Raven turned her back on him and urged her sons towards Caleb and Vicky. But he soon guessed her strategy. She was ensuring that she placed no extra emphasis of their meeting with him, than with any other member of the family.

That might be working for them, but it's doing nothing for me. He wished he could signal that fact to Raven as she stood quietly behind her sons, an arm around each shoulder.

His panic might have relayed itself to her, or was she just being kind? It didn't really matter, the encouraging smile she flashed in his direction freed his tongue and he managed to speak as he solemnly shook each boy's hand. "I've been looking forward to meeting you. Your mother's told me a lot about you." He felt an invisible band tightening around his chest. How was he doing? His eyes darted quickly to hers. The twinkle he saw eased his anxiety a little. "She's been missing you a lot."

"We missed her too." Scott, was that the younger one? hugged her tightly. "But it wasn't too bad."

"Our new Granddad took us to Knott's Berry Farm. Have you ever been there?" Tane's question was directed at his new 'cousins', not Greg. Any interest they may have had in him had lasted all of a few seconds.

Greg turned bewildered eyes to Raven. *What did I do wrong?*

"It's okay." She managed to whisper as they moved off, en masse, towards the luggage area. "Relax."

"Relax! How can you expect me to relax?" he growled. "I feel as useless as a spare…"

He didn't need her warning glance to know Scott had heard the frustrated tone in Greg's voice and mistaken it for anger—anger at Raven. He watched as Scott moved from the opposite side of Raven until he was between them. He took his mother's hand and glared up at Greg, as if daring him to upset her.

Greg felt his heart plummet at that look. What a great start he'd made! Before he could even formulate something to say to this champion, he found himself being nudged aside.

"Go walk with Dad and Joy," Abby hissed, "before you really start to mess up."

He was relieved to reach the baggage claim area. He hadn't found any words to join the general conversation. He was tempted to offer to go and get Tony's SUV and bring it to the door but realized that could have sent the wrong signals to Joy. Perhaps he needed to concentrate on making her feel comfortable. After all if she was happy and at ease, at least he would have done one thing right.

He looked around. Tony and Brad were in deep discussion about how business had been in the last few months, while Abby watched her two children talking with Tane. Scott had not left his mother's side. In fact, as Greg watched Joy and Raven quietly speaking together, he noticed how the little boy's head flopped back against his mother, while he tried valiantly to keep his eyes from closing. Greg flicked his eyes back to Tane. While he seemed animated by the long flight, Scott was totally zonked out.

Poor little guy. Greg took a shocked breath, *Maybe there's hope for me yet?* He felt like picking that little boy up and telling him he could go to sleep, right here in his arms. He realized that if he'd ever taken notice of such a scene before, his reaction wouldn't have been a swell of sympathy. More likely he would've put down the mother about her laxness at allowing a child out so late at night. He felt a glimmer of hope. *Do I actually have some paternal instincts after all? Oh God, I hope so.*

He was pulled out of his thoughts as Tony and his father started to heave suitcases off the carousel and push them in his direction. He quickly grabbed them and moved them onto the luggage carts they had waiting further back. As he pushed one full cart towards Raven and Joy, he heard a gasp from Joy and looked up to find her grasping first one of Raven's hands and then the other.

"Raven?" He clearly recognized the concern in her voice before the tone changed. "What's been going on?" He could believe she had been a teacher all her life. Her tone indicated she expected a response—an immediate response.

He watched, almost mesmerized, as Raven pulled her thumbs away from her mother's hold and hid them behind her back. He waited to hear what she would tell Joy. However, Joy's tone seemed to have the same affect on Raven as it would likely have on some errant school child. She remained silent, although she seemed to be searching for words.

Finally Raven appeared to give up, and turned beseeching eyes towards him. Greg found himself pierced on the spot by a set of begging eyes and dark blue shivers of ice that seemed to freeze him to the very core.

He felt his face heating up. Guilt rose in him as he stared back at Joy. He felt his face heating up. He knew exactly why Raven had not been able to answer. He couldn't find words either, not when Joy had him pinned under that freezing gaze. She was demanding an answer and she was going to get one.

"Is that all of them, honey?"

Never had he welcomed the sound of another man's voice so much. His father's question sidetracked Joy, but not before she had left them in no doubt that this subject was not closed, merely postponed.

****

"I think we have some talking to do, young lady."

Late though it might be, Raven had been waiting for her mother, guessing her concern would have only kept her awake half the night anyway. Greg had offered to stay with her, once she'd told him that her mother would want an explanation tonight. She'd declined his offer. It would be so good to be able to pour her heart out. Her mother would understand all her doubts and anxieties. Perhaps even manage to help her find a solution to her dilemma.

She'd suggested to Greg that perhaps he would like to spend some time with his father, although whether he was going to or not, Raven didn't know.

"Did the boys get off to sleep?"

"They just crashed." Raven smiled as Joy settled down on the end of her bed. "I've missed them so much. It's so good to have them with me again." She tried to put off the inevitable. "Have they been all right?"

"Of course." Joy smiled, knowing while these might be delaying tactics, Raven also needed to be reassured about her sons. "In fact, they've been wonderful. I'm not sure if Brad and I will ever be the same again, though." She laughed at a memory. "Many's the time over the last few days that I'd wished we missed out Los Angeles altogether. Or at least that Brad could have come up with something a little less energetic to do with them."

"Oh, you poor things. Did they run you ragged?"

Joy laughed. "I absolutely refuse to ever go on an upside down roller coaster again." She winked. "Until next time, that is."

"You never?"

"Only a few times."

Raven joined in the laughter. Would everyone have trouble imagining their parents flying around a fun-park upside down? Or was it just her?

"You're only as young as you feel." Joy obviously felt much younger than her years.

"So how's Brad?"

Joy gave a saucy wink. "Brad's just wonderful, thanks very much."

"Oh Mum." Raven leaned over and hugged her mother tightly. "It's great to see you so happy. You look terrific. Being in love suits you."

"Thank you darling." Joy smiled into Raven's eyes. "Now tell me about these." She lifted up Raven's hands and gently caressed the plasters on each thumb. "You haven't done this since you were a child. Things haven't been so great here, have they?"

"It's okay now," she started, and then paused. "Well, almost okay." Then she stopped. Why pretend? Why beat about the bush? She wanted to talk this out with her mother so why not cut straight to the chase. "No, actually it was awful." She blinked rapidly. Tears were not going to help. "But it's better now."

"Why not just start at the beginning? Has Greg been giving you a hard time about your tricking him?" Joy asked. "He did have reason to be annoyed at you."

"Yes I know." Raven sighed warily. "But we got all that sorted out, finally."

"Finally?" her mother cut in. "I told you ages ago to straighten out that silly mess."

Raven avoided the accusing eyes for a moment. "Yes I know you did, but it wasn't so simple." She stopped as her voice began to break, but then took a deep breath and began to pour the whole sorry story out. She watched Joy's face registering a myriad of emotions as the story progressed.

"You silly girl." She clasped Raven tightly in her arms for a moment. "You allowed such a mess to develop in an attempt to protect me," she murmured. She laughed gently, "Surely you know by now that I can look after myself?"

"I know, but I was so mad. You were so happy with Brad, I couldn't bear for anything to happen that could change that." They shared a smile. "But you're right, a lot of heartache would have been spared if I'd just marched into that room and told him to pull his woolly head in."

"I'm thinking that your story is far from over," Joy guessed gently. "Now fill me in on the rest."

This was so much harder even though Joy already knew the bare bones of how it all started. How was she going to tell her mother the rest? Perhaps she could leave a few of the details out.

"Something has happened between you and Greg. Am I right?"

Trust her mother to guess. It must have been all those years of first guessing unruly teenagers that seemed to give her a knack of always knowing what was going on.

Raven nodded wordlessly.

"You've fallen for him, haven't you?"

Again Raven merely nodded her head.

"So what's the problem?" Joy pried. "He doesn't feel the same way?"

"No. Yes." Raven's words stumbled out. "He wants us to get married."

Raven was astonished to see a look of such pure happiness flash across her mother's face, but it was replaced so quickly by an expression of polite interest that she wondered if she might have imagined it. She decided to ignore the dawning certainty that Joy was privy to something that Raven had missed.

"I don't know what to do, Mum? Please tell me what I should do."

Joy frowned. "I can't decide for you, Raven. You know that. But I don't see what the problem is. If you're in love with him, and he loves you too, then what is there to decide? You'll need to give the boys a chance to get to know him, of course. But they'll take to him I'm sure. He's so like Brad, and they love Brad."

"Greg is nothing like Brad, believe me. They might share the same looks but that's where it ends."

"Well anyway, they would welcome a man into their lives, I know that." She held up a hand to quiet Raven's next words. "They really responded to having Brad around. They've blossomed under his attention."

"I know, I know," Raven muttered. "It's not only the boys. I know they need a dad." She smiled sheepishly. "I've been given a pretty comprehensive lecture by Justin as well. So, plenty of people are telling me the same thing."

"Then what's wrong?"

"We live in Auckland," she burst out. "I love living in New Zealand. I don't think I want to shift over here. I never thought about living anywhere else but Devonport, let alone leaving the whole country." She gripped her mother's hands urgently. "Why does it always have to be the woman who's supposed to give up everything? Whoever made that silly decision hundreds of years ago, it doesn't need to apply now." Raven wondered if her mother thought she was being childish.

She couldn't help how she felt. It really grated that the idea of Greg giving up everything in his life and coming to New Zealand never seemed to have entered into anyone's mind, but hers. It was always just assumed that the woman would make all the sacrifices. She had a home, maybe not as flash as his, but it was comfortable. And a good job.

Why should it just be expected that she throw all that she'd ever known away and move herself and the boys thousands of miles to a huge new country, where she didn't know if she could ever feel at home.

"Oh sweetheart." Raven found comfort clasped in her mother's arms. "So that's what's worrying you."

Raven rested her head on her mother's shoulder for what seemed like ages. She listened to her mother's soft voice, crooning nothings in her ear as she was rocked gently back and forth, just as she remembered from years gone by. Just as she murmured to her own children when they were hurt or upset. She felt so safe, so secure. For these few moments she relished not having to worry about anything, not thinking about painful decisions that soon had to be faced. For a moment she could feel like a little girl again.

Raven didn't know how long she lay there. Joy made no move to release her, just allowed her to take the time and comfort she needed. It was Raven who finally moved, silently brushing at some escaping tears that had rolled down her cheeks.

"How did you decide, Mum?" she queried. "How did you know that it was the right thing to do? To give up everything? Your home, your job, your family, your country, everything you ever knew, to come over here?" She turned beseeching eyes on her mother. "Please help me so I can make the right decision too," she begged.

"I never thought of giving up my family, darling. You will always be so very precious to me. We might seem far apart, but New Zealand isn't really that far. Brad assured me that we could come, I mean go, home every year. I am going to miss you all so much, but I wanted to be with Brad." She smiled gently. "You ask me how I knew?" she shrugged. "I think I just felt that being with Brad was the most important thing in my life. Everything else just slipped into lesser importance."

She grimaced for a moment, embarrassed at how she had worded her reply. "My only concern was you and the boys. Nothing else matters very much. I love New Zealand, there's nowhere else in the world that could hold a candle to our little country, but I'm not deserting it. I'll always be a Kiwi, and a mighty proud one at that. I'll be an ambassador, telling anyone who wants to listen just how wonderful the place is. And I will be going back often."

She leaned forward earnestly. "So you see leaving New Zealand never really entered my mind. It's only you and the boys that made my decision difficult." She smiled mistily. "You wouldn't have to consider leaving family behind."

Raven examined her mother's face closely. The niggle she'd felt was growing, but could she put her finger on it? "Is there something I should know?" she asked suspiciously.

"Whatever do you mean?" Joy's response was so without guile Raven became even more wary.

Then the penny dropped.

That look on Joy's face, which she had quickly covered up, the underlying suggestion that a decision to live in America shouldn't be too hard to make, the couple of looks she had noticed Brad and Joy sharing.

"This is all Brad's doing, isn't it?" she accused. "He sent me over here to recuperate. Recuperate? Ha! He had far more devious motives in mind. He was hoping that something might happen between Greg and me!"

She sprang off the bed in her agitation and paced over to the darkened window. "How could you, Mum?" She couldn't stop her voice from breaking as she swung around to confront her mother. "How could you allow him to manipulate me like that?"

"He wasn't manipulating you, Rae. He loves you." Raven shrugged off the hand Joy tried to place on her arm. "You needed the break. Anyone can see it's done you good—"

"Has it?" Her mind raced ahead. What if Greg was to think that she'd been part of this scheme? Would he believe she hadn't? Would he ever trust her again?

"Of course it has. You're alive again, Rae. Isn't it good to feel again? To come out of that cocoon you've been hiding in for years and actually feel?"

"Mum, you don't know Greg. He's not like Brad." Raven tried to explain her agitation. "If he thought that I was part of a matchmaking plot—"

"That can be easily explained. You weren't part of it." Raven detected the determination in her mother's voice. She felt no sense of guilt, and was not going to allow Raven to blame Brad.

"Brad did something for you out of the kindness of his heart. You needed to get away and heal, and he gave you the opportunity. Any thought that you and Greg might hit it off came purely as an afterthought."

Joy faced Raven, defending Brad proudly. "In fact it was something you said days later that put the idea into our heads. Ours, Raven, not just Brad.

I admit that it would make me the happiest woman in the world if you were to settle here with us. We couldn't do anything to manipulate a relationship between you." She took a deep breath. "You seem to have managed to do that all by yourself."

Raven was bewildered. "What on earth could I have said that made you suddenly turn into matchmakers?"

"Remember telling us that if you ever saw anyone who looked as good as Brad?"

Raven did remember using those words. "For heaven's sake, Mum, that was just a joke. You must have known that?"

"Of course I knew that, darling. But it didn't stop Brad from suggesting the possibility. From then on—" Joy looked at her closely. "—I just hoped and prayed."

"Oh Mum. What if Greg ever realises? He spent ages thinking I was trying to beguile Brad." Raven found her thumbs travelling back up to her mouth. "He might think I'm part of this. He'll think I was after him, after his money."

"Then he doesn't love you," Joy spoke starkly.

Raven glared at her silently for a moment before the routine of pacing recommenced.

"You don't think Brad would allow Greg to think poorly of you, do you?"

"No-o" Raven murmured, "but I wish I never knew what you two had been up to. Next thing I know you'll have your witch's cauldrons out mixing up potions for other lovelorn single mothers."

Joy chuckled as she rose from the bed. "Forget about it, darling," she advised. "No harm will come of it, I promise. Brad will see to that."

Raven pulled a face as her mother moved toward the door.

"Better get some sleep now, you have to fill me in on all the wedding arrangements tomorrow." Joy winked at her daughter, "Not to mention getting Greg and the boys together—you're going to have a full day."

She exited Raven's room giving a very credible rendition of a witch's cackle, leaving Raven smiling. Perhaps she was being too sensitive. She had spent almost every waking moment with Greg this week, and felt she knew him so well. He knew her well enough by now to know she could never have pursued him for his material assets. Didn't he?

****

Greg looked up eagerly as he heard Raven and her sons approaching the dining room. He hadn't gone and talked to his father last night. He wanted to savor the mystique of his relationship with Raven. He shook his head. Mystique! What a stupid thought. There was no mystique.

He hoped he'd been understanding while cutting through her arguments. But he hadn't yet achieved his objective—her acceptance.

He was encouraged by her obvious enjoyment of his company, and the longing he saw in her eyes as he wished her goodnight each evening. While that longing had taken all his determination to ignore, it had bolstered his flagging confidence.

He watched her closely as she settled the boys at the table and arranged their food. Raven seemed different, quieter. Hadn't her meeting with Joy gone very well last night? Or was it just that he had never seen her in the role of mother before? He found himself keenly observing her, intrigued at the interaction between her and the boys. She talked quietly to them, answering questions, talking about things they might do to fill the day.

They seemed quiet for children. Or were kids always quiet until they had their bellies filled? They were good-looking kids, and Greg was impressed by their impeccable manners. Raven's love for them showed, making her look even more beautiful in his eyes. He knew how much she'd missed them. Watching her fuss over them, intent on focusing her attention solely on her sons, caused him no rancor. The quick glance she had thrown his way as she arrived at the table had been enough to sustain him—through the whole day if necessary. In that quick look he had seen her love for him.

He knew he had to take a back seat now. His only resentment was that he couldn't expect Raven's exclusive company any more. He knew he'd need to be patient. Greg had to rely on Raven's intuition and follow her lead, if the boys were going to accept him as a member of their family.

Greg knew Raven well enough to realize that something was bothering her. She was on edge, tense. Even more tense than last night waiting for the plane. Something had happened since he'd said goodnight—another very chaste goodnight—to her. He wouldn't bring it up now. After breakfast he'd try to get her alone for a moment to find out what was troubling her.

Greg's gaze flew to the end of the table as his father lay down his utensils and cleared his throat. He frowned at the quick glance that flashed between Brad and Joy. What's going on?

Brad slowly turned to Raven. "Raven..." There was meekness in his voice Greg couldn't remember ever hearing before. Despite his friendly, outgoing nature, his father was a very forthright man.

"This isn't a good time, Brad." Greg detected nervousness in Raven's voice.

What was going on?

"It's exactly the right time," Brad contradicted.

"I don't think so."

Greg watched a thumb travel up to her mouth. Hadn't she taken the Band-aid off her left thumb yesterday? Now there was another in its place.

She was hurting. "Have I missed something?" he asked, trying to keep his voice casual.

"It's all right, Greg," Raven jumped in quickly. "Nothing you need to worry about."

He shook his head at her, knowing she was trying to keep her problems to herself. When was she going to learn that her worries were his now?

"Raven found out last night that I sent her over here hoping you two might make a match of it," Brad cut in.

Greg's eyes were still on Raven and he caught the terrified glare she threw at Brad. He felt his lips twitch. "Is that right?" he mused.

"She's scared you'll think she was party to our hopes," Joy spoke quickly. "That you'll go back to thinking she's a gold digger."

Greg let his eyes move over his father and Joy. They were both looking at him directly, openly. They were making no excuses, not denying the accusation that hung in the air.

He caught a twinkle in his father's eye, and realized Brad already knew something had happened between them, and nothing would make him happier than for Raven and Greg to marry.

Slowly Greg turned back to Raven. He recognized the uncertainty on her face, the concern.

"Oh, Raven." He left his chair and crouched down beside her, an arm around her shoulder. "I knew that day we went to Washington that you couldn't be a gold digger. I had no idea what you saw in my father, but I knew it had nothing to do with money."

Leaning closer, he gently kissed the open lips. "When are you going to start trusting me, babe? I hope it's before we get married." He kissed her again, more firmly this time and was rewarded for his faith in her by the lips that clung to his, just for a second.

It was Greg who remembered they had an audience and broke the embrace. The shining eyes that smiled brightly into his assured him of her love and trust. She seemed oblivious to the significance of their embrace to the others as she ran a finger lightly down his cheek. Glancing back at his father and Joy, he saw the delight in their faces.

The face he turned to the other occupants at the table was much more hesitant. Here were his nemeses. His whole life, his happiness, rested in the hands of these two little boys who were now staring at him with wide, shocked eyes.

His heart pounded. This was not what he'd intended, how they had talked about telling the boys. They were going to wait until after Brad and Joy's wedding, giving the boys a chance to get to know him more.

He gulped as he felt the tension return to Raven's body, as she tried to withdraw from contact with him. He tightened his hold around her, forcing her to face her sons from within his arms. They'd blown the plans they'd made. Now was the time to make the best of the situation they found themselves in.

"Guys," he started doubtfully. As their eyes centered on him, he cleared his throat and continued. "I know this is a surprise to you, but I need you to know that I love your mother very, very much, and I hope that one day she'll agree to marry me."

As he watched a host of expressions chase across their faces, Greg hastened to reassure them. "She's not going to do that until we've all had a chance to get to know each other—to see if we can like each other." He swallowed the lump that was threatening to choke him. "I really want to be part of your family, if you'll have me."

"You want to be our Dad?" Tane asked.

His pulse leapt. Should he be encouraged? He wasn't sure yet. "Actually I don't know very much about being a dad. I would sure like to be your friend though, at least to start with. Then maybe you could help me learn to be a dad, if that's what you wanted."

Feeling Raven's fingers entwine with his, gripping them tightly, he continued, "Or we could just be friends." He hoped she approved of his tact. He daren't look at her yet, he had to plead his case to her sons.

"You got angry last night." Greg's heart plummeted at Scott's words.

Greg cleared his throat again. So he had frightened Scott at the airport.

"I wasn't angry at your Mom, Scott. I was scared."

He saw disbelief on the little face.

"Grown-ups don't get scared," scoffed Scott.

"Oh, yes, they do." Greg wasn't sure how well he was doing, but was encouraged that Raven still clutched his hand. "When something is very important, and they think they've blown it, that's really scary." He took a deep breath. "Meeting you two was very scary for me."

The boys were confused. He could see that.

"Why?" asked Tane starkly.

"Because I love your Mom very much, and I don't think she'll marry me unless you guys say it's okay."

He watched their eyes moving between him and their mother, even saw them glance toward his father and Joy, then at each other.

The silence was lengthening. "I guess that might be okay." Greg's heart raced at Scott's words, even as he knew they still held a certain amount of doubt. Did he really understand what it would mean? Probably not.

259

He had never had to share his mother with a man. Greg watched as Scott spoke to his mother. "Billy Watkins in my class got a new dad. He's got two dads now."

Greg was aware of Tane's continuing silence. He was the more sensitive of the two according to Raven, and would be hardest to convince. He was also older, and more likely to realize at least some of the ramifications of having their mother remarry.

"I'd really like it if the four of us could spend some time together during the next few days, see if we could become friends." He was a little perturbed by Tane's silent shrug, but at least he hadn't voiced any real objections.

Greg returned to his seat, glowing under the light in Raven's eyes. She seemed happy with his stance and to have no worries about it succeeding. He prayed she might be right.

The resumed conversation between the adults at the table was noisy and excited. While no one made any formal announcement, or referred to a second wedding, it was as if this was a family reunited and complete. There seemed no doubt that there would indeed, be another wedding.

As they were finalizing plans for the forthcoming day, a small voice broke in with a thoughtful question. "Where would we live?" All eyes flew to Tane.

There was deadly silence. Greg noticed Raven fidgeting with the tableware as she sought to answer the query her son had aimed at her. "I—"

"We'll live wherever we want to," Greg cut in. "Here, Auckland, Timbuktu, who cares? As long as we're all together and love each other. That's what's really important."

Greg felt Raven's eyes on him, questioning. He shrugged, smiling happily.

He had never voiced such thoughts before, but

these last couple of days had forced him to seriously consider the possibility. He found himself believing his own words. He really didn't care where they lived. If Raven wanted to continue to live in New Zealand, then that's where they would live. What was a house, but a shelter from the weather? It only became a home if love abounded there. He no longer felt the need for material things to bear witness to what he could achieve in his life. He needed Raven's love and companionship. Nothing more, nothing less.

Chapter 16

What an exhausting day. Greg felt as physically weary as when he spent long hours filling in as part of one of his construction crews. Where do these kids get their energy? This afternoon they had ended up at Abby's again where there'd been a fierce game of football prior to the sun finally going down. Greg couldn't remember a day when he'd been so pleased to see the daylight fading from the sky.

He'd found it easier than he expected, relating to Tane and Scott, following Raven's advise to play things by ear and not force any extra pressure on the boys. They'd responded willingly enough, offering a reserved but friendly approach.

Talking readily he'd tried to join in with any conversation they might be having. This had proved interesting as he'd been introduced to the latest names in television, the latest video games; all of which sounded very foreign to him. He was relieved to note Tony display the same amount of confusion when the topics continued at his house. He knew Tony was an excellent parent, taking a lot of time and effort to involve himself with his children. If Tony didn't know what they were talking about, well he, Greg, didn't need to feel like he was failing to communicate.

After four days in their company, Greg supposed he was making some headway. But was it enough? Did they actually like him? Or were they just polite and friendly little guys who'd forgotten the bigger picture here? Greg's apprehension fluctuated between outrageous hope and bleak despair.

Although he hadn't yet been invited to join in the lengthy bedtime ritual Raven shared with her sons, Greg had been encouraged tonight when they'd insisted on sharing some loud and boisterous 'high fives' with him before they joined her to head upstairs. The smile she shot across at him was bright enough to set his heart pounding. He scrubbed a hand across his face as he was left alone in the family room. He hoped to get this sorted out soon. The chaste kisses that were all he'd been able to share with Raven were driving him crazy.

He needed her. Alone.

He needed to feel her body, to touch her, to share his passion with her. Even if she wasn't ready to consummate their relationship, he needed more of her than he was getting now.

He felt himself grinning. Guess this is what being a family is all about, he found himself thinking. He'd never had to share a woman before, or at least be in the position of having to put his own desires on hold while she looked after someone else's needs.

He wasn't sure if he liked that much. Who was he trying to kid? Did he for one moment imagine that if she hadn't gone upstairs with her boys right now, she'd have been locked in a passionate embrace with him? Ready to throw all her morals to the wind, right here on the rug in front of the fire? No way.

But it didn't hurt to dream.

He was as frustrated as hell, sick of standing under a cold shower every night in the vain hope that he might actually be able to get to sleep. He jumped to his feet, impatiently waiting for her to return. At least they should be able to have a little time alone tonight. Joy and his father were at the Zimmermans'. They wouldn't be too late, he knew. After all, tomorrow was their wedding day.

He figured there would be an hour or two

between Raven being able to settle the boys for the night, and them returning to the house. Surely he and Raven could grab a couple of hours alone.

****

Raven hurried down the passageway into her room. She was in a hurry tonight, wanting the boys to settle quickly. She'd even taken the risk of telling them their goodnight story was a little rushed because she wanted to spend some time alone with Greg.

She breathed a sigh of relief that it hadn't misfired. In fact she was most impressed with her sons. They'd rolled their eyes and made loud smooching noises across the room at each other, which had earned them a severe tickling from her.

She quickly brushed her hair and applied some perfume. Looking in the bathroom mirror, she was not surprised to see a flush on her cheeks and a sparkle in her eyes. How long would they have? Two hours maybe, if they were lucky. Maybe longer?

Raven hugged herself tightly, feeling goose bumps all over her body. She was nervous, as nervous as a kitten. But as she caught the look of tenseness on her face she forced herself to smile. She might be nervous but she was no longer afraid.

She almost felt like breaking into song as she ran lightly down the stairs. She wasn't sure how this was all going to work out, but she knew that it would. She felt that she and Greg belonged together and that everything was going to be okay.

He swung around as if he sensed her presence. Seeing the way his face lit up as their eyes met caused her heart to skip. She continued to run right into his open arms, wrapping herself tightly around him. The urgency as their lips met highlighted the frustration they were both feeling. It had been days since they'd been alone. Raven revelled in the feel of Greg's fingers sliding through her hair, holding her head firmly as he plundered her mouth. Their tongues parried back and forth, searching, finding— immediately building a tension so high that they were both panting for breath as their lips broke apart.

"Oh Rae," he breathed. "I've missed being alone with you. I think I'm jealous of your sons." He pulled away slightly and searched her face. "Is it wrong of me to say that?" The words had just popped out but he needn't have worried.

"I think I'm a little jealous myself," she murmured. "I don't know of who, but whoever it is keeping you away from me."

Her lips flickered across his neck. He swallowed and she caught the movement of his Adam's apple with her lips. Her hands moved of their own volition, slipping under his sweater and grasping the lightweight material that kept her from touching his skin. She could feel his hands, touching, caressing, and causing the blood to pound through her veins. He left her for a moment. Her eyes followed him as he quickly shut the door and switched off all the lamps. She watched him moving slowly back towards her in the glow of the gas fire. It threw subtle shadows across the room, heightening her awareness of him and of her own feelings of anticipation. Her senses erupted into their own flaming fire as his fingers lightly touched her cheek.

She was so aware of him. Her whole body tingled with desire for his touch. She felt no reserve as she reached up and slid her fingers through his hair, pulling his head down until their lips touched. For just a moment she was in charge, wriggling her body close to his as she fenced with his willing tongue.

She could feel the effect she was having on him as he urged their bodies even closer, his hands digging into her hips. The very magic of his touch, his closeness was sending her into a spiral of sweet temptation, where time stood still and nothing existed except for each other and the feelings they needed to share.

His lips seared a path across her throat before settling on her ear. The flickering tongue soon had shivers running up and down her spine as she clung to him. Her body was answering the most basic of all questions. It was ready, ready for the fulfilment that only he could give.

She knew he'd not take the incentive. He loved her enough to want her happiness, and if that meant an abstinence from the most intimate of contact, he'd shown his willingness to wait. He would allow this petting to go only so far. As far as he was able to remain in control, then she knew he would call a halt.

It was up to her to show him the time for waiting was over. She was committed to loving him forever.

Could she find words? Somehow it seemed cold, so calculated to just invite a man into your bed. Even when his lips were driving you crazy, heightening every nerve ending in your body. It was so much simpler to show him, to allow the body total abandonment.

Her hands returned to caress him under his sweater, only this time the thin cotton of his shirt was too much of a barrier. She needed to feel his bare skin. She pulled and tugged at the shirt even as his lips moved across her throat to start an assault on her other ear. She shivered again as a renewed set of emotions erupted, sighing as her fingers finally touched his hard-muscled back. She thought she heard him moan as she lightly ran her fingernails across his back.

She moved so her hands could slip between them as she felt for his belt. Immediately her hands were caught and pulled away.

Raven smiled faintly, so that is the area of no return, is it?

She felt a momentary disappointment that his hands remained firmly on the outside of her clothing, although he did allow them to wander over her breasts, teasing them through their cotton covering. She knew it was in deference to her attitude towards casual sex, but their lovemaking would be anything but casual.

Raven took a deep breath and pulled herself out of his arms. She felt his reluctance to release her but with a shuddering sigh he finally did so. He moved towards the large sofa in front of the fire and held out his hand, inviting her to join him.

Raven shook her head slowly and turned towards the door. She could sense his disappointment that she intended to end the evening so soon, but didn't attempt to change her mind.

"Goodnight, my love," he murmured as his eyes left her to stare into the leaping flames.

Her heart swelled with the love she felt for him. She must have done something right in her life to deserve such unselfish devotion.

"Good night? No, I don't think so. I was anticipating something much more. Spectacular, unbelievable, incredible—" She pretended to muse as his head swept around. "—didn't you once use the word 'magnificent'?" she teased. "I think I'd like to try and live up to that—" She eyeballed him across the room, watching the dawning awareness lighten his eyes. "—now."

Opening the door, she moved towards the stairs. "Coming?" she whispered across the darkened foyer.

Her outstretched hand was swiftly grasped in a warm firm hold. So swiftly she wondered how he had moved across the space so quickly.

"You're sure?"

Raven looked at him through misty eyes. "I'm sure."

His fingers tightened around hers before they turned together and slowly mounted the stairs.

She paused outside her room but he smiled and murmured. "Too close to the boys." He led her further along the corridor.

"They're very sound sleepers." All her senses where alive with anticipation, she was loving this moment. She was tingling under the smouldering looks she was catching in the hallway's dim light. The teasing eagerness was building, her senses were becoming more and more acute.

"I'll have to remember that."

"I wish you would," she murmured saucily, as he led her into his room and firmly shut the door.

****

Later he held her tightly against his side, enjoying the feel of her skin against his. He could never remember feeling so sensational, so fulfilling. He knew he needed Raven to stay exactly where she was—forever. Curled up like a soft kitten, sated for now, but already promising more delights with those sparkling eyes.

"I'm going to hold you to it, you know." His lips brushed across her cheek.

Raven looked everywhere but at him, blood rushing into her cheeks. Greg shifted hurriedly so he could better see her face. His whispered words hadn't been to embarrass her but to remind her of his ill-timed proposal. Her screamed acceptance while pleading for fulfilment had filled him with a heady elation he'd struggled to control. But now he could savor the knowledge she was truly his.

"That was emotional blackmail, pure and simple," she countered as she pulled away from him ever so slightly, "and you know it."

He grinned across at her, completely

unrepentant.

"I know it," he agreed. "But I'm still going to hold you to it."

"And just how do you intend to do that," she queried, her eyebrows raised.

"Oh, I'm not sure yet." His finger started to trace a circle around her navel, getting larger and larger, going lower and lower. "I'm sure I can come up with some pretty persuasive means."

"Is that right?"

"Mmm." For a moment his fingers showed her just how his efforts were likely to proceed.

Raven arched her back, pushing herself closer. "I might need a lot of persuasion," she teased.

"I've got my whole life," he assured her as his lips moved to entrap an already peaking nipple.

This was fun, but he was beset by doubts.

He'd pulled a dirty trick and he would never try and hold Raven to the promise she gave during the heat of passion. Did he dare risk asking her again, seriously? What if she didn't give the answer he wanted? Now that he had sampled a taste of Heaven, his life wouldn't be worth anything if it were to slip away.

He took a deep breath and allowed some space to separate them. He watched Raven's eyes fly open as his touch left her body. He saw concern cloud the sparkle in her eyes. She seemed to be marshalling her defenses against his abandonment. He hastily reached over and grasped her hand, slowly moving it to his lips and kissing the palm.

He forced himself to speak, his heart pounding with the fear of possible rejection. Maybe formality would impress her of his seriousness, albeit verbal formality. Two naked bodies lying amongst jumbled bedding could not really lend themselves to formality.

"Raven," he began, finding he had to clear the

obstruction in his throat that threatened to mangle his words.

He tried again. "Raven, I love you very much. Would you please consent to be my wife?" He hurried on, not caring if he might seem to be begging. He was. Begging for his life. "To live with me from this day forth, in any house, in any town, in any country of your choosing. Please marry me and make me a whole person."

He watched expressions dart across her beautiful face, still flushed from the heat of their passion. He held his breath, never doubting her love for him, but was that enough? His heart began to race as he watched the sparkle come back into her eyes.

"Are you really sure you know what you're asking?"

"I don't care where we live, Raven, as long as you'll be by my side."

"It's not only that though," she pointed out gently. "You'd be taking on a family, not just me."

She was still using the wrong tense, what could he say to persuade her? Hopefully his honesty and sincerity would be enough.

"They're your sons, Rae—your flesh and blood. If I love you, how can I avoid loving what's part of you? I know it's early yet but already I feel a connection. I feel closer to them than I ever have to Caleb or Vicky. I'm not kidding myself that it's going to be all sunshine. But if you're there, I won't even see the clouds."

"And if I asked you, you reckon you could give up all this?" Her arm encompassed only a portion of his room but he understood the symbolism.

"If you asked, I would give up my life," he pledged solemnly.

His heart soared as he watched the smile that began in her eyes and slowly spread across her face.

"Thank you Greg. I'll be very proud to be your wife—" His whoop of delight almost, but not quite, drowned out her quickly tacked on. "—not yet though."

He didn't care. The smile they shared was almost like a benediction. Now he could face anything knowing that their lives would be interwoven through to their old age.

"Tomorrow, before the wedding, we go out and buy a ring." He paused, uncertainty reigning again. How long was the 'not yet' likely to be? Did she want their commitment to remain a secret? "Okay?"

"Deal!"

He looked down at the hand she stuck out towards him and laughed.

"Oh, I think we can do better than that," he whispered as he drew her more-than-willing body back into his arms.

The seal they put on that deal was one so full of shared fulfillment and ecstasy, they were likely never to forget its passion.

Epilogue

Shouts from outside the window caused Raven's eyes to rise from her easel. She grinned as she watched the melee out on the lawn. After two years, Greg still insisted on applying American football rules to any game of rugby the boys might try to have. As always, his complete disregard for the finer points of rugby met with physical retribution from her sons.

As she watched the all-out wrestling match taking place, Raven again remembered Justin's advice. Tane and Scott had desperately needed a father figure. And Greg was filling that role admirably. While she had been able to supply all their emotional needs and support while they were young, she saw how important a father was in their lives now.

And what a father Greg was turning out to be.

Her sons idolised him. Since they'd first realised her feelings for this quiet, younger version of their new grandfather, the boys had slowly gravitated towards him, each learning in his own way how wonderful and important such a relationship could be.

Raven had been so proud of her sons. Their quiet acceptance of Greg into their lives, their willingness to share her with him had surprised Raven. The jealousy and heartache that could have torn her apart never eventuated. She never gave herself the credit for having raised two fine young boys.

She winced as she saw fists flying, pelting into

that body she loved so much. Greg was cowering on the grass under an onslaught by the fast-growing boys. She saw them pause and guessed either Brad or her mother, who were sitting alongside the pool, had said something to them. The pause was enough for Greg to regroup and renew his own assault. Within seconds, he had bundled them across the paving and all three went into the pool with an enormous splash. The screams of shock and threats of retribution began a continued combined attempt to overpower and dunk. Raven watched until Greg laughingly called a halt to the assault.

The shared laughter coming from the pool area sent warmth through her that she constantly felt now—the joy and happiness of a complete, loving family.

Despite Greg's arguments, Raven and the boys had returned to New Zealand shortly after Brad and Joy's wedding. Although totally convinced of Greg's love for her, and his pledge to spend the rest of his life making her happy, Raven had still been filled with doubts. She had begged him for some time alone, away from his always-distracting presence, to sort her feelings out. The fulfilment of her teaching contract gave her the necessary impetus.

Greg had argued long and hard, offering to buy her out of any contract, but she had insisted. She'd needed time to consider all the ramifications of marrying Greg, away from him. Even now she still had trouble concentrating whenever he was near—concentrating on anything other than him, that was.

Greg had given her exactly one month. One month of long expensive phone calls, of busy days but oh-so-lonely nights. She had arrived home from work after a particularly harrowing day to find him sitting on her doorstep.

She smiled at the memory. It had been hours before they'd got the boys to sleep; long, frustrating hours.

Stunned, when he calmly announced that he'd told his father he was coming to New Zealand to live; and that Brad and Tony could sort out the business any way they wanted. She'd been speechless. If any doubts had existed about his commitment to her, that move had quelled them all. He seemed to have happily given up everything he'd ever worked for, everything he knew, just to be with her.

She had watched horrified, as he started taking odd labouring jobs advertised in the local paper.

She'd carefully monitored his faltering steps as he continued to build a relationship with Tane and Scott. Initially she'd suggested he was trying too hard, but his efforts never ceased. Gradually his efforts began to pay off and the boys started turning to him for help and advice. Soon it had been his presence they had looked for at their rugby matches almost more than hers.

He had filled their home with such happiness and contentment that Raven knew she could never let him go, never risk losing his love or support.

They'd been married in a simple ceremony at Raven's local church. Brad and Joy's unexpected arrival the night before explained some sneaky phone calls Greg had made, and filled Raven's heart with delight. The following surprise reception put on by her friends, and secretly funded by Greg she found out later, had gone long into the night. Greg had quickly made friends both within her own circle, and outside it. He'd settled into the household routine set many years earlier by Raven, and seemed to enjoy his job as a builder's labourer.

While they were ecstatically happy and her home was now filled with love and laughter, Raven worried about her new husband.

Would he ever regret his decision to live in New Zealand? She did not doubt he was happy, but one day, he would surely get sick of labouring, and remember all he had given up. Would he slowly start to resent her?

He had assured her that would never happen. He'd said he would start building some sort of business for himself when he was ready. He told her he enjoyed the physical work without having the worries of planning and organizing.

She believed him. Their life was wonderful, but self-reproach kept resurfacing. She hadn't been fair to him.

If only Joy had been there for more than a flying visit. Raven needed her support. She needed someone calm and sensible and always able to give the very best advice. Raven missed her Mum.

Their many regular phone conversations hadn't helped her to stop missing Joy. Raven missed them being together to talk and argue, to laugh and cry. Tane and Scott asking when Nana and Brad were coming home didn't help either.

She had had the opportunity of uniting this family, and instead she had torn it apart. She'd forced Greg to leave everything and everybody he knew to live on the opposite side of the world, and turned him from a successful businessman into a labourer. And if that wasn't enough guilt to deal with, Raven knew Joy was missing her grandchildren dreadfully although her mother tried to hide this. While initially Raven kept her emergent thoughts to herself, slowly her insistence at remaining in New Zealand dwindled.

It was just after the confirmation of her pregnancy that she made a serious decision to look at the alternatives.

Grimacing, she gently rubbed her extended stomach as she was subjected to a kick that seemed equally as hard as the punches she had watched the boys inflicting on Greg.

The family meeting she'd called had not lasted long. The boys showed no hesitation in voicing their desire to live in America, and while Greg had remained non-committal for a while, Raven knew him well enough by then to recognize the faint flicker of hope that he'd quickly quelled.

Once the decision had been made, everything had fallen into place so simply that Raven knew she was doing the right thing. She had advised the school she would not be applying to renew her contract; and had set about sorting out a house full of memories, packing lots, reluctantly getting rid of lots more. Greg had suggested she keep the house, saying that it would be a second home for them all, one they would use frequently on holidays back to New Zealand. It would also be available if and when the boys wanted to return to their homeland to live. In the meantime they'd placed it in the hands of a real estate management firm who would rent it short-term to tourists wanting to enjoy Auckland's North Shore without the sterility of hotels. She had been assured its location would mean a steady income, a small portion of which would be used for its maintenance, the rest was being deposited in a trust fund for the boys.

She stood up slowly, rubbing her back. The discomfort was beginning to get worse. She glanced out of the sunroom windows to find Greg watching her from where he was talking to their parents by the pool.

His face mirrored the concern that she was beginning to feel. Is it time?

She'd wanted to finish her current project before the baby arrived. She smiled across at Greg, waving his concern away. Although, perhaps she should tell him to get out of those wet clothes, just in case?

No, everything is fine yet.

She picked up a brush and studied the likeness

on the canvas.

Ever since Chris's death she'd regretted never having painted him, preserving his features on canvas for eternity. She'd never been able to bring herself to start until one day recently, when his face had begun to emerge as if by magic from under her fingers. She had worked on his portrait solely for the last few weeks, putting aside her intentions of capturing the delicate features of the cardinal she had been studying and photographing at the bird feeder in the back yard. The cardinal could wait. She needed to get Chris finished before the baby arrived. It was as if finally, she was ready to say goodbye to him.

She'd needed no photos to remind her, her painting had come from the heart. She thought this probably bothered Greg. He often sat and watched her painting, but he'd never brought the matter up. She'd given him the option of looking at the portrait as she worked, but he'd always declined, saying he'd wait until it was finished.

She sighed, feeling another uncomfortable twinge at the base of her abdomen. She hadn't wanted to upset Greg—he knew her love for him filled her heart—but she'd had a burning need to commit Chris to canvas. Whether it was to capture his likeness for Tane and Scott, or to lay his memory to rest, she wasn't really sure. She just knew she had to finish before Greg's baby arrived.

She stood back, studying her work in the dying daylight.

"Isn't it time you took a break?" Her mother was at the door.

Raven shook her head, and silently gestured for Joy to come and look. The involuntary gasp that escaped Joy's lips was praise enough for Raven.

****

Greg appeared at the doorway. "You finished?"

he asked as he watched the two silent women gazing at the canvas. For a moment he felt a twinge of jealousy as he studied the face of his wife, staring down at the image of her late husband.

The idea that Chris's face was still so fresh in her mind all these years later, had reinforced the realization that Greg wasn't the only love in her life. He pushed the jealousy aside as Raven turned to him, a smile of triumph lightening her face.

"Come see," she invited, holding out a hand. She snuggled comfortably into his arms as they closed around her.

Greg was silent as he stared at the painting.

He'd only seen a few snap shots of Chris. For some reason he'd never wanted to put a face to the man who'd sometimes seemed like a ghost between him and Raven. But as he had his first good look at Chris, he felt a weight lift from him. The painting was so detailed and lifelike, it could almost be taken for a photo.

"What do you think?"

Greg realized that Raven was waiting for some comment from him, but he found it hard to formulate words. He just tightened his hold on her and gently brushed his lips against her hair.

The image surprised him. He could see the strong resemblance between Chris and the boys, particularly Tane, whose coloring favored him. And Chris had the same quirky smile that Scott flashed around. He recognized the battered guitar, the same one Tane cherished.

But the image he was looking at was that of a boy. Well, maybe not a boy, he amended quickly to himself; but a young man, a man barely out of his teens. If Raven's memories of Chris were as she'd portrayed him, he had no reason to fear that memory. For here was a picture of a young, carefree man; his cocky smile signaling his eagerness to take on the world, and laugh in its face. His eyes sparkled, as if he had enjoyed every second of living. Greg felt a moment of sadness, as he realized the sparkle had been extinguished far too soon.

"I needed to say goodbye to him before the baby." Raven couldn't quite keep the quiver out of her voice.

Greg suddenly realized that his silence was probably sending all the wrong messages to Raven but he was unsure what to say.

"Where are you going to hang it?" Joy broke the silence.

"In the attic, in the boys' play area." Raven replied immediately.

Greg knew she wanted to keep Chris's memory alive for his sons, but countermanded that idea instantly, "I think we'll hang it in the family room, where it belongs." He smiled at Raven's reaction, the light in her eyes as she turned to him. "He is part of our family, after all."

He wasn't even aware of Joy leaving them, of her shooing away Brad and the boys as they came to see what was going on. All Greg knew was the delight of his wife in his arms, raining teary kisses all over his face.

The swell of emotion in his chest was indescribable. His once empty life was so perfect now. He had found his new stepmother, mother-in-law, whatever you wanted to call her, a true delight. He had two fine sons, a baby due any day now, any hour maybe. But most importantly the beautiful, talented, comical and very sexy lady he had wrapped in his arms.

A word about the author...

Anne Ashby grew up in a very small coastal town in Southland, New Zealand. An eagerness to see the world, fostered by her amazing mother, led her to join the Royal NZ Navy where she enjoyed a very satisfying career. She has travelled extensively and lived in Singapore and in Maryland USA.

Worlds Apart is her first novel and depicts some of the cultural and language differences she encountered whilst living in that "back to front" country, America.

A true Pisces, Anne loves the water and gets much of her inspiration while swimming. When not reading or writing, Anne finds plenty to occupy her time with her family commitments and an intense interest in genealogy. She currently lives in Wanganui, with her husband and two of their four children.

Anne would love to hear from readers. Visit her at www.anneashby.com

.

Thank you for purchasing
this Wild Rose Press publication.
For other wonderful stories of romance,
please visit our on-line bookstore at
www.thewildrosepress.com

For questions or more information,
contact us at
info@thewildrosepress.com

The Wild Rose Press
www.TheWildRosePress.com

9 781601 547224